LOVE
AND
SHAMROCKS

....

A BALLYBEG ROMANCE

(BOOK 5)

ZARA KEANE

Beaverstone Press LLC
Switzerland

Beaverstone Press
CH-5023 Biberstein
Switzerland
www.beaverstonepress.com

Publisher's Note: This is a work of fiction. Names, characters, places, and incidents are a product of the author's imagination. Locales and public names are sometimes used for atmospheric purposes. Any resemblance to actual people, living or dead, or to businesses, companies, events, institutions, or locales is completely coincidental.
Book Layout ©2015 BookDesignTemplates.com
Ordering Information:
Quantity sales. Special discounts are available on quantity purchases by corporations, associations, and others. For details, contact the "Special Sales Department" at the address above.
Love and Shamrocks/Zara Keane. -- 1st ed.

ISBN 978-3-906245-14-0

For April.
Thank you for all your support over the years.

A NOTE ON GAELIC TERMS

....

Certain Gaelic terms appear in this book. I have tried to use them sparingly and in contexts that should make their meaning clear to international readers. However, a couple of words require clarification.

The official name for the Irish police force is **An Garda Síochána** ("the Guardian of the Peace"). Police are **Gardaí** (plural) and **Garda** (singular). They are commonly referred to as "the Guards". I've kept the use of these terms to a minimum but I do use them in reference to Garda Brian Glenn's rank and when naming the local police station (Ballybeg Garda Station).

The Irish police do not, as a rule, carry firearms. Permission to carry a gun is reserved to specialist units, such as the Emergency Response Unit. The police in Ballybeg would not have been issued with firearms, hence there are no references to holsters, guns, or shooting ranges.

While I have used American spelling conventions in this book, I haven't changed the spelling of **Traveller** or **Travellers**.

A halting site is a facility constructed and maintained by local authorities for Travellers to park their caravans on. Halting sites are controversial among the settled community.

PROLOGUE

....

DUBLIN, IRELAND

For the first time since completing her twelve-step program, Clio Havelin regretted rehab. If she'd been high, she could have ascribed the entire situation to a drug-induced hallucination. Not having so much as a drop of caffeine in her bloodstream, she didn't have that luxury. This was happening. This was real. And the reality of being in a tiny police interview room listening to pat reassurances made her blood boil.

Clio pushed back her chair from the cheap plastic table and struggled to breathe. "What do you mean you're not pursuing the investigation further? How can you *not?*"

The fleshy police inspector seated opposite exchanged a significant glance with his younger female colleague. The blond woman adopted what Clio assumed was her standard expression of bland sympathy and leaned forward in a confiding manner. "We've done everything we can do, as has the school. Without Tammy's cooperation, the case won't stand up in court. There's no physical evidence and no eyewitnesses. In short, there's absolutely nothing to support your claim that Mr. O'Leary engaged in improper relations with your daughter."

"Improper relations?" Clio's nails dug into her palms. "Call a spade a spade. Trevor O'Leary had *sex* with his fourteen-year-old pupil. How can you sit here and tell me you're not going to charge him? What about the other girls he's done this to? What about the girls he *will* do this to if you don't stop him?" An icy trickle of fear made the hair on her nape stand to attention. "If you don't charge him, the school will have to lift his suspension. He'll be back teaching impressionable teenagers."

The blonde's practiced calm faltered, and she exchanged an uncertain glance with her superior officer.

Inspector Fahey loosened his tie and cleared his throat. "I understand your dismay, Ms. Havelin," he said. "We take allegations of abuse of minors seriously, believe me, but the only evidence we had to present to the judge was your statement. No one else has come forward to make allegations against Mr. O'Leary. And as we've already clarified, even your own daughter refuses to make a statement to support your claim."

"But you believe me." She looked from one to the other. "I can see it in your faces. You know what I'm saying is true."

"It doesn't matter what we believe." The inspector gave a weary sigh. "It doesn't even matter what the judge believes. The prosecution can't build a case without something to create sufficient probable cause at the very least. O'Leary denies everything, and Tammy says you're lying." He shoved his chair back and stood, his junior officer following his lead. "If your daughter changes her mind about making a statement, give us a call."

The recycled air in the interview room tickled the back of Clio's throat, bringing forth an asthmatic cough. The nagging suspicion that had plagued her since the start of this disastrous interview came to the fore. "Is this because I have a criminal record?"

The man hesitated in the doorway. "It certainly didn't help me sell your story to the higher-ups, that's for sure."

She swore beneath her breath. No matter how many years had passed since her trial, no matter how many honest jobs she'd held since, she'd always be a convicted thief and drug addict in the eyes of the law. Meanwhile, Trevor O'Leary was considered a respectable music teacher without so much as a speeding ticket to besmirch his good name. *Bastard.* Clio's hands balled into fists. She itched to punch the fecker's smug face and to kick him where it truly hurt.

"Your friend is waiting outside," Fahey said, holding the door ajar.

Still reeling, Clio got to her feet and followed the police officers out to the lobby.

Both the police sergeant and his junior colleague proffered hands. Clio shook them with barely concealed distaste.

"I'm sorry we couldn't be more help," the woman said with genuine regret. "If anything else crops up, give us a call."

Clio gave a stiff nod and shoved open the door of Rathmines Garda Station. Outside, Emma was leaning against a metal railing, tapping a restless foot against the pavement. Today's ensemble screamed New Age hippy, complete with a tie-dyed hair band that did little to control her wild blond curls. Emma straightened the instant she spotted Clio. "Oh, no," she said, searching her face. "It didn't go well."

"No, it did not." Clio wound her scarf around her neck and marched down Rathgar Road at speed, forcing her friend to scramble to keep up with her furious pace. "They're going to let the bastard get away with sexually exploiting a minor. He's even going to get his job back."

"Clio." Emma panted. "Slow down and talk to me. I know you're upset—"

"Upset doesn't even begin to cover it." The pulse at the base of Clio's throat throbbed.

"—but you shouldn't do anything rash."

Their eyes locked. Emma had known Clio since the bad old days, back when Emma's family had fostered Tammy for a couple of years before Clio got clean. Insofar as it was possible to know everything about another person, Emma knew everything there was to know about her, and vice versa.

"I'm not letting O'Leary get away with this. He's thirty years old, for goodness sake. What sort of a sick bastard takes advantage of a fourteen-year-old?" Hot tears stung Clio's eyes. She brushed them away with the back of one hand while flipping out her phone with the other. "Tammy is still in touch with him, and I don't trust her not to meet him, even if she changes schools."

Emma sighed. "She thinks she's in love with him."

"Even worse." Clio gave a bitter laugh. "She thinks *he's* in love with *her*."

They came to a halt outside the redbrick Edwardian house where she and her daughter shared the top-floor apartment.

Emma toyed with a stray pebble on the pavement. "Maybe you should consider taking your mother up on her offer."

"What?" Clio's jaw dropped. "You're advising me to drag Tammy to a spit-and-you-miss-it little town in Cork? And move in with *my mother*? What about the agency?"

Her friend grimaced. "Reilly Investigations isn't inundated with business at the moment. I'd cope on my own. A fresh start might be exactly what you and Tammy need."

"Moving back to Dublin from Barcelona was supposed to be our fresh start." *What a mess that's turned out to be.*

Emma tossed her windblown hair over her shoulder. "Think it over. It would put over three hundred kilometers between O'Leary and Tammy. Much harder for them to meet. After all that's happened, a new environment and a new school might be what she needs."

Clio squeezed her eyes shut for an instant and shook her head. "The sticking point is my mother. We've taken tentative steps toward a reconciliation, but living together is a whole other level."

"Only on weekends, right? You said she'd be away filming her show Monday through Friday."

"Yeah…"

"In other words, you'd be living in the house on your own with Tammy five out of seven days." Her friend's blue eyes burned with earnest conviction. "I don't think that's a bad deal. Helen can be a pain, but she's not a monster. If she's willing to pay the fees for Tammy to attend a private school, they're likely to provide extra tuition to help her catch up on the work she's missed over the past couple of months. She has the Junior Certificate coming up in June, doesn't she?"

"Yes, she does." If Tammy didn't get good grades in the first set of state exams, her options for the final three years of secondary school would narrow. "I hear what you're saying, but I'd have to be seriously desperate to move into my mother's house, even if she'd only be there for part of the week."

"Just consider it, okay?"

"I promise I'll talk it over with Tammy," she said with reluctance, "but I don't think she's any more keen to live with Helen than I am."

Emma's phone beeped an insistent reminder. "Two o'clock already? I'd better get moving."

Clio nodded toward her friend's cell phone screen. "The O'Brien case?"

"Yeah. Fortunately for their marriage, but unfortunately for our bottom line, I don't think Gerry O'Brien is cheating on his wife. This case is likely to wrap up quickly. Until I can confirm my gut feeling, though, I'm supposed to trail the husband. He's due to meet friends at the organic market in Temple Bar." Emma tugged at the tie-dyed headband. "Hence the outfit."

"At least you get to put your acting skills to good use," Clio said. "Your years on the stage make it easy for you to slip into a role and follow someone without them noticing."

"I set up the private investigation agency because I was struggling to find acting jobs. Who'd have thought I'd spend most of my time in disguise?" Emma stepped forward and gave her friend a hug. "Don't think I didn't notice your attempt to deflect the conversation onto me. Will you be all right on your own?"

Clio hugged her friend back. "I'll be fine. Go and catch errant husbands."

"Take care of yourself," Emma said, concern forming a frown line on her otherwise smooth forehead, "and don't do anything stupid."

She gave a wan smile. "You know me too well."

As soon as her friend's wild curls disappeared down the street, Clio switched on her phone and scrolled through her list of contacts. Her index finger hovered over one particular name. If she called Tammy's father, Trevor O'Leary would never bother Tammy again. Hell, if she called her ex, Trevor O'Leary would never bother *anyone* ever again.

She shut her eyes and dragged oxygen into her lungs. No, even O'Leary didn't deserve such a fate. All she wanted was for him to stay away from her daughter, not wind up dead. Who else did she know with the power to scare the crap out of a person? Swallowing past the lump in her throat, she dialed a number not saved on her phone but imprinted on her memory. It was time to call in an old favor.

CHAPTER ONE

....

S ergeant Seán Mackey weighed the weapon of mass destruction in one gloved hand and surveyed the scene of the crime. "Let me get this straight. Armed with an air rifle and a bottle of Jameson, you shot a bird through your *closed* living room window? While *naked*?"

Seán's Uncle John-Joe, aka the Swimming Elvis, hiccupped, swayed, and groped for the mantelpiece. He was clad in tight swimming trunks and a grubby wifebeater, his graying Elvis quiff limp and screaming for shampoo. John-Joe was none too clean, none too sober, and none too cooperative. At least he was no longer in his birthday suit. "Bit of a mess, eh?" he said after another hiccup.

"Bit of a mess" was an understatement. On the other side of the broken window, feathers, pellets, and broken glass lay strewn across the patio of the Fitzgeralds' tiny garden. Some joker had drawn an outline of a robin redbreast in the snow, CSI-style.

Seán rubbed the back of his neck with his free hand. *Jaysus.* He needed a Dublin transfer pronto, preferably to vice. He'd take prostitutes and drug dealers over outlaw

9

relatives any day. "How did you get your paws on a high-end air rifle?" he asked in the tone he usually reserved for recalcitrant rookies and crooks. "I didn't have you pegged as a small-game hunter."

The older man's tongue darted between his lips, reptilelike. His beady eyes swiveled toward his wife.

Aunt Nora was kneeling on the living room carpet, surrounded by broken glass and pulverized porcelain. Firing the air rifle at close range against the hard, flat surface of the window had caused glass to shatter and pellets to ricochet. All but one of her beloved knickknacks had been blown to smithereens—the statuette of the Virgin Mary remained intact, her expression serene amidst the chaos. Seán's mouth twitched at the incongruity.

"My Dalmatians," she moaned, clutching a severed porcelain head to her fluffy peach bathrobe. Although her impossibly black hair was still in curlers, Nora wore full war paint. When they were kids, he and his brother, Dex, had speculated their aunt must either reapply her makeup before going to bed or wake up at an ungodly hour to ensure she looked her best.

Instinct drove Seán to touch her shoulder. Experience made him recoil. For a millisecond, he was hurtled back twenty-five years to happier times. The nostalgic taste of his aunt's apple tart, the sugary smell of his tenth birthday party, and the sweet sight of his mother's smile. His mother...A dull ache of grief settled between his shoulder blades, erasing the happy memories in an instant. He flexed his spine, shrugging off the past. He had no time for sentimentality. "Nora, where did John-Joe get the gun?"

His aunt placed the broken china dog on the carpet and pushed herself to her feet. "From that fool, Buck MacCarthy," she said through pursed scarlet lips.

Seán knew Buck. He was a fisherman with more hair than sense. Which, in Buck's case, wasn't saying much. "Why does Buck need an air rifle?"

John-Joe shrugged, his tongue poking a bulge in one cheek. "How should I know?"

"What did the bird do to warrant you firing several shots at it and turning your living room into a disaster zone?"

"It was plaguing me. Kept banging against the window and causing a racket."

"So you decided to shoot it?" Seán's eyebrow arched north. "Bit extreme, don't you think?"

His uncle's scowl created a unibrow. "Not right away. Not till it flew inside and shat all over my costume." He pointed toward the rhinestoned monstrosity slung over the sofa.

Seán squinted. Like its owner, the costume had seen better decades. It was white—or had been in a previous life—with fraying cuffs and a velvet trim. Its appeal was not enhanced by bird excrement.

"Times are hard." The older man's shoulders sagged the slump of defeat. "I had a gig, see. First one in months."

"The Elvis impersonation business slow in West Cork?" Seán asked, deadpan. A nation in the depths of recession was unlikely to have much call for professional performers at private parties, let alone a sexagenarian gyrating in Speedos.

His uncle's mouth formed a petulant pout. "No money to pay the mortgage ain't no joking matter. I got a wife to support."

"You wouldn't be financing the mortgage by taking on a few side jobs of, shall we say, dubious legality?"

"Eh?" John-Joe danced a nervous jig on the thread-worn carpet, like a toddler fighting the urge to pee. "Don't know what you're talking about."

"Someone has been shooting out tires at the Travellers' caravan site," he said with icy casualness. "With an air rifle." He took a step closer to his uncle. "Don't suppose you know anything about that?"

John-Joe appeared to shrink inside his swimming trunks. "I don't have anything to do with the Tinkers."

"Travellers," Seán corrected, "or Pavee. Gypsies, if you must."

The man's nose wrinkled. "I don't go in for politically correct shite. They're Tinkers to me."

He took another step closer to the man who'd once been his favorite uncle. "Has your un-PC self been taking potshots at their caravan tires?"

John-Joe's head gave an uncertain shake.

"In that case, I'll be having a word with Buck."

The man's Adam's apple bobbed. "So...we done here?"

He gave him a tight smile. "No, we are not done. I'm charging you with possessing a firearm without a license, discharging said firearm in a residential area, and for generally being a blight on society."

John-Joe's jaw slackened. "You can't do that!"

"Not the last part," Seán said with regret, "but the rest I can."

"Air rifles are legal. Have been since...since...they changed the law."

"Since 2006, air rifles with a muzzle energy less than one joule don't require a license." He placed the bagged-and-tagged weapon by the sofa. "This air rifle exceeds the limit. Even if it didn't, you're only allowed to fire them in designated areas. Newsflash, John-Joe: that excludes your living room."

"How was I supposed to know?" John-Joe's voice rose in a panicked whine. "Buck said he bought it off the Internet."

"I'll be asking Buck about that when I invite him to join you at Ballybeg Garda Station for a lecture on the Firearms Act."

John-Joe's feet stopped their nervous shuffle. "Down the station? Do I have to?"

"Yes, you do." His voice held a note of steel. When he'd been disgraced, demoted, and sent to rusticate in a country police station, Seán had been determined to keep his distance from his estranged family. Within days of moving back to Ballybeg, his uncle's propensity for petty crime had scuttled that plan. "I'll need a statement from you, too, Nora," he said in a gentler tone.

His aunt glared at her husband, cheeks quivering. "You blaggard. Because of your tomfoolery, I'll be hauled off in handcuffs."

"Don't be daft," Seán said with a touch of impatience. "All I need is a statement. You're not being charged with anything."

"Handcuffs!" Nora screeched as if she hadn't heard a word he'd said. "What will the neighbors say? I'll never live this down."

John-Joe was clearly at the end of his hungover tether. "Ah, would you ever quit your moaning, woman? Only peace I get is when you're at mass."

Nora's hands fluttered to her forehead, and then to her chest, in a subconscious sign of the cross. Her gaze flickered toward the swimming trophies on the mantelpiece, souvenirs of John-Joe's days as a champion swimmer.

Seán regarded the trophies with a pang of regret. Hard to believe his uncle had once been the town hero, before his drunken antics and Swimming Elvis act had turned him into the town joke. "Stop arguing. Let's go and get this over with. If John-Joe cooperates, you'll both be home by noon."

If Seán's hunch was right—and they usually were—he finally had a lead on their mystery shooter. He gave a mental fist pump. This was the part of the job he loved. If he solved the case quickly, his Dublin transfer was in the bag, but he hoped to goodness the culprit didn't turn out to be someone close to his uncle. John-Joe had neither the patience nor the brains to carry out a stealthy operation over a period of months, but one of his regular partners in crime might.

Out of the corner of his eye, he spotted movement. Before he could react, Nora grabbed a swimming trophy from the mantelpiece and chucked it at her husband, hitting him square in the beer belly.

"Ow," Joe-Joe roared. "Have you lost your mind, woman?"

"Yes," she screamed, tears of anger running down her face in mascara-tinged rivulets. "I lost it the day I was stupid enough to marry you."

Ouch. Seán placed a steadying hand on his aunt's arm, but she wrenched it free, hysterical by this point, cursing and flapping and whacking John-Joe with whatever missile came to hand.

"For crying out loud, Nora."

She ignored him, moving down the row of trophies with impressive speed.

Patience had never been Seán's strong suit, and the little he possessed had run dry. "That's it," he snapped. "I'm cuffing the pair of you."

After a short struggle, during which John-Joe's undershirt developed another rip, he managed to slap handcuffs on his aunt's and uncle's wrists. "You have no one to blame but yourself, Nora. I told you I only wanted a signed statement from you."

He dragged one air rifle and two protesting relatives down the hallway and out the front door. On the way, he grabbed a Mack for John-Joe and chucked it over his shoulders. The combination of tight swim trunks, wifebeater, and raincoat made the man look like a flasher. Sweat beaded on Seán's forehead. *Jaysus. What a start to my day.*

A crowd had gathered by the gate of the Fitzgeralds' two-up two-down terraced house. Several pairs of eyes unpeeled Seán's layers as though he were an onion. Heat burned a path from his scalp to his toes. Too many people in Ballybeg knew his family history. What he wouldn't trade for blissful anonymity...

Seán pictured the baton in his utility belt. He missed his SIG. He missed Dublin. He missed a lot of things. With a bit of luck, Frank—his former partner—would have news of a place on the vice squad. Their lads' weekend couldn't begin soon enough.

A second squad car pulled up behind Seán's. Garda Brian Glenn climbed out of the vehicle, a beam of delight spread across his freckled face. "Quite a turnout. I haven't seen a crowd this big since Ben Driscoll held up the post office with a banana."

"This sort of caper always brings out the curtain-twitchers." Seán wrestled John-Joe and Nora into the backseat of his squad car.

Before he closed the door, Nora put a hand on his arm. It was warm, solid, familiar. "You don't have to arrest us," she said in a beseeching tone. "Please,

Johnny." Her breath floated in ghostlike wisps through the crisp February morning.

He dragged cold air into his lungs, past affection warring with everything that had happened since. Had the maternal look she was giving him not reminded him of what he'd lost, he might have caved. "I ceased to be Johnny twenty-five years ago, Nora."

He slammed the door. If only shutting out the past was as easy as shutting a car door. Cutting short the question hovering on Brian's tongue, Seán added, "If that pair of eejits represent domestic bliss, I'm staying single."

The younger policeman rolled with the deflection and turned his attention to the air rifle. "I'll lock the gun in my car. There are five registered firearms in Ballybeg, and this isn't one of them."

"John-Joe got it from Buck MacCarthy. I'll haul him in for questioning later. Hopefully, it's a viable lead on the Travellers case."

Brian's grin faded. "Speaking of the Travellers, there's been a development."

Seán was instantly on the alert. "Another incident?"

"One of the caravans had its tires blown out with the occupants sitting inside. As you can imagine, they're none too pleased."

"That brings the tally to four attacks this month." Seán frowned. "Hell on wheels, no pun intended. When was this latest attack?"

"Twenty minutes ago."

He exhaled in a hiss. That put John-Joe in the clear. Was that a disappointment or a relief? He jerked a thumb at his car. "I'll drive by the Travellers' site once I've dealt with the miscreants."

"It's all happening today," Brian said, waggling his red eyebrows in an exaggerated fashion. "While you're dealing with drunken Elvises and mystery shooters, I'm on my way to meet our local celebrity with Superintendent O'Riordan."

He tilted his head. "Local celebrity? I didn't know we had one."

"Indeed we do. It's that ultra-conservative talk show host who used to write a silly advice column for *The Tribune*."

Seán's heart rate kicked up a notch. *No*, he thought. *Please, no.* "Not Helen Havelin?" The words came out in a croak.

"Yeah, that's the one." Brian rolled back on the balls of his feet and grinned, seemingly oblivious to his partner's inner turmoil. "She's the new owner of Clonmore House."

Seán's world tilted on its axis. The acrid sting of bile rose in his throat.

Helen Havelin. The woman who'd helped destroy his childhood was living in Ballybeg.

CHAPTER TWO

....

CORK CITY

Delivering money to a gangster with a Napoleon complex was not what Clio had planned for her Friday evening. One lousy favor. That was all she'd asked of Ray Greer, part-time crook and full-time arsehole. Instead of ensuring that she and Tammy would be left in peace, Ray and his goons had managed to both screw the job up and screw her over.

Clio stood on the pavement before the impressive façade of the Sheldon Hotel, feeling snowflakes melt on her nose. Friday night revelers jostled her as they passed. Traffic whizzed by in a blur of taxis, buses, and flashing lights. Cigarette smoke wafted from furtive smokers huddled in doorways, who were bouncing up and down in an effort to keep warm. Laughter spilled out of pubs, taunting and beckoning. These were happy people. Good people. Hadn't-just-robbed-two-thousand-euros-from-their-mother people.

To think she'd assumed calling Ray for help with Trevor O'Leary would be a smarter move than contacting her ex. Clio's lungs burned with rage. In the aftermath of the debacle, she'd swallowed her pride and had accepted her mother's offer of a fresh start for her and Tammy in

Ballybeg. Yet within a week of moving into their new home, Ray had smashed her plans to smithereens. *The double-crossing toad!*

Taking a ragged breath, she pushed through the revolving doors and entered the hotel. The lobby was a kaleidoscope of shifting shapes and colors. Families carrying luggage more expensive than her car. Elegant couples arriving for a luxury weekend break. Businessmen with smartphones glued to their ears. Clio's frozen hands clutched her handbag. She did not belong here.

Through the moving mass of people, she spied the designated meeting point. An oversized stone fountain with water gurgling up and over the carved fish center. Obscenely ostentatious, but it fit the general ambience. Her mother would love this hotel.

At the thought of Helen, guilt clawed its way from her stomach to her throat. Why had her mother not answered the phone earlier? She could have talked to her. She could have said she needed to borrow the money urgently, for Tammy's sake. Helen might not have listened, might have refused, but it would have been worth a shot. Yet every time Clio dialed her number, she was greeted by a tinny voice mail message. With an hour's notice to deliver the cash, there was no time to wait for her mother to respond to a panicked text or e-mail.

Which had left her with precisely one option, and it was a bad one—rob her mother's safe and race to Cork City to deliver the money.

Pulse pounding, she placed one leaden foot in front of the other. The voices in the lobby rose and fell with snippets of conversation. Luggage carts and feral children darted in front of her. She dodged them, keeping her focus on the fountain.

If she'd had any other option, she'd have told the blackmailing scumbag where to stick his demands. But what choice did she have? The weasel knew he had her over a barrel. The instant Ray had threatened Tammy, she had panicked. She'd put her daughter at risk once before and had to live with the consequences every minute of every day. This time, she'd do anything to avoid putting Tammy in danger.

A hand grabbed her arm, twisting painfully. The man squeezing her arm was big and burly with a walrus moustache. Clio registered his badge. A security guard. *Feck.* Sweat beaded on her upper lip.

The security guard's piggy eyes raked her outfit, pausing at her shoes. When his head jerked up, he wore a smirk. "Are you sure you're where you need to be?"

In other words, was she sure a woman wearing a ratty winter coat, a vintage Ramones T-shirt, ripped jeans, and hooker heels belonged in the lobby of one of Ireland's most illustrious hotels? *Hmm...*she was pretty certain the answer to that question was no.

"I'm meeting someone." She wrenched her arm free.

Another smirk, wider this time. "The Sheldon is not *that* type of establishment."

With her heart pounding against her ribs, Clio glanced at her watch. Five minutes. If this idiot kept delaying her, she'd be late for the meeting with Ray. "I'll be out of here in a few minutes," she said, pointing to her watch. "Ten, max."

Beefy arms folded across his chest. "I'm asking you to leave."

"For feck's sake," she snapped. "I'm not a prostitute. I'm here to drop something off."

Too late, she realized the implication of her words. *Damn.*

The security guard's smirk evaporated. "We don't tolerate drugs on the premises."

"It's money," she said in a rush. "I'm...delivering it to my employer. He's staying at the hotel."

The unibrow reappeared, and his lips parted as if to argue further.

Clio plunged her hand into her bag and whipped out the envelope. "See?" she said, opening it a crack. "Can I go now? My boss is the impatient sort, especially when it comes to his hard-earned cash."

"What's your boss's name?" he asked, hesitating. "I need to check our register."

"Bollocks. If a guest has a delivery of cash he doesn't intend to put in the main safe, the hotel staff have no business knowing his room number."

He dithered a moment, uncertainty flickering over his fleshy features. "Go on with you," he growled, "but if I catch you selling anything you shouldn't, I'll have you arrested faster than you can run in those heels."

She pushed past him and hurried toward the fountain as quickly as her shoes allowed. Trust her to rush out of the house barefoot, leaving her with the only footwear she could find in the couple of moving boxes still in the back of her car—scarlet open-toed stilettos she'd bought for a costume party.

She clattered over the slick marble floor and slid to a stop in front of the fountain. She stared down at swirling blue. Koi darted through the water, bright orange and white, glinting like goldfish on steroids.

And then her mind reached back, and the fountain blurred in her vision. Tammy had owned a goldfish when she was little, back in the days before she'd morphed into a moody teenager. *Tammy...Oh, God.*

There was still time to change her mind before Ray arrived. Not much. A minute, maybe two. She'd retrace her steps, return the money to the safe, and come clean —to her mother and to the police.

She squeezed her eyes shut and let out a ragged breath. Who was she trying to kid? She could never go to the police. If she hadn't been let down by the Irish judicial system, she wouldn't be in this mess.

The clock chimed the hour. Six o'clock. Clio's witching hour. She opened her eyes and dragged air into her lungs. Last chance to save her soul. Heart hammering an unsteady rhythm, she spun around and headed for the exit.

At that moment, someone knocked into her, sending her reeling. She grabbed the edge of the fountain to break her fall but lost her hold on her handbag. It fell to the floor, the contents spilling over the marble tiles.

"Sorry," said a gruff Dublin-accented voice.

The hairs on Clio's nape sprang to life. *Of course.* Ray wouldn't come in person. He'd dispatched a minion.

The stranger shoved stuff back into the handbag and thrust it at her.

No, I've changed my mind. The words lodged in her throat.

"Ta," he said and melted into the crowd.

Hands trembling, Clio opened the bag and reached inside.

The envelope containing the money was gone.

***

Seán weaved his way through the teeming lobby of the Sheldon Hotel, mobile phone pressed to his ear. "You can't make it to Cork this weekend?"

"Nah, no chance." His friend's tone was morose. "If I leave the missus in the lurch, she'll castrate me."

"Far be it from me to put your balls in jeopardy, Frank," Seán said dryly. Speaking of balls, he needn't have busted *his* getting to Cork City in time to meet Frank at the Sheldon.

"Maybe next month, eh? When the kids are better and Shelia's mum can help out."

"Yeah, no worries. Our lads' weekend can wait. Give me a call when the kids are over their flu. Is there's any news on—"

Frank's impatience crackled down the line. "If I knew anything about the Greer bust, I'd tell you, buddy. You know that. No one knows anything. Or if they do, they're not talking."

"Okay. I might have a lead on a decent case in Ballybeg." A stretch, but Seán was an optimist. "Maybe I'll get a transfer back to Dublin sooner rather than later."

"Yeah." The other man sounded distracted. "Listen, I'd better go. The little one's roaring her head off."

"Go play daddy. I'll talk to you soon."

He rang off and slipped his phone into his pocket. *Damn.* He'd been looking forward to spending a couple of days with Frank. Although he'd seen his former partner several times since he'd moved to Ballybeg eleven months ago, their plans for a weekend in Cork City kept falling through. Given the date and its implications, Seán had prayed it would work out this weekend. He craved the distraction of an old friend's company.

He stared ahead, unseeing. What now? Stay in the hotel room they'd booked for the weekend? Go back to Ballybeg? If he went home, he'd spend the evening staring at the four walls, too wound up to sleep, too tired to concentrate on a book or TV show. Being in Ballybeg made him antsy at the best of times, brought memories to the surface that he'd rather suppress.

Tonight was definitely not the best of times. It was the anniversary of the greatest fuckup of Seán's life. Weird to think that this time last year, he still had a couple of hours before his career imploded. And young Alan Brennan still had a couple of hours left to live...

A shudder of revulsion coursed through him. He didn't want to be alone. Not tonight. Learning Helen Bloody Havelin was living in Ballybeg had been the crowning glory to what had already been a crappy Friday. It was as if all his ghosts had colluded to ambush him on the same day. If Frank wasn't around to talk work and rugby, he'd down a few pints in splendid solitude. Maybe even pick up a woman for a night of mindless, no-strings-attached sex—the only variety of sex he was into. He didn't do relationships. And judging by past experience, relationships didn't do him.

The hotel bar would do as well as any other for pints and flirtation, and it had the added advantage of not being far from Seán's hotel room. Decision made, he moved toward the wooden doors of the bar.

A flash of red snared his attention. A small strawberry-blond-haired woman stood beside the fountain, clad in impossibly high heels. From the red stilettos, Seán's gaze meandered north. Slim, denim-clad legs, tiny waist, and firm breasts accentuated by a form-fitting T-shirt underneath a winter jacket. He let out a low whistle and slowed his pace. Not bad. Not bad at all.

His eyes moved toward her face, and his breath caught. She was fine-boned with full lips, high cheekbones, and a narrow nose. Memory tugged his brain. She was familiar. Had he seen her somewhere before? Or someone who looked like her?

At that instant, a man in an ill-fitting suit crashed into her, sending her handbag flying. Its contents spilled over the marble floor. The man bent to help her. The hairs on the nape of Seán's neck stood as he watched the guy shove some of her things back into the bag and give it to her. At first glance, there was nothing strange in this scenario, and yet...and yet, he'd swear he saw the man slip something into his pocket.

He stepped forward.

"Look out!" An elderly man bore down on him, struggling to retain control over his heavily laden luggage trolley.

Seán leaped back to avoid a collision. By the time the trolley passed, the man at the fountain was gone. He scanned the crowd, but the guy had vanished. The woman kneeled on the floor, ashen-faced, shoving the last stray items into her handbag while staring into space.

He closed the space between them. "Did he take anything?" he asked gently, crouching beside her.

She glanced up, startled. Their gazes locked. Up close, she was a couple of years older than he'd first calculated.

Maybe early thirties. Her fine features and pale skin were offset by a pair of startlingly green eyes, a trifle too close-set for beauty, but striking nonetheless. Seán's stomach did a flip. He ventured a small smile. A red stain crept up her cheeks, and she lowered her lashes.

"No," she said in a low voice thick with emotion. "He didn't take anything."

Her nose twitched, and her hands shook. *She's lying. And she's afraid.*

Seán bent down to scoop up a pen that had fallen out of her bag. He handed it to her, feeling her cold fingers against his warm ones. A zing of awareness made his pulse race. "Are you sure he didn't take anything?"

"I...Yeah." She shoved the pen back into her handbag. "I'm positive."

He took her hand and helped her to her feet. His large hand encased her small one. She was tiny, even in those ridiculous heels. They didn't match her faded jeans and T-shirt or her makeup-free face. In comparison to every other female in the lobby, she was underdressed, but she outshone them all.

She looped the bag over one shoulder and made an effort to steady herself. Whatever had gone down with the guy, she was visibly shaken.

"Do you want to get a drink?" he heard himself ask. He should run. He had enough on his mind without taking on other people's problems, and this was not the sort of woman he'd been planning on picking up tonight. A single glance sufficed to inform him that this woman came with strings—strings so tightly knotted they'd require tweezers to unravel. But Seán was a fixer, and a sucker for a damsel in distress. There was something that drew him to this particular damsel, some clue in a puzzle he had yet to solve.

She turned those fabulous green eyes toward him and his breath caught. "I told the security guard that I'd be out of here in a few minutes."

He gave her a measured look, then a smile. "You here to do something illegal?" he asked in a teasing tone.

Her laugh was broken and half hysterical. "No."

"In that case, let me deal with the security guard, if need be." Seán propelled her forward, his palm burning against the small of her back. "Come on. Let's get that drink."

CHAPTER THREE

....

Inside the hotel bar, music of the bland top-ten variety drifted from the speakers. Men in slick designer suits chatted up women accessorized with shoes and handbags that cost more than Clio earned in a month. Her gaze dropped to her ratty outfit and the ridiculous red heels. She stood out like a flickering neon sign.

Warmth crept up her cheeks, and she crossed her arms over her breasts. Her feet itched to flee, but where could she go? Her mother was filming in Galway, and Tammy was spending a couple of days with Emma's parents in Wexford. Neither of them was due back in Cork until tomorrow. The idea of returning to an empty house after the run-in with Ray's minion made Clio's stomach clench and twist. She wanted to be amongst people, to bask in their carefree Friday night revelry. Anything to distract herself from what she'd done.

"Stools okay? There are a couple free at the bar."

Her rescuer's deep voice wrenched her back to the present. She looked up at him and gave him a brief once over. A reluctant flutter tickled her abdomen. He had a Rugby player's build—tall, broad, muscular. Laugh lines framed his bright blue eyes, giving the impression a smile was never far from his lips. He wore his dark hair close-cropped. Chiseled cheekbones and a square jaw added to the impression of classic beauty, but his face was saved from the tedium of perfection by a nose tilted slightly to the left.

"Rugby accident?" she asked, slipping off her coat.

"Eh?" His hand flew to the bridge of his nose. A slow smile curved his lips. "Yeah. Keep meaning to get it fixed."

"Don't. It adds character."

He chuckled, a rich sound that sent tingles skittering over her skin. "I'm glad you like it."

She shouldn't, but she did. And she rather liked him. She wasn't in the market for a man, but a bit of harmless flirtation would take her mind off her problems, keep her from dwelling on her worries.

Clio cocked her head to the side and stared directly into his electric blue eyes. "You in the habit of rescuing damsels in distress?"

His grin grew wider. "Only ones wearing sexy shoes."

Heat prickled her neck, and she shifted her focus to the hint of dark stubble grazing his jaw. This guy was too sexy by half. In an alternate reality—one excluding the turmoil of the past few months—she'd have been all over him. She swallowed past the stubborn lump of regret lodged in her throat.

Mr. Sexy took her bare arm. The searing heat from the skin-to-skin contact made her breath catch. "Come on," he said. "Let's nab those stools while they're still free."

He maneuvered a path through the crowd, past the well-dressed drinkers fumigating the atmosphere with warring designer scents. Clio's nose itched, and she felt the familiar asthmatic catch in her chest. Given the stress of the evening, it was a wonder she hadn't yet needed her inhaler.

"Here we are." Mr. Sexy stopped before two vacant stools by the bar's chrome counter. The warmth of his palm on the small of her back was reassuring. He guided her to one of the stools, and she clambered up, her torso brushing his as she sat. Her cheeks grew even hotter.

Gosh, she had to get a grip. She was acting like a teenager with her first crush, not the world-weary cynic life had chiseled her into. Besides, any man of sense would run if he knew the trouble she was in.

Clio inhaled sharply and focused on the bottles behind the bar. They were arranged on frosted-glass shelves, artfully lit to draw attention to the most expensive. Her mother would love this joint. It would appeal to her delusions of grandeur.

The thought of Helen precipitated another wave of panic. Clio's heart pounded, and she reached for the inhaler in her jeans pocket.

Her fist closed round the inhaler when a barman slid into view, resplendent in a crisp white shirt and black bow tie. "What can I get you?" he asked, studiously ignoring Clio's disheveled appearance.

"A pint of Guinness," Mr. Sexy said. He turned to Clio. "What are you drinking?"

She took another look at the display of bottles and exhaled wheezily. They represented a past she'd abandoned twelve years ago. Avoiding alcohol when she was stressed was one of her unwritten rules. Avoiding spirits altogether was another. Her nails dug into her palms. One drink. One drink wouldn't plunge her back into her former lifestyle. Alcohol had been the least of her issues, after all. And her past problems faded into insignificance when compared to her current predicament.

"I'll have a G&T, please. With Bombay Sapphire." The name tripped off her tongue in near reverence. She hadn't tasted its sweet bitterness in over twelve years and had sworn never to do so again, but it wasn't every day you put yourself beyond redemption.

"Not going local with Cork Dry?" Mr. Sexy asked, anchoring her in the present. His voice was very deep, very masculine, and sounded like its owner gargled with the finest single-malt whiskey.

Clio's skin tingled in giddy anticipation. She'd always had a thing for voices. Unfortunately, that thing for voices had gotten her into trouble a time or ten. She took deep, steady breaths, but her gaze slid over the muscles rippling under her companion's black silk shirt. Accepting his invitation had been an extremely bad idea. What was she thinking? The security guard would go ballistic if he found her in here.

"I don't do local," she said in a tone sharp enough to slap.

"Men or booze?" he asked, a glint of mischief in his intense blue eyes.

"Both."

A wicked grin spread across his face. "Then it's just as well I'm not local."

She'd been so distracted by the events of the evening that she hadn't registered the absence of a Cork dialect. A Dublin accent, she guessed. The north side of the River Liffey. The wrong side, as her mother would say.

She drummed her fingers on the counter, flexed them over a beer mat.

"You want to shred that mat," he said, laughing. The deep, throaty sound made her blood hum.

She ripped the cardboard, one neat slice at a time. "You a cop, a lawyer, or a psychologist?"

He quirked an eyebrow. "Not a fan of those professions?"

"Right now, I'm not a fan of men."

"Yeah? Right now, I'm not a fan of humankind." His cheeky grin softened his words. "Present company excepted, of course."

"Of course." This guy was a charmer, albeit with an edge.

She glanced up when the barman pushed their drinks across the counter. For a moment, Clio was mesmerized by the cool perfection of the drink with its glistening slice of lemon. She tapped the glass once, then twice. Her years of partying were behind her. Long before she'd moved back to Ireland, she'd made the conscious decision to focus on her daughter, to be the sort of mother she'd always wanted. And she'd failed. God, how she'd failed. A hard lump formed in her throat, forcing her to blink back tears.

"We never introduced ourselves," Mr. Sexy said, cutting through her thoughts. "I'm Seán Mackey."

"Orla O'Brien." Orla was a good, nondescript name and so common in Ireland that it blended with the damp air. O'Brien was equally commonplace and a far cry from her cursed unusual surname. Her lip curled. The last thing she needed right now was him connecting her to Helen Havelin, Ireland's Number One Advice Columnist. Or Ireland's Number One Nutcase, depending on where you fell on the political spectrum. Upon hearing her name, people either reacted with revulsion or with mirth. She wasn't in the mood to deal with either.

Seán raised his pint glass. "*Sláinte*, Orla."

"*Sláinte.*" She clinked her glass against his and returned it to the counter without taking a sip.

"What brings you to Cork?"

"Holidays," she lied. "You?"

The merriment in his eyes dimmed. "I was supposed to spend a lads' weekend with a friend from Dublin. Canceled, unfortunately."

A tourist. Excellent. Her resolve not to succumb to her libido was dwindling by the second. She stole a glance at his ring finger for a glint of metal or a telltale indent. He had neither.

"I'm guessing you hail from the same part of the country as me." He flashed a sexy half smile that made her blood hum.

"Yeah. I'm a Dubliner, born and bred." At least that part of her story was true.

He leaned back on his barstool. "What do you do, Orla?"

Discussing jobs bored Clio. *Share as little information as possible* was her motto. If people were persistent, fib. "It's the weekend. Time to forget work."

"True," he said, taking her cue with good cheer. The teasing twinkle in his eye bolstered her impression that Seán was a man with a sense of humor. The fluttery feeling in her stomach gathered pace.

"Have you seen much of Cork?" she asked.

"A fair bit. If you're interested in history, the Old Gaol's worth a look."

Clio wasn't, but Tammy would love it. "So far, I haven't been farther than the shopping district."

Strangely, the mindless small talk was a soothing distraction. There was something about Seán that relaxed her, something in his relaxed posture and easy smile that told her he wasn't a threat. Slowly but surely, her heart rate was returning to normal.

"I went on one of those hop-on, hop-off bus tours," Seán said, taking another sip of his pint. "Not usually my thing, but it was great fun."

That did sound like fun. It was something she could do with her daughter. Try to repair the broken bridge of their relationship.

Tammy. Dark memories surfaced with the viciousness of rubbing alcohol in an open wound. Clio shuddered. If she'd been more alert, more open to communication, she'd have guessed the truth about Tammy's relationship with her music teacher.

And if she'd guessed the truth, he'd never have had the opportunity to hurt her daughter. Barring the invention of a time machine, she couldn't change the past. What she knew for certain was that she would do everything—anything—to keep her daughter safe from further harm.

"Everything okay?" Seán asked, his tone laced with concern. "For a moment there, you looked haunted."

"I'm grand," she said with more determination than conviction. "Nothing to worry about." She needed to shove her daughter out of her mind, at least for tonight, but if she wanted a night of mindless small talk and mild flirtation, she had to get into character. What would a generic girl named Orla do on a Saturday night, seated next to a hot guy? Clio angled her knees oh-so-subtly in Seán's direction.

Suddenly, her mobile phone vibrated, turning the fluttering in her stomach into a churning sensation.

Clio's hand flew to her pocket. A sense of foreboding made her pause. With a trembling hand, she pulled out the phone.

Caller display confirmed her fears. Ray. *Oh, shit.* She'd have to take the call. If she ignored him, he'd phone the house. No one was home tonight, but Ray was persistent. He'd call tomorrow, and Helen might answer. Or, worse still, Tammy. The last thing Clio wanted to do was worry her daughter on the weekend before she started her new school.

"Problem?" Seán asked, brow creased.

Clio scanned the bar. It was packed. There was nowhere quiet for her to take this call. If she went back out into the lobby, she'd risk running into the security guard. Her heart thudded in her chest, and the fingers clutching her phone had pins and needles.

The phone continued to vibrate.

Shit, shit, shit.

She slid off her barstool with more speed than grace. A spiky heel caught on one of the bars, causing her to stumble.

Seán's strong hands steadied her. "You okay?"

He was close enough for her to smell his cologne. Something subtle and spicy, and a hell of a lot sexier than the heavy scents worn by most of the men in the bar. She drew in a breath, fought back tears. "I'm fine, but I have to take this call."

She turned her back on him and pressed the phone close to her ear, covering her other ear to block out the noise.

"Clio." Her former boss's voice was sweetly insidious, the high-pitched tone belying the steel underneath.

"What's up, Ray?" She moved to the end of the bar counter, well out of Seán's earshot. "Your man has the envelope. I consider our interaction at an end." *Keep calm, keep casual. That's the trick.*

"Two thousand euros doesn't even begin to cover what you owe me."

"I don't owe you *anything*. I paid you when I hired you. All I asked you to do was..." She glanced around and dropped her voice a notch. "Jesus, Ray. I didn't ask you to do what you did. Your men screwed up. Be happy with the money I've given you, because I'm not in a position to get you any more."

His hyena laugh made her jerk the phone away from her ear. "I'm not interested in money, Clio. I wanted to see if I could still make you jump when I snapped my fingers. It seems I can."

So he *had* been yanking her chain over the money. She'd suspected as much when he'd called earlier. After the risks she'd taken getting him the money at an hour's notice. If she ever had the misfortune to meet the psychotic troll in person again...She ground her teeth to stop from screaming. "What's this really about? We've established you don't need the m—contents of the envelope your man took—and I've been out of the *business* for far too long to be of any use to you on that score."

"All right," he said smoothly. "I'll get to the point. I want you to acquire a valuable antique for me."

The words hit her like a punch to the kidneys. She'd been expecting this. Of course she had. She wasn't foolish enough to think he'd let her wriggle out of his clutches without making her squirm, but she hadn't expected him to hit her up with an indecent proposal *tonight.*

"I haven't done a job in years. To say I'm rusty is an understatement. Why can't you find someone with more recent experience?" *In other words, someone skilled at cracking modern alarm systems.*

"Because you have easy access to the item in question." He paused as if to give his next words the appropriate gravitas. "Your mother's thirteenth-century leopard aquamanile. I want it."

"My mother's *what?*"

"Oh, Clio," he mocked. "Your mother went on a spending spree at a Sotheby's auction last week, didn't she?"

"She mentioned an auction, but I still don't know what item you're referring to."

"Tsk," Ray said. "That's what you get for dropping out of school. The name is self-explanatory. *Aqua* and *manos.* A vessel used to carry water for washing hands."

She heard, if not saw, the smirk. If the condescending little creep were in front of her, she'd be tempted to slap him. "Whatever that thing is, I don't know where to find it."

His laugh was a cackle, high-pitched and nasal. "I suggest you start looking. The piece is worth a quarter of a million euros."

A quarter of a million? Holy hell. She knew her mother was wealthy, but she'd no idea she was rich enough to drop that kind of cash on an ornament. "How do we do this?" Her fingers were numb around the phone. No way in hell would she go through with it. She needed to buy herself time, string him along until she figured out a way to fix this problem.

"You locate the antique and give us access to your mother's new house."

Icy-sharp cold spread through Clio's limbs, the sensation as sudden as a dive into a freezing plunge pool. This could not be happening. "If you only want one antique, why do you need to..." She trailed off, conscious of her surroundings.

"I never said I was only interested in *one* antique." She could visualize his smug smirk spreading across his wide face. "Apparently, your mother has quite the collection."

Clio gripped her mobile phone tight. Helen did have a lot of ornaments, but were they worth so much money? Well, Clio had never claimed to be an art expert, had she? "Right," she said, desperately needing to end the conversation before she lost the remaining vestiges of self-control. "I'll be in touch when I've found it."

"You'll be in touch by Sunday evening."

Ray was enjoying this. Clio could picture him sitting behind his enormous desk, smug and self-satisfied in a pinstripe suit and loafers. She wanted to scream. She wanted to rant and rave. She wanted to tell him he was a despicable weasel. But she couldn't. He held the power cards, and they both knew it.

"Fine. Talk to you soon." She cut the connection and stared blankly at the display screen. The cacophony in her ears grew louder. How was she going to get out of this pickle? Replacing the money was child's play in comparison to warding off this disaster. Shaking, she returned to her barstool.

"You still going to tell me there's nothing wrong?" Concern creased the corners of Seán's intense blue eyes. He'd rolled back his shirtsleeves, exposing strong forearms sprinkled with dark hair. He looked solid, dependable. The sort of guy Clio would consider boyfriend material if she were in a position to date.

Tears stung her eyes. For a crazy moment, she debated confessing all. Instead, she grabbed the G&T she'd ordered earlier and brought it to her mouth.

In the milliseconds before the tart liquid hit her tongue, she contemplated putting it down, walking away. She took a swig, felt the burn as the alcohol snaked its way to her stomach. Torture at its finest.

It went down far too quickly.

Seán watched her, curiosity still reflected in his eyes, but no judgment. He drained his pint and cocked an eyebrow. "Another round?"

"Yeah," she said. "Same again for me." If she was going to get wasted, she might as well do it in the company of a handsome man.

Two G&Ts later, Clio felt good. More than good. Finally, the horror of the past few months was receding, even if it was a temporary reprieve.

Seán took her hand, his fingers curling protectively around hers. With his other hand, he caressed her arm, tentatively at first, then with more pressure. Lust, hot and achy, spread lower. Her breathing was slow and steady without a hint of a wheeze.

"Do you want to get out of here?" He stroked the crook of her elbow in a movement so sensuous she almost gasped aloud. "I have a hotel room for tonight."

A hotel room. X-rated visions danced before Clio's eyes, and her heart skipped a beat. How long since she'd had sex? A year? Longer? The thought of Seán's fingers working their magic on more skin than she could expose in a public place made her shiver in anticipation.

"Well?" he prompted, looking directly into her eyes. "What do you say? If you're not interested, no worries. I can call you a taxi."

He was giving her an out, but where would a taxi take her? To her mother's empty house? She had nowhere else to go. Her skin crawled at the thought of being alone in the house and a night spent tossing and turning in terror. In contrast, the idea of a night spent in a warm bed with a gorgeous companion was seductively appealing.

"Yeah," Clio said, "why not?"

If her path to hell wasn't paved with good intentions, she'd settle for good sex.

CHAPTER FOUR

....

Orla was trouble. Seán had suspected she was trouble when he met her by the fountain, oozing sex appeal and vulnerability. He'd known she was trouble when she slid onto the barstool next to his, wafting perfume and attitude.

He had a nose for troubled females and an instinct for avoiding women encumbered by baggage. He'd bet his vinyl collection that Orla was both. What was it about her that made him throw his usual caution to the wind? The reckless, restless feeling that had been building inside him all day? Or a more primitive instinct?

His stomach somersaulted as he watched her sashay across the lobby, her spiky heels clicking against the marble floor. The subtle swing of her hips emphasized her firm, denim-clad buttocks. *Oh, boy*...Seán's mouth was dry as parchment. Since the afternoon, thoughts of Helen Havelin had intruded on his peace of mind. He needed to quash them with a sledgehammer. What better way to forget than in the arms of a sexy woman?

And Orla was sexy. She wasn't beautiful, not in the classic sense. Chin too narrow, nose too large. *But those eyes*...He let out a low whistle. They were the nearest thing to jade he'd ever seen.

One of her heels skidded on the slick marble. He reached forward and grabbed her arm, steadying her.

She turned, raised those fabulous green eyes, and his breath caught. "This is the second time you've stopped me landing on my face."

A hint of a smile teased the corners of her mouth. Her full lips were a natural dusky pink hue. He wanted to kiss them, to nip her delectable little earlobes, to explore the soft skin of her neck.

He enveloped her dainty hand in his large one, tentative but possessive. "You sure about this? If you'd rather go home, I can make arrangements."

"Getting cold feet?" Her voice was low, sultry, teasing, and—in direct contrast to her shabby clothing—flavored with an accent acquired at an exclusive private school.

"Hell, no. Merely trying to be a gentleman."

She looked him straight in the eye, chin tilted. "I'm not looking for a gentleman tonight."

*Okay...*The crotch of his trousers strained against his zipper. "In that case, let's get to my room so I can behave in an appropriately ungentlemanly manner."

Orla laughed. Her fingers intertwined with his felt oddly right.

They reached the elevator and squeezed in with a group of Italian tourists. Her body pressed up against his in the crowded space made his blood hum. His fingers lingered on her shoulders, and he had to restrain himself from touching her more than was publically acceptable. It was a challenge, even for someone as PDA averse as himself.

"Whew," said Orla as they stepped out of the lift on the third floor. "That was tight."

"Claustrophobic?" he asked with a wink.

"A little." She still wore a greenish tinge. "I'm terrified of getting stuck."

"Oh, I don't know." He let his fingers dance across her shoulders. "Being stuck might have its advantages."

"Not with half Italy as an audience."

He laughed and guided her down the corridor to his hotel room. She was a head shorter than him, even in those crazy heels. He was looking forward to removing the shoes one by one. He'd bet the wild packaging hid dainty feet.

They reached his door, and he put the key card into the slot. "Ladies first," he said when the door clicked open. He pressed the palm of his hand against the small of her back, sensed a prickle of awareness in his chest.

Orla laughed when she saw the bed. "Some room. I didn't have you pegged as the four-poster type."

"I'm not," he said. "Perk of the job, I guess." The room was impressive and way beyond his cop salary. One of the advantages of being a Guard was getting hotel accommodation at a bargain rate. The Sheldon was glad to have law enforcement on the premises, especially on weekends.

Orla turned and smiled up at him. If her eyes held a hint of mischief, those soft pink lips were tinged with sensual promise. Hopefully, he could persuade her to make good on that promise. If the sultry look she was giving him was an indicator, she would.

"Come here." He bent to claim those sexy lips. The kiss was soft, hot, and flavored with promise. She gave a little moan, slipped her arms around his back, and pulled him closer. His tongue found hers. She tasted of gin, peppermint, and something uniquely her own. Seán increased the pressure, intensifying the kiss. His breathing shifted from labored to short, sharp bursts. This felt so good. Too damn good. His hardening erection strained the front of his trousers.

He ran his hands through her long red hair, marveling at its color as it slipped through his fingers. Against his chest, he could feel her heart beating as wildly as his own. When he nipped her earlobe, she gave a little yelp. "Not good?" he asked, then trailed angel kisses down her neck to the base of her throat.

"Very good," she gasped, and her head fell back to allow him easier access to the rapidly beating pulse in her throat. "Bite me again."

"With pleasure." He retraced the route from her throat to her ear, nipped the lobe, and toyed with her loop earrings. She gave a little moan of pleasure before tugging his shirt free from his trousers and smoothing her palms up his bare torso.

It was his turn to gasp when her fingertips performed an erotic dance across his skin, slowly at first, then gathering pace. She moved her hands upward, toward his nipples. She tugged hard on his nipples, and his groan turned into a growl. "You like?" she asked with a sly smile.

"Hell, yeah." He slid his hands beneath her T-shirt, and his heart skipped a beat when he reached her bra. It was of the sports variety, plain and practical, and held her small breasts tight and taut. He toyed with the strap. He'd always had a thing for plain women's underwear. He had no objection to their lacy counterparts, but the clean lines and simplicity of a sports bra was a major turn-on.

She fumbled with his shirt buttons, and one bounced off the glass mirror.

"Steady on," he said with a laugh.

"Sorry. They're fiddly." Another button ricocheted off the mahogany dresser. "Oops."

They stumbled against the wall, him tugging up her T-shirt, her fiddling with the clasp of his belt. They might be tipsy, but their bodies knew what to do.

His belt opened, and she shifted her efforts to the button and zip. He groaned as she slid into his trousers and touched his erection through his underwear.

"Well, well," she said in a breathy voice.

Slipping her fingers through the slit of his underwear, she stroked the tender flesh beneath. Seán let out a low hiss. She slid to her knees, and his balls ached. "No," he gasped, catching her arm. "I want to kiss *you* first."

Her eyes widened, then a smile curved her full lips. "Then I'd better get naked, hadn't I?"

She took a step back and, in one fluid movement, pulled her top over her head and flung it to the side. His eyes widened, and he licked his lips. Underneath her T-shirt, as he'd ascertained during his exploration, Orla wore a black sports bra.

"Had I known I'd be stripping off for someone this evening, I'd have worn something sexier."

He shook his head. "Trust me. It doesn't get sexier than that."

Her eyes met his and held his gaze. Slowly, deliberately, she unbuttoned her jeans. She tugged them over her slim hips and down her legs.

Seán's blood pounded. Her simple Brazilian-cut knickers were as black as her bra and equally sexy. *Jaysus.* His night was getting better by the second.

Biting her bottom lip, she reached for the clasp. She slid the straps down her upper arms and revealed what lay beneath the bra.

Seán's heart rate kicked up a notch. The V of her top had given a glimpse of the barest hint of creamy cleavage, but nothing beat the real deal. Orla's small breasts were high and firm with nipples the same dusky pink as her lips.

"Well, hey," he said, his voice husky with arousal. If this was the road to temptation, Seán was pressing the accelerator.

Orla let the bra dangling from her fingers drop to the floor. Her mouth smiled an invitation.

Seán closed the distance between them, and his fingertips met silky skin. *Damn.* He was a lost man. "Lose the panties."

Her eyes widened, and her mouth opened and shut. For a moment, he thought she'd argue the point. Instead, she laughed and hooked her thumbs into the sides of her underwear. She slid the knickers over her hips and tight little bum, let them drop down her legs, then kicked them off her feet in an elegant dance.

"On the bed," he said in a growl.

This time, she didn't hesitate. She lay on the floral cover, one arm flung out to the side, the other teasing a pebbled nipple. Her breathing was low and shallow and made his pulse pound.

"And now?" she asked, her eyes cloudy with desire.

"And now," he replied, settling between her legs, "relax."

He kissed her breasts, nipping her nipples. She gasped and pulled on his hair, the fingers of her other hand tracing the vertebrae in his neck.

He kissed a path to her abdomen, then drew his tongue in an erotic circle around her navel. Her belly was perfect. Slightly rounded, but with little excess flesh, and decorated with the odd silvery stretch mark.

Seán let his tongue slide south, exploring her soft, neat curls while his fingers kneaded her firm buttocks.

She arched when he bent to tease her clit. "Oh. Oh, my," she exhaled in a breathy moan.

Her taste was a delicious mix of sweet and salty. He nibbled her clit, making her gasp.

"I want you inside me."

"Patience is a virtue."

She laughed. "I don't do virtues."

Despite her obvious impatience, she fell silent and allowed him to tease her to distraction. Her every moan made him harder, his breath more shallow. He wanted her bad.

Finally, she arched away from him. "Now I want. You. Inside. Me."

"That's more like it." He reached for the foil packet he'd had the foresight to toss on his bedside table before they'd gotten too hot and heavy and rolled a condom over his shaft.

Orla helped him position himself at her opening. She felt warm, wet, ready. He pushed inside her, relishing her slick tightness, and paused to allow her to become accustomed to his size.

She arched her hips and wrapped her legs around his waist. Seán pushed deeper and began to thrust.

It felt good. Amazingly good. Her lips parted. She licked them, and he bent to claim them in a passionate kiss.

Each movement brought him a little closer to heaven.

Orla wrapped herself tighter around him, kneading his buttocks, exploring the contours of his back. Her breathing grew rapid and shallow.

Playfully, he nipped her ear, laughed at her sharp intake of breath. Her beautiful green eyes grew cloudy before she gasped as she orgasmed. Seán kept the pressure up until the last wave receded.

"Oh, wow," she murmured against his neck. "Don't stop now."

He dropped a kiss onto her throat. "I don't intend to."

Then he ceased to think, succumbed to the rhythm and increasing pressure, until he came in an explosion of searing hot ecstasy.

Gasping, they fell back on their pillows.

"Wow," he said, discarding the condom.

"Wow, indeed." Orla rolled over and propped her head up with her elbow. She ran her fingers down his chest. "Could you be persuaded for a second round?"

He laughed. "I might be."

"Then I'd better do my best to convince you." Trailing her fingertips over his penis, she bent to take it into her mouth.

Orla's powers of persuasion proved to be most effective. Seán was on the verge of another orgasm when his phone rang.

And not just any ring, either. A particular ring designated for a particular person.

The boss.

Damnation. Seán raised his head and stilled his hands on her shoulders. He wanted to ignore the call, let it go to voice mail. Already, he felt himself deflating. A call from the super at this hour on his night off didn't herald good news.

He swore under his breath. "I'm sorry, Orla. I have to take this call."

She looked up at him, her lips forming a small O of surprise before drooping into a frown.

Her expression of hurt and disappointment was like a sucker punch to the gut. He raised himself off her, hopped off the bed, and began rooting through his trouser pockets for his phone. He wanted to hurl the damn thing against a wall.

"Don't move a muscle," he said over his shoulder with a forced grin. "I'll be back in a few minutes."

At least he hoped he'd be able to continue where he'd left off. It depended on whatever the super had to say. He stepped into the bathroom and closed the door. Finally silencing the insistent tone of Meatloaf's "Bat Out of Hell," he said, "Sir?"

"Seán?" The super's voice was grave, confirming Seán's hunch that this call wouldn't bring good news. "There was a fire at the halting site. The fire chief says it looks like arson. A couple of the Travellers are at Mercy Hospital with smoke inhalation and burns."

He let out a sharp breath. "Any leads?"

"No. The Travellers are keeping tight-lipped, as per usual. You said you were in Cork City for the weekend. Any chance you're near the hospital?"

"I'm at the Sheldon Hotel. Not far to walk."

"Then I'd like you to go by the hospital. Try to get the family to talk to you."

Seán paced the narrow parameters of the bathroom. "What makes you think I'll have more luck than the Guards on duty?"

"You're not from this part of the country. The Travelling community has less of an issue with Dubliners."

In his experience, that was debatable—as was the super's assumption about Seán's origins—but he let it roll.

He placed his fingers to his temples. "All right. My uniform is at home. You'll have to take me dressed in civvies." Then he remembered the flying buttons. "Actually, could you lend me a shirt? Mine is... buttonless."

The super laughed out loud. "Did I call at an awkward moment?"

"Yeah, sir, you did." Why the hell couldn't the super call Brian? Or Tom Doyle? They mightn't have been in the middle of hot foreplay with a gorgeous woman.

"Sorry, lad," the super said, sounding not the least bit contrite. "I'll have one of the local Guards leave a shirt for you at the reception desk."

Great, thought Seán, sitting on the hard edge of the bathtub. *They'll laugh their arses off.* "One more thing, sir," he said slowly, "I'm not exactly sober."

The super fell silent for a moment, then gave another laugh. "In that case, I'll tell the Guards to serve your shirt with an extra shot of espresso."

Ha, ha. No, he'd never live this one down.

"Seriously, Seán, I need you there. Brian's on another case, and I can't get hold of Doyle." The super pronounced Doyle's name with a snarl, making his opinion of the reserve policeman clear.

Seán massaged his temples and cursed the collapse of the Irish economy. Cuts had left the Irish police with a skeleton staff and made them reliant on reservists like Tom Doyle, some of who were next to useless. "I'll be there in ten, sir." If he sprinted, he'd make it in five.

"You sure I shouldn't send a car?"

"No need. I'm not far from Mercy University Hospital. I'll get there quick enough." The walk wouldn't make the missing buttons magically reappear on his shirt, but the cool evening air would cure him of his erotic regrets.

He hung up and went back into the bedroom. Orla was sitting on the bed, putting on her bra. She glanced up when he shut the bathroom door and started pulling on his own clothes.

"I'm sorry," he said, reaching for her bare shoulder. "I have to go."

"No need to apologize." Her casual tone was belied by her wobbly smile.

"It's work," he said, surprised by his genuine regret. "I'm..."

She pulled her T-shirt over her head. "No need to explain. Thanks for a fun evening."

Seán dropped his hand. "Right. Can I have your phone number? I'd like to invite you for dinner. Make it up to you for taking off like this."

Her face was a blank mask. "Sure." She rattled off a series of digits.

As he typed them into his contacts and pressed Save, he wondered if the number was genuine or if she was fobbing him off with a fake. "I'll call you tomorrow, once I've checked my work schedule."

Orla nodded and scrambled for her shoes. He spotted one by the door. Retrieving it, he handed it to her, their fingers brushing for an electrical instant.

The heat of sexual awareness coursed through his veins. He closed his hand around hers and dropped a kiss onto her wrist. The throb of her pulse sent a lightning bolt of arousal direct to his groin. "I'd have liked to spend the night with you, Orla. I'm sorry I have to leave."

She nodded, eyes shuttered, the flirtatious demeanor of earlier replaced by an air of awkward distraction. She tugged her hand free and scrambled for her handbag.

"Where are you staying while you're in Cork? I'll call you a taxi."

"Oh, no." Her eyes met his—calm, cool, direct. "There's no need for a taxi."

Seán frowned, his eyes sliding over her worn jeans and T-shirt to the red heels. "You have somewhere to go, right? I don't want you wandering round town this time of night. It gets rough down by the quays."

"No worries. I'll be fine." The quaver in her voice said otherwise.

He wrinkled his brow, a suspicion forming. "You didn't book accommodation before you came down to Cork?"

Her eyes darted to the side. "I was going to look for a room but then I got...distracted."

Distracted by him. She was unlikely to find a vacant bed at the Sheldon. Even if they had a spare room, it was probably more than she could afford, if her clothes were anything to go by. Hell, if they didn't discount for law enforcement officials, it was more than he could afford on a cop's salary. "Stay here," he insisted. "I doubt I'll make it back, but you're welcome to have the room in my place."

She hesitated a fraction of a second before answering. "I can't take your reservation."

"Of course you can. Knowing you're safe in a warm bed will make me feel less of a heel for taking off like this."

"Well...thank you." She tugged at neckline of her T-shirt, reminding him of the silky skin of her cleavage.

"No problem," he said, keeping his voice even. He placed the key card on the dresser. "Breakfast's included. Just drop the key at reception when you leave."

She blinked, drawing attention to the eyes that had riveted him when he'd first seen her in the hotel lobby. "Bye, Seán."

"Bye, Orla. Thanks for a fantastic evening. Hope to see you again soon. In the meantime, enjoy your stay in Cork."

He clicked the door shut.

CHAPTER FIVE

······················

CLONMORE HOUSE, BALLYBEG

C lio leaned one hip against the granite kitchen counter of her mother's new weekend home, surrounded by moving boxes and bad vibes. She downed the last dregs of cold coffee and wished her hangover to Hades. This was why she'd sworn off spirits. From now on, she was sticking to the odd glass of wine and avoiding the hard stuff.

She massaged her aching temples with her free hand and fought a wave of nausea. Last night, she'd tried to forget her crazy situation using gin and Seán as distractions. This morning, she was plagued by reality and regret.

She placed her coffee cup on the counter and squeezed her sore eyes shut. Thank goodness Seán had been kind enough to let her stay in his hotel room. To her amazement, she'd managed to sleep in until it was almost time to collect her daughter from the train station.

When she woke up, her first act had been to call Emma. She'd poured out the whole sordid story, starting with the phone call to Ray six weeks ago and its unforeseen consequences. To her credit, Emma hadn't said, "I told you so." She'd simply agreed to transfer two thousand euros from her bank account to Clio's so that

Clio could replace the cash she'd taken from her mother's safe. Emma was the best friend any woman could ask for. Plus she was a private investigator. She'd promised to try to ferret out a nugget of information Clio could use to get Ray off her back and out of her life.

Looking for a part-time job in Ballybeg hadn't been on Clio's immediate agenda. She'd been hoping to put out feelers for translation work she could do from home. However, paying back Emma meant she'd need to pick up work as soon as possible, preferably a job in a pub or a restaurant where the pay came weekly and could be augmented by tips.

In addition to finishing unpacking moving boxes, today's to-do list included figuring out a way to stall Ray over the burglary. That was going to be a lot more complicated than replacing the missing cash. *Oh, God.*

A crash jolted Clio back to the present, sudden as whiplash. Her eyes flew open.

Shards of broken glass lay scattered across the terracotta kitchen tiles, shimmering defiantly in the pale sunlight. Framed by a mountain of empty moving boxes, Helen and Tammy stood on either side of the broken vase—her mother regal in a tailored suit, her daughter channeling Marilyn Manson on a bad day.

"You stupid girl!" Helen's screech was like a banshee on acid. She dropped a small traveling case onto the kitchen floor and pointed a scarlet-lacquered talon at the slivers on the floor. "Vintage Waterford Crystal. Vin. Tage."

Tammy shrank inside her oversized shirt, shoulders hunched. Clio's stomach muscles clenched to see her daughter so nervous. Harsh memories surfaced of a childhood spent weathering Helen's glacial gibes.

"Sorry, Gran." Tammy's normally strong voice was low enough that Clio had to strain to discern her words.

"Hello to you too, Mother," Clio said dryly. "Given your mood, I take it filming in Galway didn't go well?"

Ignoring her daughter, Helen danced a five-inch heel against the hard stone floor. "Do you have to be so clumsy, Tamara?"

"I'm not clumsy." The girl crossed her arms over her thin chest and ran a nervous tongue over her braces. "Not usually. You startled me."

Helen raised a tweezed eyebrow. "This is the second item you've broken since we started unpacking. Perhaps you'd take care if they were yours. Since you and your mother are living under my roof rent-free, I suggest you pay more attention."

The girl's face crumpled.

Clio's anger hit like a blow to the abdomen, then soared in pace with her pulse. "Mother," she said, voice low but determined. "It was an accident. I'm sorry the vase got broken, but Tammy didn't smash it deliberately."

Helen peered at Clio over the top of her designer spectacles. "Deliberate or not, she should be more careful. Given the state of *you*, I'm surprised you can form a coherent thought, let alone give it voice."

Was her hangover obvious? Clio caught sight of herself in the gilded mirror by the kitchen door. *Ouch.*

Why had she downed that G&T? Not to mention the two subsequent ones? She should have resisted. She should have stayed strong. Shoulda, woulda, coulda. *Yeah, right.* "Never mind me. Stop picking on Tammy. She's worked hard unpacking boxes since we got home two hours ago." She stepped forward and reached out to give her daughter's shoulder a reassuring squeeze.

Tammy recoiled, her expression morphing from upset to resentment. "If you cared about anyone but yourself, you'd never have brought me to this dump." With a choked sob, the girl fled the kitchen. A few moments later, her bedroom door slammed.

Helen drew herself up to her full five-foot-six-inches, including heels. "The girl needs to respect her elders. You're far too lenient with her."

Clio jittered with the urge to smash every tissue-paper-wrapped piece of porcelain in the house. "While I'm grateful for the chance to start afresh in Ballybeg, I'm not prepared to let you bully me or Tammy."

Helen blinked, her haughty expression crumbling. "I'm not bullying anyone. I just want things done correctly." She paused, uncertainty marring the immobility of her usually frozen features, and then heaved a sigh. "Perhaps my reaction was a little hasty. It's been a trying weekend. Everything that could go wrong did go wrong while filming the episode of my show. A veritable case of Murphy's Law gone wild. And I was fond of that vase."

"Tammy is sorry she broke it. She can pay for a replacement out of her pocket money."

Her mother brushed invisible lint from her pencil skirt. "Don't be silly. I don't expect the child to give me her pocket money. It would take her years to pay back what the vase cost."

"She can make a token contribution at the very least." Clio placed her empty coffee cup in the dishwasher and fetched the brush and pan from underneath the sink. "I realize living together is difficult for all of us, but Tammy's recovering from a traumatic experience. She needs support, not constant criticism."

Helen's mouth hardened into a thin line. "If you'd paid more attention to where she was going and who she was seeing, none of this would have happened."

Clio's breath caught on a retort so delicious she could taste it. Her nails dug into her palms. Only the reminder she was dependent on her mother's goodwill stopped her from exploding. "Like you kept an eye on me?"

Her mother looked tired all of a sudden, her true age showing briefly beneath the careful mask of makeup. "That's precisely what I mean. I don't like to see you making the same mistakes with Tammy that I made with you."

"There's no comparison," Clio snapped, her resolution to keep her cool evaporating. "I got pregnant when I was seventeen by a younger boy. Tammy was attacked by a thirty-year-old man."

"He didn't attack her." Helen's tone was clipped, impatient. "He seduced her. Tammy says she loves him."

"I know what she says." Her voice raised a notch, wobbly with emotion. "But she's not yet fifteen. He's an adult." How obtuse could her mother be? How could she not see a major problem with a teacher persuading a minor schoolgirl to have sex?

"Be that as it may, your handling of the situation leaves much to be desired."

Hysterical laughter gurgled in Clio's throat. If only Helen knew just how much her handling of the situation left to be desired.

"I'm saying this because my reaction to your pregnancy drove you away." Her mother's tone was tired, resigned. "I don't want to see you create a rift with Tammy that takes years to heal."

"How can you compare our situation to my relationship with Tammy? I'm there for her. I'm being supportive. I haven't rejected her for making a mistake."

Helen raised an eyebrow. "Are you really there for her, though? You're very quick to dismiss her emotions. Telling her she can't possibly be in love with Trevor O'Leary isn't respecting her feelings."

"He abused her. What she thinks she feels isn't real. It can't be."

"It is to her. In any case," continued Helen with an imperious sniff, "the man is in a coma. I suppose one can consider his being mugged a sort of karmic justice."

Karmic justice delivered at the hands of Ray Greer's thugs. Clio shuddered. Violence was *not* what she'd had in mind when she'd asked Ray to scare O'Leary off. Why he'd taken it upon himself to beat the living daylights out of the man was a mystery.

The throb in Clio's head turned into a drumroll. She knelt on the floor and brushed up broken glass. A crazy impulse to tell her mother everything hovered on the tip of her tongue, but mutual trust was in short supply. *With good reason*, she thought, the image of the two thousand euros fresh in her mind. "I tried calling you yesterday," she said carefully, "but I couldn't get through."

"Oh? Did you leave a message?" Helen scrutinized her phone's display. "Or did you speak to my PA? Phoebe didn't mention your call."

"No message. It wasn't something I wanted to discuss with your assistant."

Helen lowered her gaze, and a hint of a frown line appeared on her forehead. "If this concerns Tammy's issues, I contacted the psychologist I mentioned. She'll be in touch next week."

"Thank you, but that's not what I wanted to—"

Helen's mobile phone buzzed, instantly claiming her full attention. "It's my producer. We'll talk later. In the meantime, can you finish cleaning up this mess? And maybe start unpacking the living room?" She moved toward the door, phone to her ear, heels clicking across the hard stone floor.

"I...Yeah, sure." Clio's legs were as unsteady as a building during an earthquake. *Damn.*

She leaned over and resumed clearing up the shards of glass. Why had she had an impulse to spill her guts to her mother? A few minutes of semicivil conversation couldn't erase years of mistrust. Besides, she'd soon have the money back in the safe. And, however she managed it, she'd prevent Ray and his gang from ransacking the house.

A shard of glass pierced her finger, making her wince. Crimson blood beaded at the tip. Cursing, Clio sucked it furiously, catching another sight of herself in the mirror. She looked haggard, a pitiful rendition of the fresh-faced girl of yesteryear. The stress of the past few months was taking its toll.

Clio dumped the broken glass into a plastic bag and tossed it into the bin. She straightened her spine and flexed her shoulders. Next up were the living room boxes. Clio's stomach did a flip, and her mind shifted into gear. The living room boxes were amongst the few Helen had deigned to unpack herself. Most of the valuable ornaments were in there, hence her reluctance to let Clio and Tammy near them.

Clio's heartbeat accelerated into a sprint. If Ray's coveted aquamanile was in Clonmore House, it would be in one of those boxes.

***

Seán popped a painkiller and downed it with an energy drink. After a night spent questioning taciturn relatives and sifting through the charred remains of the caravan, he was exhausted, headachy, and red-eyed, not to mention tormented by memories of a naked Orla. God, she was one sexy woman. He felt awful for running out on her. He didn't usually do follow-up dates, but he owed her one. And it would be no hardship, frankly. She was sexy, funny, great in bed. Exactly what he needed to take his mind off the job.

He eyed the mountain of paperwork on his rickety desk, topped by a cheeky Hello Kitty Post-it note courtesy of Brian Glenn. Buckets had been strategically placed to catch the drips from Ballybeg Garda Station's leaky roof. *Drip, drip, drip.*

Seán shivered and buttoned his uniform coat closed. The building's heating system had broken down yet again. In keeping with the general tone of his morning, he'd lost the coin toss with Brian to see who got the station's lone portable heater. Screw the budget. He was buying another couple of heaters to tide them over until they escaped this cesspit.

In the spring, the staff of Ballybeg Garda Station was due to move into temporary digs while this building was bulldozed and another constructed in its place. The move couldn't come soon enough for Seán.

He fingered his phone with frozen fingers. Maybe he'd send Orla a quick text message before he tackled the admin. Invite her to dinner. He typed fast and hit Send. Almost instantly, his phone pinged. *Message undeliverable.* His heart sank. He'd wondered when she'd given him the number if it was the real deal. Seán chewed the top of his pen. Perhaps he'd give her a quick call, just in case.

A tinny automated voice droned, "This number is not in service." So she *had* given him a fake number. Seriously? Okay, he'd had to cut and run, but he'd had a great time up until that point. He'd thought she had too. Ah, well. It wasn't as if he had time to spare on wining and dining a woman, however sexy she might be.

He massaged his temples and tried to focus on the mountain of paperwork on his rickety desk. *An Garda Síochána* was strapped for cash at the best of times, and at Ballybeg Garda Station, funds for office furniture were nonexistent.

At the knock on his office door, he looked up.

"Morning, Seán." Superintendent O'Riordan stood in the doorway, dapper in his police uniform, his silver-gray hair neatly combed off his broad forehead. Although he must have barely met the height requirement that had still been in place when he joined the police force forty years ago, the super's confident posture and straight back made him appear taller than he was in reality. He looked cheerful and rested. Unlike Seán, *he'd* had a full night's sleep.

"Sir," he grunted in greeting.

"That bad a night?" The super cocked a bushy gray eyebrow. "I come bearing coffee." The older man placed a tall paper cup on the desk. The tantalizing aroma of freshly brewed coffee was sufficient to bring a smile to Seán's face, however fleeting.

"Ah," he said, "the coffee smells divine. Thank you."

"I wouldn't drink the swill in the machine out front if my life depended on it." His boss gave an exaggerated shudder. "This is from the Cottage Café on Curzon Street."

Seán knew the place. It was the newest café in Ballybeg, and served a decent espresso. He took a sip of the strong black brew and sighed in appreciation.

"No news on the fire?" the super asked, sitting on the edge of the desk.

"No news," Seán said with a grimace, "and no one's talking."

"In that case, I need to borrow you for a couple of hours."

He gestured toward the stack of papers. "Much as I'd love to escape this freezing office, can't it wait, sir? I'm way behind on admin."

The super's smile widened to Cheshire cat proportions. "No, lad, it can't wait. I have a job for you."

Seán sighed and pushed his chair back from the desk. "Does this involve John-Joe Fitzgerald and an air rifle?"

The older man laughed. "No. It involves Helen Havelin and a stalker."

"A stalker?" Seán frowned. "Who'd she piss off this time?"

It was the super's turn to frown. "I don't think Ms. Havelin is in the habit of pissing people off."

Seán begged to differ but opted to keep his trap shut. This toeing-the-line business was a bitch. Facing Helen Havelin wasn't on his bucket list, especially not with a pounding headache, but he had his Dublin transfer to consider. He toyed with his cup. "At least the coffee is portable."

"Indeed it is." The super grabbed Seán's hat and scarf from the stand by the door and tossed them on the desk. "Come on, lad. Let's go."

CHAPTER SIX

....

C lio found the aquamanile in the last moving box. She kneeled on the plush carpet, staring at the copper piece in her hand. It was smaller than she'd expected and heavier than it appeared. The delicate face was exquisite, each detail lovingly carved. The copper was polished to a fine shine. The aquamanile was over eight hundred years old, yet the expression on the leopard's face was so lifelike, it could have been made yesterday.

Clio placed it on the ground with trembling hands. *A quarter of a million euros.* That amount of money could buy a person freedom.

"Are you finished unpacking?" Helen appeared in the doorway, making Clio jump. She'd changed into a figure-hugging dress and strappy sandals. Her dark red hair was pulled back into a ponytail, and her makeup was flawless. She could pass for Clio's sister. Helen claimed her youthful looks were thanks to good genes. Clio suspected they were thanks to good docs.

"Yeah, I'm finished." Clio pushed herself to her feet and positioned the aquamanile on the mantelpiece. "This was the last box."

Helen clucked her disapproval. "Not there, Cliona. Put it on the display table by the window."

Walking toward the table was akin to wading through seawater. Clio's limbs didn't seem to work as they should, and her hands refused to stop trembling.

Her mother didn't notice.

But when had Helen ever noticed when Clio was upset? She'd spent her childhood trying to connect with her mother, desperate for her attention and approval. It wasn't until she fell pregnant with Tammy that the full force of her mother's attention was turned on her—and that was with anything but approval.

Helen stood before the window, stroking the leopard aquamanile, a rare expression of contentment across her face. "A lovely piece," she said. "As soon as I saw it, I had to own it."

Clio tasted the bitter dregs of resentment. When had Helen last touched her in affection? Or Tammy? Never.

Guilt gnawed at her insides. Okay, her mother might be a pain at times, but she didn't deserve to be robbed. Not of the two thousand euros Clio had taken from the safe, and certainly not of something this valuable. She'd phone Ray and tell him they were still waiting for the rest of Helen's belongings to be delivered to Clonmore House. Anything to stall him and buy time for Emma to dig up info that Clio could use against him.

She bit back a scream of frustration. What demon had possessed her to take justice into her own hands? Why hadn't she done what everyone else had advised, namely let it go? She caught sight of the photo of a two-year-old Tammy perched on the mantelpiece, all chubby cheeks and sweet-faced innocence.

Her heart swelled. She hadn't let it go because she'd wanted to keep her daughter safe.

She took a deep breath and forced her feet into motion. Time to contact the devil himself.

***

They took the super's car, a sleek black BMW. With a cynical smile, Seán slid into the passenger side. Despite being strapped for cash, the Irish police force managed to find the money to supply its senior officers with cars befitting their rank. Seán should know. Up until last year's debacle, he'd been among them.

Ballybeg Garda Station was located on the outskirts of the town and a mere five-minute drive from Clonmore House. During the short journey, Seán stared vacantly out the car window, willing the painkiller and the caffeine to do their respective jobs. The sun was making a valiant effort to penetrate the dark cloud cover, but with limited success. Down on the beach, the red warning flags were at full mast. In addition to the heavy rain, the wind was strong today and the currents strong. Out in the foaming, crashing waves, Seán could make out two wind surfers. Suicidal eejits. Every year, there were several drownings in the bay. Most occurred while the flags were flying. They'd had two over the summer, both tourists. Why anyone would want to brave the cold February water was beyond his powers of comprehension.

74

The frost-tipped fields whizzed by as the super applied pressure to the accelerator. When they approached a set of tall, wrought iron gates, the knots in Seán's stomach unraveled to perform a jig. The super rolled down his window and spoke into a monitor. Presently, the gates creaked open, and in they drove. The tree-lined driveway meandered for a kilometer before a final curve revealed the house. Seán let out a low whistle. As country houses went, Clonmore House wasn't overly large, but it was in good nick for its age. Seán was no architectural expert, but he'd hazard a guess the place was built in the Victorian period.

His mouth twisted in a grimace. A career built on bullshit and bad advice was lucrative.

They pulled up in front of a short flight of steps. Seán stepped out onto the gravel and rolled his shoulders to release the tension. It didn't work. The super bounded up the steps and lifted the brass knocker. A sudden vision of his father made Seán falter. He squeezed his eyes shut, blocking the image, then followed his boss up the steps to the front door.

***

At the jangle of the doorbell, Clio's heart leaped. Her step faltered.

Helen peered through a gap in the lace curtains. "Oh, good. The police are here. That was quick."

"Police?" Clio's voice was barely a squeak. Her heart lurched and thudded. Had her mother noticed the missing money already? If so, why hadn't she mentioned it?

"The regional superintendent came by yesterday." Helen's face glowed with animation. "What a lovely man. I'm confident he'll take care of it for me."

"Take care of what?" Clio struggled to breathe. *Please, please, please don't mention the money.*

"I fear my Dublin stalker has found my Ballybeg address. I made the local police aware of the situation."

"What stalker?" Her voice rose to a squeak. "You never mentioned this before."

Helen sniffed. "When would I have mentioned it to you? We barely talk."

"Every time I try to talk to you, you have something more important to deal with."

Her mother raised one pencil-thin eyebrow. "Do you think this house, this lifestyle, pays for itself?"

The doorbell rang a second time.

Clio wiped dust from her T-shirt with shaky hands and blew out a breath that didn't calm her. The police might not be here about Ray, but they soon would be if she couldn't figure out a way to prevent the burglary. Would the police see guilt in her eyes? Weren't cops trained to read body language? And what was this stalker business? If her mother had mentioned having an obsessive lunatic on her trail, Clio would never have consented to bring Tammy down to Ballybeg. Her heart pounding an unsteady beat, she walked toward the front door.

With a bit of luck, the employees of Ballybeg Garda Station were clueless country bumpkins. If not, she'd have to be an incredible actress.

Two figures were visible through the stained glass paneling. The superintendent had brought a lackey. She took a deep breath, then wrenched open the door.

A handsome man of sixtyish with silver-gray hair and a friendly smile stood closest to her. Superintendent Whatsit, she assumed. Her gaze traveled to the left. The second man was taller, closer to Clio's age. She registered a muscular torso that filled the blue shirt of his uniform to perfection. Then Clio's eyes trailed up to his face.

It was Seán from last night, and he was wearing an expression of horror.

The shock was as sharp as a blow to the stomach. Of all the men she could have hooked up with, she'd gone and had sex with a Ballybeg policeman.

CHAPTER SEVEN

···

Seán's heart did a slow thump and roll. Framed by the door's ivy surround was Orla from last night. She wore a wraparound cardigan over an old T-shirt bearing the logo of a rock band, faded denim jeans, and Snoopy slippers. She looked good. More than good. And that was despite the I-want-to-kill-myself expression on her face.

But what the hell was she doing at Clonmore House?

"Ah," boomed the super's cheerful voice. "You must be Ms. Havelin's daughter."

Daughter? I had sex with Helen Havelin's daughter? The ringing in Seán's ears drowned all sound. Orla's lips moved in response to the super's question, but she might as well have been miming. It wasn't until Seán sucked air through his teeth that he realized he'd been holding his breath.

He'd known Helen Havelin had a daughter, but not in a million years would he have connected this casually dressed, makeup-free, wild-haired woman with the airbrushed celebrity who'd wrecked his parents' marriage.

Courtesy of the Irish tabloids, he was certain of one fact. The daughter's name wasn't Orla.

He stared at the woman frozen on the threshold. Her face mirrored his horror, green eyes wide, pink mouth parted. A flush crept up her shock-drained cheeks. When she bent her head, strands of silky strawberry-blond hair brushed her cheekbones, just as they had last night in a rather different situation.

Her hair was a lighter shade of red than her mother's —although in Helen's case, it was almost certainly helped by colorants.

The reminder of Helen Havelin brought a bitter taste to Seán's tongue. No wonder she'd given a false name.

"You'd better come in," said Orla-Cliona. Her voice was low, flustered. A far cry from the vivacious woman he'd seduced last night.

With leaden limbs and a leaden heart, Seán stepped inside Clonmore House.

Cliona led them through a small entrance hall then down a narrow corridor. At the end of the corridor, a door stood slightly ajar, a slit of light spilling out in an ominous glow.

Helen Havelin was in that room.

Seán's feet dragged across the slate floor. He forced oxygen into his lungs and tried to ignore the hammering in his head. If it hadn't been for that selfish bitch, his parents would still be alive.

Cliona pushed open the door, revealing a large room stuffed with art, ornaments, and fussy furniture.

Helen Havelin served as the room's centerpiece, reclining gracefully on a sofa. If memory served right, it was called a chaise longue. Why did his brain latch on to such an insignificant detail? Was his subconscious trying to distract him from focusing on the chaise longue's occupant?

"Superintendent O'Riordan. Lovely to see you again." Helen's melodious posh accent grated against Seán's nerves. To listen to her plummy tones, you'd never think she'd grown up on a farm near Cobh.

Hatred rolled over Seán in waves, and his fingernails dug wedges into his palms.

Helen swung her slim legs to the floor and rose to greet them. She shook the super's hand, holding it a moment too long for such a short acquaintance, then gestured for him to take a seat on an adjacent armchair.

With the fluidity of a robot, Seán forced one foot in front of the other and unclenched his right hand. If he didn't offer it to the woman, the super would have his hide.

He needn't have bothered. Helen kept her focus on his superior. She reclaimed her seat on the sofa, leaving Seán with an outstretched hand. If anyone else had snubbed him, he'd have been irritated. In this case, relief was his primary emotion.

Thoughts churning, he claimed the chair next to the super's.

"Cliona will get us coffee," Helen said and for the first time shifted her attention to Seán. "Or would you prefer tea, Sergeant?"

Her haughty tone and arched eyebrow dared him to ask for such a plebian beverage. He was tempted to ask for tea, just to annoy her.

"Coffee's fine." The words came out in a hoarse croak.

"Cliona?" Helen's eyebrow arched even higher.

Her daughter blinked a few times before a flush crept up her cheeks. "Oh, right. I'm on it."

Even though she'd lied to him and given him a fake phone number, Seán couldn't help but a feel a pang of sympathy for the woman as she hurried toward the door, her gait unsteady. Being landed with a harridan as a mother couldn't be easy.

The gentle sway of her hips drew attention to her firm backside, outlined by tight denim jeans. Memories of last night danced before his eyes, as tantalizing and seductive as Cliona's tipsy striptease.

The vision sent a shot of lust straight to his groin. Seán swallowed a groan. Why the hell did the sexiest woman he'd met in years have to turn out to be Helen Havelin's daughter?

***

Clio sagged against the kitchen door. Seán was a cop. And he was sitting a scant five meters from the leopard aquamanile.

His expression was unfathomable, but he recognized her. How could he not? Damn him for making that uniform look sexy. She buried her head in her hands and moaned, her red-hot cheeks burning her palms. When she was younger, she'd often used fake names and never once been caught out. Why now?

Straightening, Clio held her hands out in front of her. They wouldn't stop shaking. She clasped them together in the hope the tremors would subside, but no such luck. Grabbing a glass from the kitchen counter, she forced water down her throat.

"Why is a police car outside?"

Clio's heart leaped in her chest. "Jesus, Tammy, you scared me."

"Sorry," the girl said, not sounding the least contrite. She slouched toward the fridge, wrenched open the door, and took in its contents with a moue of distaste. "There's feck-all to eat."

"There's plenty to eat. And watch your language."

Tammy cast her mother a scornful look. All rage and bitterness were directed her way these days. However heinous Tammy might find Helen, Clio bore the brunt of her frustration. "Why are the Guards here?" the girl demanded as she extracted a carton of milk.

"Helen mentioned problems with a stalker."

Tammy's expression radiated skepticism. "Who in their right mind would want to stalk Gran? She's ancient."

Clio suppressed a smile. "She's in her sixties. Please try to get along with her. I know she can be difficult, but we are living in her house."

"Only because *you* insisted on dragging us down here. I don't see why we couldn't have stayed in Dublin. Now I'll see even less of Dad than before." Tammy unscrewed the cap and drank the milk directly from the bottle. It was an exercise in provocation. Tammy knew Clio hated it when she did that.

"Your dad isn't the best influence in the world, pet."

Tammy glared at her. "And you are?"

"I know I've made mistakes, but your father..." She trailed off. What was the point in dragging up her ex's dodgy friends and even dodgier family? For all Clio knew, calling him over the O'Leary situation instead of Ray might have been the smarter move. "We'll arrange a visit after your exams," she said, plastering a smile on her face. "How does that sound?"

"June is months away. Why can't I see Dad on my birthday?"

Clio sighed. "We've been over this before. Please let's not fight."

The girl crossed her arms over her thin chest and treated her mother to her trademark death glance. "I'm going for a walk. We're done unpacking, right?"

"I unpacked the last few boxes before the Guards arrived, but I'd rather you didn't go outside alone until we know more about this stalker story."

Her daughter raised an eyebrow in a facial expression so similar to Helen's that Clio nearly cried. "You're taking her seriously?"

"The police are here. *They're* taking her seriously." Clio grabbed the sugar bowl from the cupboard and flipped the switch on the coffee machine. "See this as your cue to catch up on schoolwork before Monday."

Tammy's belligerent expression slid back into place. "I don't want to go to that school. The principal is a snob. A sure sign the kids will be too."

"Maybe they will, maybe they won't. Regardless, you're going to be attending Glencoe College as of Monday. You might as well get used to the idea."

The girl seemed to shrink in her oversized black sweatshirt. "I'll hate it."

"If you start with that attitude, you probably will." She brushed a stray lock of hair from her daughter's face. Being a responsible adult sucked. Watching her child struggle with insecurities and depression was a painful reminder of her own teenage years. She didn't want Tammy to be miserable at her new school, but they'd already been in Ballybeg for over a week. The girl couldn't hide at home forever. "Tell you what. Why don't you brainstorm ideas for a mural on your bedroom wall, and we can start working on it next weekend. It will be a nice treat after a hard week at school." Since the move, she hadn't had time to sketch or paint. She was itching to get her hands on a brush. Plus a mother-daughter art project would do them both good.

"I'll consider it." Tammy replaced the milk in the fridge and paused as if willing herself to say something. "I'm sorry I broke the vase. Did Gran give you hell?"

"Don't worry. I told her you'd pay her something out of your pocket money."

The girl nodded. "Fair enough. I guess I'll go read in my room until the police leave."

"Happy reading, pet. I'll pop up once they're gone."

After her daughter left the kitchen, Clio finished preparing the coffee tray. Left to her own devices, Clio was fine with a packet of sugar and a milk carton, but Helen would freak if she didn't bring a sugar bowl and a milk jug.

*Helen...Ray...the police...*The tremors in her limbs returned. She had to pull herself together.

Focus. Breathe. Think.

Neither Seán nor Superintendent O'Riordan was a mind reader. They couldn't know what she'd done—or rather, what Ray's men had done. All she had to do was remain calm. Times were, she'd had a knack for turning every situation to her advantage, no matter the odds.

Since Ray and his gang had attacked O'Leary, she'd lost her nerve. Time to sharpen her mettle and kick some gangster arse.

CHAPTER EIGHT

....

Time dragged while Cliona was gone. Seán shifted uneasily in his chair, hearing the creak of antique wood. Until she'd left, he hadn't realized how Cliona's presence acted as a sandbag for his resentment toward his father's former mistress. Now she was gone, he was struggling to maintain his professional demeanor. Helen's coy banter with the super was enough to make him hurl.

His eyes roved the room—anything to avoid looking at the woman. She sure had a lot of ornaments. Most were hideous. All were expensive. She'd better have good insurance.

His gaze settled on a display table by the window. He stood to take a closer look. These pieces were older than the others. Exactly how old, Seán couldn't say, but they reminded him of stuff in a museum. He liked the little copper cat. He bent to take a closer look.

China rattled, and Seán jerked round. Cliona was back, bearing a coffee tray and looking less frazzled than before. Their eyes clashed. If this were a staring contest, she'd give him a run for his money.

"How do you take your coffee, Sergeant Mackey?" she asked, all cool efficiency.

"Black, no sugar." He stepped away from the display table and reclaimed his seat.

Cliona had long lashes, he noted while she poured his coffee. And she smelled divine. He caught another whiff of her perfume when she leaned over to give him the cup. Thank feck she was careful to avoid skin-to-skin contact during the handover. Lack of sleep had addled his wits. He couldn't afford to do something daft...like kiss her.

When everyone had a cup, the super extracted his notebook. "Now," he said, businesslike, "I've brought Sergeant Mackey up to speed on the situation, but if you could sum it up for him in your own words?"

Helen inclined her neck a fraction. She had poise, he'd give her that. She perched on the edge of the sofa, hands folded on her lap, legs crossed at the ankles, knees angled slightly left. Beside her, Cliona slouched awkwardly. She had neither the perfect symmetry of her mother's bone structure, nor her confident bearing. That must have been tough growing up.

"It began six months ago," Helen said. "I received the first in a series of poison pen letters. Nasty missives are an unfortunate byproduct of fame, and it wasn't the first time I'd been the recipient of one."

If she made a habit of shagging other people's husbands, he wasn't surprised she got hate mail. It was a wonder no one had put out a hit on her.

Now, Seán. Behave. Pushing personal bias to the side, he concentrated on doing his job.

"What makes these letters different?" the super asked.

"The sender knows a lot about my private life. They delight in sending photographs of me at the gym, out shopping, or dining with friends. They've also made reference to personal information to which few are privy."

Cliona's shoulders stiffened.

Interesting reaction. What's she hiding? Seán found his voice. "Do you think the sender is someone who knows you personally?"

Helen's hard eyes focused on him. He had the impression she was annoyed he'd had the temerity to address her without an invitation. She gave a lazy one-shoulder shrug. "I don't know, Sergeant. I'm not in the habit of socializing with psychopaths."

Seán scribbled a few notes, more to stop himself from making a sarcastic retort than to record information. "Ms. Havelin, can you think of anyone with a particular grudge against you?"

Apart from me.

She examined her red fingernails. "I've made a few enemies in my time. In my line of work, it's inevitable."

Seán's fingers stiffened around the pen. "There's no one you suspect of writing these letters?"

"No." Her answer came a fraction of a second too late.

Seán made another note.

"There's been a further development," Helen said, "hence my request that you stop by today."

Cliona's head shot up. Clearly, mother and daughter did not communicate.

"A black car keeps following me. One of those four-by-fours with tinted windows. The police in Dublin are aware of the situation. Until this morning, I'd hoped it was a coincidence and had nothing to do with the threatening letters."

Seán leaned forward, instincts alert. "What happened this morning?"

"I saw the car loitering outside the gates of Clonmore House."

"You're sure it wasn't a tourist? Checking a map?" Cliona's tone edged into frantic.

"No." Helen's headshake was emphatic. "I know that car."

"Did the Dublin police run the plate?" asked Seán.

Helen's laugh was brittle. "Yes, Sergeant Mackey. They ran *all* of them. The car has a different license plate each time. The only thing the plates have in common is that they're all fake."

Cliona reached for her coffee. Her hands trembled so much that she returned the cup to its saucer with a clatter. Was she freaked over the stalker? Or was her trepidation to do with whatever had spooked her yesterday in the hotel lobby? "Why didn't you mention this before?" she asked, looking at her mother.

"Because I didn't want to worry you," Helen's hands remained steady around her coffee cup, "and because I hoped it was yet another problem we could leave behind in Dublin."

A significant glance passed between mother and daughter. A warning? This time, Helen was the first to look away.

"What other problems?" Seán's tone was gruffer than he'd intended.

"Nothing that has any bearing on the letters." Cliona fiddled with her necklace, crossed and recrossed her legs.

Her mother said nothing. The blank mask was back in place.

Seán tapped his pen against the coffee table. After years on the force, his bollocks radar was highly tuned. These two were spooked. And they were lying through their orthodontically perfected teeth.

"If you're frightened for your safety, Ms. Havelin, why haven't you hired a bodyguard?"

"Because, Sergeant Mackey, I wasn't aware I needed one." The tight smile didn't reach her green eyes. Eyes the same shade as her daughter's, but in contrast to Cliona's expressive mood stones, Helen's were arctic.

"What's changed?" Seán asked.

The older woman darted a look at the super, then back to Seán. "I received this in this yesterday's post." She slid a cream envelope across the coffee table.

Seán retrieved a pair of rubber gloves from his pocket and put them on. The envelope was made from good quality paper, the address printed on a laser printer. There was no return address, but he hadn't expected to find one. The postmark gave him pause. Galway City.

Was the Galway postmark a coincidence? He didn't believe in coincidences.

Inside was a Catholic memorial card with a picture of Helen Havelin. The space for the date of death was filled with a question mark.

"A death threat," he murmured. Helen must have seriously pissed someone off this time. Seán showed the card to Cliona and the super.

The super's bushy brows frowned a V.

Cliona blanched. "Who'd send a death threat to Mother?"

"If I knew who, I wouldn't have called the Guards." Helen fidgeted in her seat, her perfect poise slipping. "I wasn't worried for my safety before, but I am now."

The super turned to Seán. "I'll need you and Garda Glenn to keep an eye on the house on the days Ms. Havelin is in residence."

His head jerked up. "What?" Surely he couldn't be hearing right.

"You're to watch out for Ms. Havelin when she's in Ballybeg. Escort her if she needs to go somewhere."

Seán forced his gaping jaw back into position. Surely the man wasn't serious. "May I have a word, sir? In private?"

The super gave him a hard look followed by a stiff nod. "Please excuse us for a moment, ladies."

Once they were out in the corridor, Seán shut the door and turned to his boss. "If you're expecting the staff of Ballybeg Garda Station to act as bodyguards for Helen

Havelin every weekend, how are we supposed to take care of everything else? We're short on manpower as it is."

"There's nothing else to be taken care of," the super said in a stern tone. "At least nothing of importance."

A hard ball formed in Seán's chest. "What about the fire at the halting site?"

"Probably a fight with a rival clan." The super shrugged, the Travellers' fate dismissed with one small twitch of his shoulder.

Frustration coiled in Seán's stomach. "With all due respect, sir, one of them has a nasty burn on his leg. So far, no one's actually hurt Ms. Havelin. That makes the Travellers case a priority."

"Your salary is paid by taxpayers' money, including a sizable chunk of Ms. Havelin's income." The older man's nostril's flared. "Since when did Tinkers bother to pay tax?"

Seán glared at his boss. "They're entitled to justice, sir, same as everyone else. I don't care how much tax Helen Havelin pays. It doesn't give her the right her to use the local police as her personal bodyguards."

The super's bushy eyebrows drew together, drawing attention to his frown lines. "How dare you show such disrespect?"

"Disrespect? I'm not her servant."

"No, but you are a servant of the state, and I'm your commanding officer. If I say you're to keep an eye on Ms. Havelin, then that's what you'll bloody well do."

He ran a hand through his short hair. This was insane. How dare one pampered celebrity commandeer the meager staff of Ballybeg Garda Station?

Seán fought to steady his breathing. "I'll do the guard duty, but I want to stay on the Travellers case."

The super was as prickly as nettles. "Ah, leave it, Seán. The Tinkers aren't worth the trouble."

"That's not the impression you gave when you called me on my night off."

"Bitter about not getting laid, is that it?" The veins on the super's nose pulsed an ugly red. "I've read your files. You're a good policeman. I know the attacks on the Travellers can't be tolerated, but their presence near Ballybeg is a nuisance. Whenever they stop at the damn halting site, a slew of petty crimes follows. If someone from the town is attacking them, it's in revenge."

Seán drummed his police boot against the stone tile. "I don't care how many petty crimes they've committed, sir. The fire could have been lethal."

His boss paused and then said, "If the situation escalates, we'll reassess. In the meantime, I want your priority to be protecting Ms. Havelin."

"So if one of the Travellers dies, it warrants police time? Good to know."

The super sighed, his features softening. "Helen is only in Ballybeg for two or three days each week. You'll have plenty of time to look into the attacks on the Travellers when she's away."

Seán's jaw tensed. "As you say, you're the boss. I can hardly refuse." Not while his Dublin transfer was in limbo, as the super well knew.

"Good lad." The older man's cheery smile slid back into place. "Let's rejoin the ladies."

With leaden limbs, Seán trudged after his boss. He had the distinct impression he was in for a long couple of months.

CHAPTER NINE

....

Clio sped up the drive to Tammy's new school and reviewed her Monday to-do list. The list was succinct: Find a job. Fob off a gangster. Avoid one sexy policeman. The last item would be the trickiest.

In the two days since the Ballybeg police force had been watching over Helen, she'd done her best to avoid Seán and his delectable dimples. He'd stayed at Clonmore House until late Saturday evening, and his younger colleague had taken over on Sunday. Clio heaved an internal sigh. How was she supposed to negotiate with criminals with the police underfoot? She needed a miracle. And barring divine intervention, a one-way ticket to South America.

Beside her, Tammy sat slumped in the passenger seat, shoulders hunched, eyes downcast. "Do I have to start today?"

"We've been over this. If you miss any more school, you won't be able to sit the Junior Cert exams."

"I'm going to fail them anyway. Starting today or next week won't make a shred of difference."

"Don't be defeatist. Glencoe College has an excellent reputation. The principal has made a special study plan for you, including extra tutoring in math and chemistry. If you apply yourself, you'll be fine."

If Tammy's truculent expression were any indication, the girl wasn't convinced. Frankly, neither was Clio. Tammy was intelligent but lacked discipline. She was clever at art and languages and got good grades in those subjects by putting in the minimum of effort. Math and science were "boring" and "only for nerds" so Tammy chose to ignore them. Math and science, unfortunately, didn't choose to ignore her.

The girl folded her arms across her chest and scowled. "If the other kids know I'm getting extra help, they'll make fun of me."

"I doubt you're the only student getting assistance in a particular subject. Any problems with your classmates, tell Ms. Cavendish."

Tammy snorted. "Yeah, right. Acting the tattletale is a great way to make new friends. I don't see why I couldn't stay home for another week and help you finish unpacking the house."

"This isn't up for negotiation. You're starting school today, and that's my final word on the matter." Clio eased her ancient car into the last available space. Hers was the only vehicle in the school car park that was more than two years old. She turned to her daughter and forced a smile. "Do you have everything?" Her chipper tone rang false.

Tammy rolled her heavily mascaraed eyes. "Mum, I can pack a schoolbag. I'm nearly fifteen, not five."

"Okay, pet. Best of luck at your new school." Clio reached out to touch her daughter's shoulder, but her hand froze when Tammy flinched.

"In other words, don't have sex with any of my teachers." The girl cast her mother a look of raw disdain. "Got the message. You never even *try* to understand my feelings."

Clio flinched. Tammy's words—and the memory of Helen saying something similar on Saturday—were akin to being doused with a bucket of ice water. "I do try to understand. Believe me, I know you've suffered over the past few months, but your feelings for O'Leary are in your head. You don't love him. You can't. When you're older, you'll realize that." *Damn.* She bit her tongue. It was coming out all wrong.

"Do you know how condescending you sound?" The girl's eyes flashed. "I confided in you, and you ran to the police."

Clio let out a raw sigh. "I had no choice. I couldn't not report what you'd told me."

"I told you I was in love with Trevor. Instead of supporting me, you dismissed my feelings and wrecked my life."

"Sweetheart," she said desperately. "It's like... Stockholm Syndrome."

"Oh, please don't start." The girl's hand was on the door handle. "He didn't hurt me. I seduced him, not the other way round."

Clio banged the steering wheel hard enough to send pain shooting up her right arm. "Would you listen to yourself? You're talking nonsense. A fourteen-year-old girl does not seduce a thirty-year-old man."

"But that's what happened. Why won't you believe me? Even Gran does. Why can't you?"

She blinked, startled. "You talked to Helen about Trevor?"

"Why not?" Tammy bit her lip. "Unlike you, she didn't dismiss my feelings as nonexistent."

"When did this *tête-à-tête* occur? Before or after she bawled you out for breaking her vase?" The notion that her daughter might confide in her mother over her stung.

"After." The girl shrugged. "She came up to my room, and we had a chat. She invited me to join her one weekend when she's filming her show."

"Did she indeed?" Clio experienced a stab of envy sharp enough to cause physical pain. As a teenager, she'd often asked her mother if she could accompany her to the TV studio. Helen had dismissed the idea out of hand, saying she'd get in the way. "That's great, Tammy. Did she finish off by telling you how you'll amount to nothing if you continue making unsavory associations and wasting your expensive education?"

"No." Tammy looked her straight in the eye. "She leaves that to you."

"What?" A coil of emotion twisted painfully in her stomach. "All I've said is you need a fresh start, a new environment. What's wrong with that?"

"Nothing. But every time you look at me, I see disappointment in your eyes."

Clio gave a shaky laugh. "No. The look you see is fear."

"You've nothing to be afraid of. I don't have a thing for older men, as you call it. I love Trevor."

She squeezed her eyes shut briefly and prayed for patience. "Okay. I don't want to argue with you, especially not on your first day at your new school."

"Don't you see, Mum? You're *still* not listening to me. You hear the words I say but refuse to let them penetrate."

"Tammy—" Clio began, but the girl had already opened the passenger door and climbed out of the car.

Her daughter hesitated before shutting the car door. Maybe, just maybe, she'd apologize for losing her temper. Maybe, just maybe, they'd communicate properly for the first time in months.

Instead, Tammy extracted a crumpled sheet of paper from the pocket of her school blazer and thrust it under Clio's nose. "Can you order these for me, please?"

Or maybe not.

Clio took the paper and scanned the e-mail printout with a sinking heart. "Another list of texts for your English class? How many books do they expect you to read?" Yet more money she didn't have to spare. "Why didn't you give this to me last week?"

"Because I forgot to print out the e-mail." Tammy cast her a black look and slammed the car door.

Clio winced. She gripped the steering wheel with taut fingers. Through the car window, she watched her daughter trudge over the cobblestoned courtyard and up the flight of steps leading to the ivy-framed entrance.

Glencoe College was a good school. Prestigious and way out of Clio's price range. The hefty tuition fees were part of the deal she'd made with her mother when she'd agreed to move to Ballybeg and act as Helen's housekeeper. With a bit of luck, the girl would make new friends soon, but watching Tammy's hunched shoulders, it was hard to be optimistic.

Releasing a raw sigh, Clio put the car in gear and wheezed out of the school car park. Time to spend more money she didn't have.

Fifteen minutes later, Clio reached Ballybeg. It was a pretty seaside town with a promenade above the strand, a pier stretching out toward the sea, and an array of brightly colored buildings that stood defiant against the relentless gray of the winter sky. A small square at the center of the town was notable for its imposing statue of Michael Collins, a local man and one of the leaders during Ireland's fight for independence.

In the ten days since she'd moved to the area, Clio hadn't yet had a chance to explore the town properly. Between unpacking boxes, she'd snatched a couple of opportunities to go for a quick jog, but time constraints meant she hadn't strayed too far from her mother's property.

She glanced at the clock on the dashboard. It was a few minutes before nine o'clock. Once she sorted out Tammy's book order, she'd ask around the local shops and cafés for a job.

She circled the town center a couple of times, eventually finding a parking space on the main street. Patrick Street was lively and bustling, despite the early hour. The Book Mark was located in a two-story terraced house painted bright turquoise. The old-fashioned bell jangled as Clio pushed open the door and stepped inside. It was larger than it appeared on the outside. The front room of the shop was divided into a small café on the right and a book display on the left. A smaller room to the back housed a vast array of new and used titles, and an even smaller alcove boasted an impressive selection of comics.

Clio paused before a massive display of mystery novels by a well-known Irish author and scriptwriter. The slick covers were sinister, yet subtle. She picked one up and turned it over to read the blurb on the back cover.

"Jonas O'Mahony is a local author," said a voice with a thick Cork accent. "That's the third book in his Detective Inspector Brady mystery series."

She looked up to see a small, round woman in her sixties beaming at her through owlish spectacles.

"I'm Bridie Byrne." The woman thrust a plump hand at Clio.

"I'm Clio Havelin." Bridie's handshake was warm and firm.

"Ah." The older woman nodded knowingly. "You moved into Clonmore House."

She braced herself for the inevitable mention of Helen and her fame, but it never came.

"I'm pleased it's finally got a new owner," Bridie continued. "It used to belong to my brother. He and his wife moved to Marbella a few months ago. Good riddance, I say. The house was empty for a few months until you moved in."

"The house is beautiful, as is Ballybeg. Although I haven't had a chance to see much of the town."

"Ah, sure you'll have plenty of time to explore. Have you found a job down here?"

"No," she replied, seizing upon the opening, "but I'm looking for one. Bar or restaurant work to tide me over until I build up my translation business. I'm a freelance translator for Spanish and French. I can work anywhere as long as I have access to the Internet."

"Ah, the Internet. Doing me out of business, so it is." The twinkle of mischief took the sting out of her words. "I'm nearing retirement anyway. Amazon and the like will merely push me there sooner. Is there something in particular you're wanting?"

"Yes." Clio fished in her handbag and pulled out a piece of paper. "My daughter needs these books for her English class."

The older woman pushed up her spectacles and examined the list. "We have four titles in stock. I'll have to order the others."

"No problem. When will they be in?"

"If I place the order today, they should be here on Wednesday. That soon enough for you?"

"Wednesday's fine."

"Anything for yourself? Maybe one of those mysteries?"

Tempting. Clio fingered an embossed cover, tracing the outline of a pistol. How long had it been since she'd last read a book? Before she'd had Tammy, she'd read a book a day, easily. These days, she was lucky to manage a book a month. The move from Spain back to Ireland had forced her to offload most of her paperbacks, and the few books Helen owned that weren't fancy coffee-table books were on her digital reader. Clio's finances wouldn't stretch to a decent smartphone, never mind a dedicated digital reading device.

"Are you doing the hard sell, Bridie?" asked a voice in the background. "Jonas will be pleased." A woman bearing a large plastic container of baked goods backed into the shop. She had rich red hair and blue eyes that twinkled with good humor.

Bridie helped her heave the box onto the counter. "Now that you're both part of the family, I have to look out for your interests."

The red-haired woman flashed a grin at Clio. "Jonas is my husband."

Clio whistled. "Lucky you. I've seen him interviewed on television."

"I'm Olivia, by the way," the redhead said. "You're new in town." It was phrased as a statement, not a question.

"That's right. We've just moved into Clonmore House."

Olivia looked her up and down in frank assessment. "You don't much look like your mother. Apart from the hair."

"That's what people tell me." In comparison to Helen's polished beauty, Clio was plain and drab.

"Know many people around here?" Olivia asked.

She shook her head. "I haven't had a chance to explore the town yet. We're still getting the house sorted after the move."

"Come by MacCarthy's pub on Friday evening. I'll introduce you round."

"Oh, thanks." She blinked, unused to such ready amiability. "I might do that." She shouldn't be planning a night out when she had more pressing concerns. Concerns that included how to dig up dirt on one of Dublin's most notorious—and elusive—gangsters. *Oh, hell.* She'd have to phone Emma later to see if she had any news.

"I'm usually at the pub by eight," Olivia said, unpacking the baked goods into Bridie's food display cabinet.

On the other hand, it *would* be nice to hang out with someone around her age and chat about meaningless stuff. It wasn't as if she knew Olivia. They wouldn't have to dwell on the more unpleasant parts of the past few months. "Okay. Sounds good. Thanks for the invitation."

"We redheads have to stick together." Olivia winked and unloaded the last of the scones and then packed up her stuff. "That's everything, Bridie. Will I see you and Granddad later?"

"Yes, love. I'll give you a call before we arrive."

Olivia strode to the door, clutching the now-empty plastic container. "Bye, Clio," she said over her shoulder. "Nice to meet you."

"Nice to meet you too. See you on Friday."

"Speaking of MacCarthy's," Bridie said after Olivia left the shop, "you might ask them if they're hiring. I have a notion Sharon, my assistant, said they were short-staffed."

Clio glanced at her watch. Nine-thirty. "It's too early for them to be open yet. I'll call round later. Thanks for the tip. Where is the pub?"

"Just off the main square." Bridie pointed through the shop window. "See the statue of Michael Collins in front of the town hall? Take the lane to the left of the statue.

MacCarthy's is down there, right beside the betting shop. You can't miss it."

"Thanks. I appreciate the tip."

The older woman popped a mystery novel from the display into the plastic bag containing Tammy's books and handed it to Clio. "This is the first book in the DI Brady series."

"Oh, I can't..."

"It's on the house." Bridie shoved her half-moon spectacles back into place and indicated the piece of paper on which Tammy had listed her required reading texts. "With a book list this long, you'll be a valued customer."

"Well, thank you. I appreciate it. I'll be back on Wednesday to collect the rest of the books."

"See you then. Best of luck with your job hunt."

"Thanks, Bridie." She turned and headed in the direction of the shop door. When her phone beeped to indicate an incoming message, her heart lodged in her throat. *Ray? Please, no.*

With trembling fingers, she withdrew her phone from her pocket with one hand and opened the shop door with the other.

And walked straight into a very broad and very masculine chest.

CHAPTER TEN

....

Seán froze the moment Cliona Havelin crashed into his chest. Without Friday night's heels, the top of her head didn't even reach his shoulders. The sound of her books hitting the wooden floor jolted them into motion. She sprang back as if he'd electrocuted her, and he bent to retrieve the book bag. When he pressed the bag into her hand, his fingers brushed hers, just as they had when he'd helped her with her bag in front of the hotel fountain. A spark of awareness crackled and fizzed. Memories of her high, firm breasts made his mouth dry with desire, and his heart beat an uneven rhythm.

"Thanks," she murmured, averting those fabulous green eyes.

"Everything all right at Clonmore House?" he asked sotto voce. "No more sightings of strange black vehicles?"

A hint of a smile tugged at the sides of her mouth. "No, Sergeant. I'm not certain I buy that story. I suspect my mother was freaked by the memorial card and is now imagining potential threats everywhere."

"Perhaps," he mused, "but we're looking into suspicious black cars all the same. And please call me Seán."

Her eyes met his, intensifying the electric current between them. "I'm Clio. Only my mother calls me Cliona."

"Clio is a nice name." Far nicer than Orla. Why had she used a pseudonym? Was it because she disliked her mother and wished to ditch her famous surname? Distancing oneself from the past was a habit with which he was familiar. Problem was, his past had caught up with him.

Brian cleared his throat and edged past Seán into the shop. "Morning, ladies," he said, smiling at Clio before turning his attention to Bridie, who was busy unloading the dishwasher in the shop's tiny kitchen.

"Hello, lads." The bookshop's owner came forward to shake their hands. "Thanks for coming by so quickly. Can I offer you a cuppa and a bite to eat while we chat?"

Coffee sounded great to Seán. "I'll have an espresso."

"Black tea for me." Brian stared at the sweet treats with a look of unfiltered lust.

"With one of Olivia's berry scones?" Bridie grinned at him. "Go on. You know you want one."

The young policeman returned her smile. "As long as it's served with clotted cream."

"That can be arranged," Bridie said and maneuvered her bulk behind the counter of the small café.

Seán turned back to Clio. "How's Tammy? First day at her new school, right?"

She bristled, suddenly prickly as a porcupine. "She mentioned that to you?"

"Yeah. She made me a coffee when I was at Clonmore House on Saturday night, and we had a chat."

Clio stiffened, her expression morphing from surprise to barely concealed fury. "I don't like strange men talking to my daughter. If you're going to be hanging around the house babysitting my mother, I'd prefer it if you and your colleagues kept your distance from Tammy."

What the feck? Seán exchanged a loaded look with Brian. Tammy was a kid, for cripes sake. Did she think they were sexual deviants? "I meant no harm. She offered me coffee, and I accepted. I thought it might make her feel less awkward having me in the house."

"Just...just stay away from her." Clio backed out the door, eyes blazing. "And stay away from me too."

"What was all that?" Brian asked after the door shut behind her. "Does she think we're pervs?"

Jaw gaping, Seán stared through the shop window at Clio's rapidly retreating form. Did she seriously think he was sexually interested in a fourteen-year-old girl? Tammy was still a kid, for heaven's sake, complete with braces and adolescent awkwardness. She'd be a beauty when she grew into herself, but that wouldn't be for another few years. He cleared his throat and addressed his partner. "It certainly sounded like Clio was accusing me of behaving inappropriately with her daughter."

"That's going to make our time in Clonmore House a barrel of laughs." Brian scrunched up his nose. "Helen

Havelin is a snob. Up until a minute ago, I'd have said her daughter was much friendlier."

"So would I." Clio's outburst stung him to the core. Why did she think he or Brian would hurt her daughter? She'd seemed on edge since the moment he'd met her, but her sudden flare of temper didn't make sense.

Bridie bustled out of the tiny kitchen with a tray bearing three cups and plates laden with berry scones and ramekins of clotted cream. "I couldn't help but overhear that exchange. There's something odd about the Havelins. I can't imagine Clio and her daughter moved in with her bitch of a mother by choice. Helen was always a pain in the arse. I had to sit beside her in class, back in the days when she was plain old Helen McMahon."

Seán's eyebrows shot up. "You went to school with Helen Havelin?"

"Don't look shocked, Sergeant Mackey." Bridie's eyes twinkled over the rims of her half moon spectacles. "I laughed myself silly when the glossy magazines printed photos from her fiftieth birthday party the same year I celebrated my sixtieth. It's amazing what nips, tucks, and fillers can do, not to mention ruthlessly erasing your past."

Seán stiffened and eyed her with suspicion. Was she dropping a hint that she'd rumbled his revisionist history? He shifted in his seat. Of course she knew. There was very little about Ballybeg and its inhabitants that escaped Bridie.

The older woman's expression gave nothing away. "Helen's daughter looks a lot like she did before she wrecked her face with all the cosmetic procedures," she said. "Pretty girl. I noticed you checking her out, Sergeant."

"None of your matchmaking, Bridie," he said with a dry laugh. "You can be content with setting Brian up with Sharon."

"Hey," his younger colleague protested, "we managed that all by ourselves."

Bridie gave Seán a sly wink and settled her large frame onto a chair at one of the tables in the Book Mark's small café. "Come on and drink up before it gets cold."

He took a seat across from Brian and Bridie. The smell of freshly brewed coffee was divine. "You'd better tell us what's been happening with the thefts."

The woman took a sip of tea and peered at them over her half-moon spectacles. "As I mentioned on the phone, someone has been helping themselves to our tip jar. It's not an enormous amount of money, and I generally let Sharon keep all the tips from her shifts, even if I'm also working. Regardless of the amount in the tip jar, it's the principle of the thing. I don't like someone coming into my shop and stealing from me and my employee."

"Do you have any idea who's responsible?"

The corners of her mouth drooped. "It's happened twice since Christmas, but on two different days. The only thing the days had in common was that groups of school kids came in to order books. Also—" She hesitated.

"Yes?" Seán prompted.

"A couple of Traveller kids came in to root through the used book section. I don't like pointing fingers, but this sort of thing hasn't happened to me before."

He sighed. Unfortunately, it was true that Travellers were often caught stealing. They had a different conception of property and possessions than settled folk. Despite the television documentaries portraying the Traveller community as wealthy gangsters, many families led a fairly hand-to-mouth existence.

"Do you know their names?" Brian asked, pen poised and notebook at the ready.

"I've a notion the boy was called Jimmy. I don't know the girl's name."

"What about the school kids?" Seán prompted. "Which schools were they from?"

"A few were wearing Glencoe College uniforms. I recognized James Jobson and Kyle Dunne. I don't want them to be involved, as you can understand."

Seán nodded. Bridie's recent marriage to Kyle's grandfather would make accusing him of shoplifting rather awkward. "Anyone else you recognized?"

"There were a couple of girls from Sacred Heart, as well as Jenny Cotter and Roisin Quirke from Glencoe College. There was another girl not in uniform. I'd never seen her before."

"Would you consider installing security cameras?"

Bridie laughed. "For a little country bookshop? Those cameras don't come cheap."

"All right. We'll ask around, but my hopes aren't high. We have no evidence that either the school kids or the Travellers were involved."

"I understand, but I wanted to report it all the same."

"You were right to do so." Seán drained his coffee cup and stood. "If you have any further problems, please let us know."

"I will. Thanks for coming round."

Outside on the pavement, a brisk wind propelled Brian and Seán down the street toward their car. He'd used his free day yesterday to reflect on his inner turmoil at being faced with seeing Helen Havelin on a regular basis. She was more the personification of what had happened to his family rather than the real problem. He knew this, same as he recognized that blaming her was irrational. Unfortunately, years of pent-up loathing every time he saw her face on the television was difficult to delete. He exhaled a sigh. Yet another reason to solve the Travellers case and push for a transfer. The sooner he left this damn town and all its dark memories behind him, the better.

CHAPTER ELEVEN

···

If Clio heard "It's off season" or "We only hire locals" one more time, she'd scream. After leaving the bookshop, she'd trudged around Ballybeg in the rain, clutching a folder containing crisply printed copies of her C.V. She'd asked in all the shops, cafés, and restaurants if they needed part-time staff, but none did. The one restaurant manager who deigned to look at her C.V. had sniffed in disapproval. "A cocktail bar? We don't serve cocktails here. Can't think of anywhere in Ballybeg that does."

"I can serve more than cocktails. I have restaurant experience too."

"Yes," the manager said significantly, "in a Michelin-star restaurant in Barcelona. A bit fancy for us. We serve burgers."

"Do you know anyone who's hiring staff?"

The man shrugged, already turning away. "You could try MacCarthy's."

The same place Bridie had suggested earlier. Clio checked her watch. The pub would be open by now. She'd head back toward the town square and try her luck.

Outside the restaurant, the wind had picked up force and the rain fell in heavy sheets. Clio pulled up the hood of her raincoat and ventured out into the elements.

Unfortunately, the hood was no match against the driving wind. At this rate, she'd be soaked before she'd walked five meters. Why hadn't she tied her hair back this morning? It would look like a bird's nest by the time she got to the pub.

A police car was parked near the town square. Seán Mackey leaned against the side of the vehicle, muscular arms folded languidly across his chest, laughter on his lips as he chatted to a blonde in her early twenties. The woman wore a faux fur coat over a green sequined top. Her umbrella was patterned with wild polka dots. Judging by her towering heels, she'd consider Clio's fancy-dress scarlet stilettos everyday footwear.

A pang of an emotion she couldn't pinpoint pricked her conscience. Was it...envy? She wasn't by nature a jealous person, and certainly not when it came to men. She'd learned the hard way not to depend on them to stick around. "Use them, then lose them" was her motto. Which meant feeling the stirrings of envy over a guy she'd had a one-night stand with was absurd, especially when she'd flown off the handle at him in the bookshop. Clio swallowed a sigh. Her impulse to panic every time she sensed a potential threat to Tammy was out of control.

She was on the verge of continuing her wet journey to the pub when the younger policeman—Garda Glenn, if she recalled correctly—strode out of the supermarket with a small plastic bag in his hand. His face lit up when he caught sight of the blonde and he caught her up in a hug, followed by a passionate kiss. Ah...so Seán was being friendly to his partner's girlfriend, not flirting. The thought shouldn't have come as a relief, yet it did. She was being ridiculous, but she hated feeling drawn to Seán.

Clio swallowed past the lump in her throat and shifted her weight from one leg to the other. She'd overreacted in the bookshop. She felt bad for snapping at Seán. It wasn't his fault that she was paranoid at the moment with regard to Tammy and older men. If they were going to be seeing one another regularly until her mother's stalker nonsense blew over, she'd need to rein it in. Hovering on the edge of the pavement, she contemplated crossing the street to apologize. However, he and Glenn got into their car, waved to the woman she presumed was Glenn's girlfriend, and drove off.

After the car disappeared around a corner, she pulled her coat tight around her chest and plunged down the side street to the left of the Michael Collin's statue.

Sure enough, MacCarthy's pub was next to a betting shop. The green paint on the walls looked recent, as did the varnish on the heavy wooden door. The sign in the window was succinct and to the point. "Help wanted. If you're literate, numerate, and semiclean, ask for Marcella." Clio laughed out loud, the first proper laugh she'd had since the odious Ray had destroyed her dreams of a fresh start in Ballybeg.

A poster on the pub's front door featured an older man with Elvis hair crooning into a microphone while wearing what looked like a pair of swim trunks and goggles. All in all, MacCarthy's sounded like Clio's kind of joint. She glanced at her watch. Just opening time. She pushed open the heavy wooden door and stepped inside.

The pub was deserted save for two older men standing sentry at either end of the bar. The counter was the old-fashioned kind, polished wood that gleamed even in the dim light. The walls were decorated with old Guinness posters and Midleton whiskey ads, along with pictures of Ireland's Republican heroes—men and women who'd fought in various uprisings in Ireland's long struggle to gain independence from Britain.

A large woman with wild, spiky hair stood behind the bar pulling a pint. She did it slowly, holding the glass at an angle and letting the foam settle before adding more liquid to the glass.

Clio approached the counter. "I'm looking for Marcella."

"You've found her." The woman shoved the pint glass toward one of the customers and gave Clio a once-over. The neutral expression on her face gave little away. "Are you here about the job?"

"Yes. I'm looking for part-time work for the next few months."

"Hmm. Any experience?"

"I haven't done bar work in a while, but I made cocktails at a club in Barcelona for several years and waited tables at a tapas bar before that." She deliberately failed to mention the Michelin-star restaurant. If Marcella wanted to familiarize herself with the full list of Clio's previous jobs, she could read the C.V.

"As you see, we're nothing fancy. Just your average country pub."

A pretty nice country pub from what Clio could tell. The furniture and deco gave the impression of a recent renovation. "I don't need fancy. Do you serve food?"

"Yeah. I take care of all the cooking. We have two hot meal options during the winter, plus snacks. I do a proper menu during the tourist season."

"So you'd need me to serve those as well? I can cook, too, if you're into Spanish cuisine."

Marcella gave a wry grin. "Most of the locals are happy with traditional Irish fare, and it's what the tourists expect."

"They wouldn't go for tapas?"

"The tourists might, but"—Marcella jerked a thumb at her elderly customers—"the only thing this crowd wants on tap is stout."

Clio beamed. "I can cope with that."

"Do you have a resume?"

Clio rooted through her handbag and slid a piece of paper across the counter.

The other woman blinked at the resume, then stared at Clio. "You're Helen Havelin's daughter. Why do you want a job pulling pints? More to the point, why do you *need* a job in a pub?"

For the millionth time since she'd returned to Ireland, Clio cursed her unusual surname. It had never been an issue while she'd lived in Spain.

"News always travels fast in a small town," Marcella said, giving her a knowing look. "A celebrity and her family moving here is prize gossip."

Clio laughed. "And I thought my neighbors in Spain were nosy!"

"Speaking of nosiness, you didn't answer my question. Why would Helen Havelin's daughter need to work in a pub?"

"Because I'm Helen Havelin's *daughter*, n o t *Helen Havelin*." She paused, debating how much she should reveal. Marcella's direct gaze demanded honesty—or at least an explanation that stuck close to the truth. "For reasons I'd rather not get into, my daughter and I needed a fresh start. In return for room and board, I'm acting as my mother's housekeeper while she's away during the week, but I still need to earn money on the side." And sooner rather than later if she wanted to pay Emma back before the spring, not to mention saving enough money to escape Ireland—and Ray Greer—for good.

Marcella nodded, clearly satisfied with, or at least accepting of, Clio's abridged version of events. "How many hours a week do you want to work?"

"I clean Clonmore House every morning until lunchtime, but I'm free after that."

"I'm looking for someone who can work the odd lunch hour in addition to evening shifts."

"I can make that happen." It would mean getting up earlier to get all the cleaning taken care of, but she'd manage. Thank feck Helen had had the good sense to hire a gardener—Clio and plants were not a good mix.

Marcella returned her attention to the resume. "Not much call for cocktails in Ballybeg."

"So I've been informed."

Marcella raised a questioning eyebrow.

"I asked around the town for jobs. The manager of the Chew and Chat burger restaurant indicated that cocktails weren't popular around here."

"Jim Green?" Marcella snorted. "The man is a prick. Big fish, little pond, entrenched opinions. Just to piss Jim off, why don't we try a cocktail hour as an experiment? Anyone in Ballybeg who wants something fancier than a pint or a glass of vino has to go all the way to Cork City."

"Sounds like a fantastic idea. We could offer a few options to start with and focus on drinks that use ingredients you'd likely have in stock in any case."

"All right. I'll need to talk to my brother first though. He's the owner and manager."

"How many people work here?"

"Mostly it's just me and Ruairí. Our sister, Sharon, does a couple of shifts a week, as does our brother, Shea. We don't usually need to hire extra staff unless it's for a one-off event, but Ruairí's wife is in the third trimester and on medically ordered bed rest. He's trying to juggle work with looking after her, and I've started a part-time cookery course. We need someone to pick up the slack."

"If you're willing to give me a chance, I'd be delighted to be that someone."

Marcella grinned. "I'm leaning toward it. Now for the crucial question. Can you pull a decent pint of the black stuff?"

"No," Clio said frankly, eyeing the Guinness taps, "but I can learn."

"In that case"—Marcella lifted the counter flap and ushered her through—"there's no time like the present."

CHAPTER TWELVE

B y lunchtime, the sweat was rolling off Clio. She was making a balls of her trial shift, that was for sure. At this rate, she'd be fired before she got hired. The sight of Seán Mackey striding into the pub didn't exactly elevate her mood. Her stomach twisted painfully. She needed to apologize to him for lashing out earlier. It wasn't his fault she was paranoid at the moment.

He stopped short at the counter, his eyes widening in surprise. "Hey. I didn't expect to see you behind the counter."

"New job." Clio threw a furtive glance over her shoulder to where Marcella's brother, Ruairí, was pulling a pint. "At least, I hope it will be my new job. Listen, Seán…" She hesitated for a second. "I'm sorry for snapping at you earlier. It's not your fault I'm sensitive where Tammy is concerned. She's…vulnerable at the moment, and I have a tendency to be overprotective as a result."

He stared at her for a moment, curiosity writ wide across his handsome face. Her breath caught in anticipation of the inevitable questions she didn't want to answer. And then he beamed—a warm, comforting smile that turned the cramping in her stomach into butterflies. "No worries," he said in his deep bass. "If you say Tammy is vulnerable, I'll tread carefully around her. I'll make certain Garda Glenn and the reserves know to do the same."

"It's—" She broke off, quelling the impulse to elaborate. "It's a long story. Anyway, I overreacted at the bookshop."

"No worries. I'm sure having us hanging around the house every weekend isn't ideal."

She choked back an hysterical laugh. He had no idea *how* awkward it was going to be. "I'm sure we'll manage."

His gaze meandered to the pint glass in her hand. "How's the new job going?"

"It's going." Clio pushed a runaway lock of hair behind one ear and gave a rueful smile. "Did you want to place an order?"

"Yeah." He perused the chalkboard menu behind her shoulder. "I'll take the cottage pie and a mineral water."

Further down the bar counter, John-Joe raised his pint glass in greeting. "Hey there, lad. Aren't you going to say hello to me?"

Seán's expression underwent a series of slow-motion changes, starting with surprise, morphing into pain, and ending with a shuttered reserve. His reaction to the older man was both strange and strangely intense. "Hi," he muttered before nodding to Clio and retreating to a table near the door.

How odd. "Not your greatest fan, John-Joe?"

A pained look flickered over the older man's fleshy features. He took a deep drink from his pint glass before responding. "He used to like me well enough when he was a boy. Times changed."

Clio blinked. How had John-Joe known Seán when he was a kid? Hadn't Garda Glenn said that Seán had moved to Ballybeg last year? His accent certainly held no trace of Cork. *Interesting...*

The next quarter of an hour flew by in a flurry of pints and food trays from the kitchen. When she brought Seán his order, he was flipping through one of the pub's copies of the local newspaper.

"Any news on your mother's stalker?" he asked, putting the paper down and picking up his cutlery.

She shook her head. "I'm becoming more and more convinced that she imagined the whole thing."

Seán paused, forkful of cottage pie halfway to his mouth. "She didn't imagine the memorial card."

"True, but the story seems farfetched. I know she has a few rivals at the TV station, but most people regard her as a has-been."

"Out of touch with the times?" The corners of his mouth twitched.

"Out of touch with reality."

"Not much support for conservative Catholicism these days," he said in a dry tone. "Not after all the Church scandals."

"No. I don't know how much my mother believes in it all, to be honest, but her old-fashioned slant on topical issues is the basis of her career." It certainly hadn't prevented Helen from having affairs, she thought cynically. Not that her stepfather had been a saint, either. If she were the marrying kind, theirs wasn't the sort of marriage she would want to emulate. Picking up the empty tray, she said, "Enjoy your meal. I'd better get back to the kitchen to collect more orders from Marcella."

She turned to walk back to the bar, and her stomach lurched. A big, burly man lacking a discernible neck slid onto a bar stool and ordered a pint from Ruairí.

He spoke not a word and barely touched his drink. His eyes were trained on Clio. She could feel their menace as she moved around the pub, taking and delivering lunch orders with shaking hands. She didn't recognize his face but she didn't need to. He had to be one of Ray's enforcers. His presence in Ballybeg could only mean one thing: bad news.

Heart pounding, she glanced at her latest drinks order. The tonic water was located in a small fridge underneath the counter—directly beneath where No-Neck was sitting. Taking a deep breath, she kept her eyes down and crouched to open the fridge. When she stood, he grabbed her arm.

"Hello, Clio." Mr. No-Neck's fingers dug into her forearm, making her grateful for the thin pullover that prevented him from touching her skin.

She tried to pull free from his grasp, but he held tight. "What do you want?" she asked in a shaky voice.

His teeth-baring sneer made her pulse pound. "Just checking up on you. My boss was wondering how you're doing."

With a quick wrench, she disentangled herself from his grasp. "As you see, I'm doing." She lowered her voice to a harsh whisper. "You can tell your boss he'll hear from me soon. If he wants this job done properly, he'd better stop breathing down my neck. I told him I'd be in touch when I had news." With a bit of luck, Emma would dig up something useful soon. Her latest text message hadn't been promising though.

"Is there a problem, Clio?"

She spun round at the sound of the deep, gravelly voice. Seán was eyeing No-Neck with suspicion.

"Nothing I can't handle." She forced a smile, aware that her wobbly tone was not giving the firm and confident impression she wanted to exude.

No-Neck took out his wallet and placed coins on the counter. "Keep the change." Although he'd lost the sneer, his threat-laced tone sent an icy trickle of fear down her spine.

Neither she nor Seán spoke until the pub door closed behind the man.

He raised an eyebrow. "Still going to tell me nothing's the matter?"

"Yep." She busied herself with swiping a cleaning cloth over the counter, avoiding eye contact.

"Looked to me like that man was threatening you."

She tossed the cloth into the laundry bag beneath the counter and straightened. "You've been assigned to guard my mother against a stalker who may or may not exist. Your duties don't extend to me."

He leaned closer, near enough for her to catch the spicy scent of his aftershave. A shiver of awareness shook her like a tremor. "That's where you're wrong, Clio. My duties extend to everyone who falls under the jurisdiction of Ballybeg Garda Station."

"I don't need protecting," she whispered.

"You sure about that?" His warm breath tickled her neck, making her nipples pebble.

Taking a steady breath, she gripped the edge of the counter. "I can look after myself."

"What are you running from?" He'd dropped his voice to a low rumble, presumably so that other customers wouldn't overhear. "Why are you back living under your mother's roof?"

Her eyes flew to meet his, brimming with fire. "What do you know about my life?"

He stared back at her, a determined tilt to his jaw. "Enough to know you're not at Clonmore House willingly."

For a moment, panic froze her tongue. Did he know what had happened in Dublin? About her accusations against O'Leary? Or even worse, what Ray had done to him?

No, he couldn't possibly know anything. She needed to get a grip and control her reactions, or she'd truly ignite his suspicions.

"What's so strange in me taking a job as my mother's housekeeper?" she parried. "The job market in Dublin isn't exactly booming." This, at least, was true. "I agree that living with Helen isn't ideal, but I have a daughter to support. I swallowed my pride and accepted my mother's offer of a home and a job."

The corners of his mouth twitched. "How's it working out for you?"

"I'm sending my daughter to a good school, and we have food on the table and a roof over our heads. I'd say it's working out fine." *For now, at least.*

He toyed with a beer mat, flipping it deftly between his fingers. "You planning on living at Clonmore House long term?"

"Define 'long term.' Once I have money saved, I'll look for a place of our own."

"Not in Ballybeg?" he asked in surprise.

"I don't know. I'm not keen on Cork, but I'm reluctant to force Tammy to move schools again."

Seán returned the beer mat to the counter. His gaze was direct, its intensity riveting her in place. "If something's bothering you, you can talk to me. On or off the record."

"Thank you," she said, touched by his sincerity.

"I'd better get back on the beat." He pushed back from the counter and replaced his police hat. Normally she

didn't like hats on men—or uniforms, for that matter—
but Seán wore his police blues to perfection. "See you
soon, Clio. Good luck with the job, and remember what I
said."

"Bye, Seán."

He strode toward the exit—strong, sexy, dependable.

Ruairí appeared at her shoulder. "Hey, Clio. Marcella
needs you to collect food from the kitchen. You gonna
serve my customers or stand here flirting?"

"I wasn't flirting, I was..." Her cheeks grew warm.
"Sorry, I'm on it."

"Steady on, kid." The big man grinned, lessening the
harshness of his strong, uncompromising features. "I
was teasing you. You did well today. If you want the job,
it's yours."

"Thanks, Ruairí. I won't let you down." She released a
breath, and her shoulders sagged with relief. Thank
goodness. She'd be able to pay Emma back soon. Now if
only finding a solution to the Ray situation were so
simple.

CHAPTER THIRTEEN

....

B y Thursday, Clio had worked three shifts at the pub and was becoming a passable pint-puller. John-Joe Fitzgerald—one of the pub's most faithful customers—took a cautious sip from his glass. "Not bad. Not bad at all. Much better than the shite you served me on Tuesday."

Clio laughed. "High praise indeed, coming from such an experienced Guinness drinker."

The man patted his considerable beer gut. "Given the amount of time and money I've invested in the company over the years, they ought to give me shares."

"Do you do anything besides drinking pints?" Clio asked, polishing glasses with a cloth and arranging them neatly on a shelf. "You've been in here every shift I've worked so far."

"I'm an entertainer." He jerked a thumb at a poster on the wall—the same one she'd observed on the day she'd first visited the pub. "I cover Elvis songs and dance."

"*You're* the Swimming Elvis?" A vision of a half-naked John-Joe performing "Jailhouse Rock" sprang to mind. *Ugh.* She reached for the mental eye bleach.

The man beamed with pride. "That's me. I was a champion swimmer in my youth and sang at all the best clubs. These days, business ain't as rosy as it once was, but I still get the odd gig."

Right. Clio gave an internal shudder. That was one act she'd pay good money *not* to see.

Ruairí emerged from the kitchen carrying a tray laden with soup and thickly cut soda bread. He seemed like a nice bloke, albeit gruff and not particularly inclined to chat. Clio put it down to stress about his pregnant wife.

"How's it going?" he asked when he returned from serving the food. "Did you figure out the cash register yet?"

"Yeah. Marcella showed me all the programs yesterday."

The man nodded, distracted by the beep of an incoming text message. A frown line formed in the center of his brow when he scanned his phone's display. "I need to get home. Jayme's not feeling well. I'll call Sharon to cover for me, but I don't know how long it'll take for her to get here. Can you manage on your own until then? Marcella prepared most of the food before she left for her course. All you need to do is warm it up."

"I'll be fine. I hope your wife is okay."

Tension oozed from his every pore. "So do I."

Soon after Ruairí left, the lunchtime rush began in earnest. Being in the heart of Ballybeg, MacCarthy's did a roaring trade with workers from nearby shops and offices looking for a quick bite to eat. Everyone wanted food and a drink, and everyone wanted them served within seconds of placing their order.

After an hour of being rushed off her feet and still no sign of the other MacCarthy sister, disaster struck. The

Guinness tap ceased to flow. Clio fiddled with it, swore, and crouched under the counter. Was a tube blocked? Or was the barrel empty? If so, how was she going to replace it? *Feck!*

"Problem?" asked a voice from above. A very familiar masculine voice.

Clio jumped in fright, bashing her head off the edge of the counter in the process. Stars swam before her eyes.

"Are you okay?" Seán lifted up the counter flap and came to kneel beside her.

"I'm fine," she lied, wincing from the pain.

He raised a questioning brow.

"Okay, I'm not fine, but I soon will be."

He touched her head gently, massaging the area she'd injured. "You'll have a bump and a headache to keep it company."

"Frankly, my head is the least of my worries at the moment." Clio nodded toward the empty beer barrel. "Ruairí meant to check the kegs earlier but he had to leave in a hurry."

"Need help?"

Clio wiped sweat from her brow. "This is my third shift, and I wasn't supposed to be working on my own. We haven't covered changing the barrels yet."

"Not a problem. My grandfather ran a pub in Dublin. I spent my teenage years changing barrels and pulling pints." Seán stood and helped Clio to her feet. "Why don't you sit down for a sec until your head settles? Brian and I can take care of the customers."

"Do you know your way around the kitchen?"

"I don't, but Brian does. Sharon MacCarthy is his girlfriend. He's helped out at the pub before."

Seán waved across the pub to his partner, and Brian ambled over to the counter. "Problem?"

"Can you help Clio serve customers while I change a barrel?"

"Sure." Brian shrugged off his uniform coat and rolled up his shirtsleeves. "Where are the food orders?"

Clio shoved the notebook toward him. "Here, complete with table numbers."

The younger man scanned the list. He wasn't as classically good-looking as his partner but there was something appealing about his earnest freckled face and soft Donegal lilt. "Okeydokey. I can manage this. Do you know where the cellar is, Seán?"

"Yeah. I helped Ruairí move barrels once before." Seán gave Clio a bone-melting smile. "I'll be back in a sec."

She stared dreamily after his retreating back. It had to be the blow to the head. She never mooned after men.

"I'll hit the kitchen," Brian said. "Are you feeling up to serving drinks?"

"I'm a little dizzy, but I'll be fine."

Brian checked his phone. "Sharon sent a text to say the bus from Cork City was delayed, but she should be here in fifteen to twenty minutes."

With the policemen's assistance, Clio managed to keep the tide of customers satisfied for the next quarter of an hour.

"Thanks for helping out," she said when the crowd finally thinned. "Am I keeping you from important police work?"

"We're on our lunch break," Seán said, "and it's been a quiet day."

"Do you have much to do in Ballybeg? Apart from babysitting my mother?"

His disillusioned expression was eloquent. "The fire at the halting site is a dead end, and not much else is happening. The odd bar fight to break up. A few stray sheep to herd. That sort of thing."

"Doesn't sound particularly exciting."

He screwed up his nose. "No."

"I love Ballybeg," Brian said, emerging from the kitchen with a neatly sliced fruitcake. "There's a sense of community here that you don't get policing a big city. Everyone knows everyone else by name, and people are willing to lend one another a hand. I'd miss that if I moved to a bigger station."

Clio smiled at Seán. "You don't agree?"

"Well...everyone does know everyone else's name, not to mention his or her business. I prefer more anonymity, you know?"

The three of them whirled round when the pub door burst open. In hurried the young blonde Clio had seen talking to Seán earlier in the week. She'd replaced the fake-fur coat with a fuchsia-pink puffy jacket and the towering heels with matching furry pink boots. "I think you're needed out at the halting site, lads," she said in a breathless voice. "I saw an ambulance drive up there when I was on the bus. There was quite a commotion."

As if on cue, Seán's phone began to play "Bat Out of Hell." He exchanged a loaded look with Brian and held it to his ear. "Mackey speaking. When was this? Right, sir. We'll head straight to the hospital."

"What's happened?" Brian asked when he rang off.

"A young Traveller boy was found badly beaten. He's been taken to the hospital with severe head injuries. The super wants us to question the family." Seán turned to Clio. "Will you be okay now that Sharon is here?"

"Yes. Thanks again for your help. Before you go, I gotta ask, what's with the funny ringtones?"

Brian snorted. Seán's worried expression turned into a grin. "It's a habit of mine," he said. "Everyone gets an assigned ringtone."

"Usually a song from his ridiculously large vinyl collection," Brian said with a chortle. "Our Seán hasn't embraced CDs, never mind downloads."

"We'd better get a move on. I'll see you tomorrow, Clio." A wry smile brought a twinkle to his eyes. "I believe I'm to escort your mother to Cork City."

Her heart skipped a beat, and a tingling sensation skittered over her skin. "I believe you are."

CHAPTER FOURTEEN

....

Seán's Friday morning began with a throbbing head, a bruised ego, and no leads. He swallowed a groan. He'd been in law enforcement too long to assume his day couldn't get any worse.

The squad car bumped over the dirt track. Each bump jolted Seán's joints, sharp reminders of his underslept, undercaffeinated condition.

"You okay?" Brian asked from the passenger seat.

"I'll be grand." He stretched his neck from side to side, hearing the stiff bones creak. "My body's objecting to my night on a hospital chair."

"Rather you than me, mate," Brian said. "So do the Travellers have any idea who attacked Jimmy Murphy?"

"If they do, they're not talking, and Jimmy's in no state to be questioned."

What an understatement. The poor lad was in a coma, his fate a hovering question mark. Getting info out of his relatives had been about as successful as a donkey winning the Grand National. In other words, they'd said sweet feck-all. Seán's fists balled in frustration. He hated feeling helpless during an investigation and having the sense that he was chasing his own tail.

"Do you think Peig Murphy will talk to us?" Brian asked.

Seán slid a glance toward the passenger seat. "Unlikely. I've been out to the halting site five times since the attacks began, but Peig's always...away." He drew out the last word, rolled it on his tongue.

"The Tinkers take the piss," Brian said. "Think they're above the law."

"In their eyes, they are. They have their own code, moral and judicial. As far as they're concerned, our laws are irrelevant. If we're to have any hope of getting info out of them, don't let them hear you call them Tinkers."

The car continued its bumpy ride. At last, the trees parted to reveal a field dotted with caravans, cars, and assorted junk. The majority of the caravans were old and shabby, but one or two modern mobile homes were perched at the edge of the field.

"Would you look at the state of the place?" Brian's tongue dripped disgust. "The county council's had over a decade to put in sanitation facilities."

A crackle of laughter bubbled up Seán's throat. "Ah, the infamous Traveller Accommodation Act. Brian, my lad, I saw very few Traveller halting sites with the promised parking spaces and plumbing before the Irish economy imploded. Now that we're well and truly screwed financially, I doubt they'll ever follow through."

Seán shifted gears and eased the car to a stop a few meters from the first caravan. He took a last swig from his energy drink, then climbed out of the vehicle.

No sooner were they out of the car than they were surrounded by a gaggle of curious children and excited dogs. The older kids hung back, wary of people from the settled community, especially those wearing police uniforms.

Seán locked eyes with one of the older boys. "I'm looking for Mrs. Murphy."

The child regarded Seán through dark solemn eyes that reflected a stoic resignation more suited to a man of ninety than a boy of ten.

Indecision flickered over his features. After a brief pause, the boy inclined his head toward the lone brightly colored caravan among the drab mobile homes.

"Good lad," said Seán. He tossed him a euro.

The boy let the coin fall to the ground. It splashed into a puddle of mud. Its intended owner made no move to retrieve it, radiating disdain.

Wrong move.

Brian cleared his throat and nudged Seán. They picked their way through debris and children and knocked on the front door of the colorful caravan.

At first, there was no response. Seán was on the verge of adding a second, heftier knock when a deep voice bade them enter.

Inside, the caravan was crammed with trinkets. Religious icons jostled for space with more exotic wares. The decor made John-Joe and Nora Fitzgerald's house look Spartan.

The caravan's lone occupant was seated at a small table, enjoying a glass of whiskey, a cigarette, and a game of solitaire. When she glanced up, the large crucifix around her neck clanked and swayed.

"Mrs. Murphy?" Seán blinked through the haze of smoke.

"Been a long time since anyone called me Missus." Her deep, phlegmy guffaw sounded like she was in danger of hacking up both lungs. "Call me Ma. Or Peig, if that tickles your fancy."

She was dressed in severe black and looked more like a nun than a gypsy. Her white hair was pulled back in a tight bun, emphasizing the grooves etched into her cheeks and forehead. Blue eyes, small and shrewd, were fixed on Seán.

He drew his ID from his pocket. "Sergeant Seán Mackey, Ballybeg Police. This is my partner, Garda Brian Glenn."

Peig scrutinized the ID, then jerked a hand toward the spare chairs at the table. "Sit."

They sat.

"We've come about Jimmy," said Seán, shifting uneasily on the hard wooden seat.

A spasm of pain rippled over Peig's coarse features, deepening the grooves. "Oh, aye," she said, taking a drag on her cigarette. "Keeping up appearances, are ye? No one bothers about the Travellers excepting ourselves, least of all *An Garda Síochána*." She leaned forward, exhaling a cloud of acrid smoke. "Lest, of course, there's a burglary in the neighborhood."

"That's not true Mrs....Peig. I'm a member of the police force, and I care about the welfare of everyone in my jurisdiction, regardless of heritage."

"Fine words, boy. I'd like to see action to back them up." Peig leaned back in her chair, stubbed out her cigarette, drew another from the pack. Sweet Afton, nonfilter. Noting his surprise, she said, "Got my own private stash."

Must be some stash. Sweet Afton ceased production several years ago. "Mrs. Murphy," he began again, but she cut him off with a curt gesture.

"We'll have tea."

Seán tapped the table with his knuckles. Rushing Peig was pointless. If she was determined to steer this interview, he'd best let her think she was in control.

Peig stood, and he could hear her creaking bones as she moved to her small kitchen. The whistle of the kettle soon followed. "I don't take sugar," she said, making it clear that Seán and Brian wouldn't either. Seán didn't care. He wasn't fond of tea and intended to drink as little as he could get away with.

Impish glee danced across Peig's face. She grabbed the whiskey bottle and poured generous dollops of amber liquid into their hot tea.

Seán held up a hand. "We can't drink on duty."

"Can't or shouldn't?" she asked, sitting her skinny frame back behind the table and shoving a mug and a challenge toward Seán. "Sure, let that young pup drive."

Brian regarded his mug as if it contained deadly nightshade instead of a serving of Ireland's finest.

Seán leaned back with his tea and took a cautious sip. *Jaysus*. It packed a punch. "So." He kept his voice normal, easygoing. "About the attacks."

Silence sliced the air sharp as a kunai knife.

"Do you know who attacked Jimmy?" asked Peig. Her glare could bore holes in cement.

"Not yet," Seán said. "We were hoping you could help us."

Her harrumph expressed her opinion of Seán, the settled community, and the *Gardaí*. Very little. "This is why we Travellers prefer to look after our own affairs. When the Guards can be bothered to investigate, they find nothing, and we're as likely to find ourselves accused of all sorts of shenanigans."

"With all due respect, Peig," Seán said, "We can't be allowing vigilante justice. If someone is trying to harm your people, let us help."

Her snort was eloquent.

Seán flexed his jaw. "Over the past four months, we've received reports of tires shot out, smashed windows, and trashed caravans. If the attack on Jimmy is connected to the vendetta against the Travellers, the perpetrator is becoming more dangerous with each incident."

Peig stubbed out her cigarette in an overflowing ashtray. "I'm not a fool, boy. You don't know the half of it."

"Enlighten me. How did this begin?"

Peig leaned back in her chair and crossed thin arms over her scrawny bosom. "It started with the dog."

"There was nothing about a dog in the reports I received."

Peig shrugged. "We hoped to sort it out on our own, but we've been no more successful than you lot."

"Tell me about the dog."

Her mouth formed a grimace. "Last May, one of my son's racing dogs was beheaded. A greyhound. Beautiful creature, she was."

"Beheaded?" The word fell from Brian's mouth in a horrified gape.

"That's what I said. They found her body the next morning, over by the woods." Peig's eyes narrowed. "The head was put into my son's bed."

"Jaysus," said Brian, awestruck. "Just like *The Godfather*."

Peig shot him a look of confusion. "The what?"

"You know, the film."

A blank stare.

"Never mind." Brian's feigned resignation failed to conceal his contempt for Peig, her home, and her lifestyle. If the lad had any ambition to rise in the police force, he'd need to work on his body language.

"You have no idea who could be behind these attacks?" Seán scrutinized her as he spoke, hoping for a flicker of emotion or an involuntary twitch. "Anyone from Ballybeg been particularly nasty to your people?"

Peig's right cheek spasmed, and she shifted her attention to her mug of fortified tea. When her eyes rose to meet his, her expression was impassive. "No one I can think of."

No one she was prepared to name. Seán opened his mouth to press her further, but the caravan door hit him in the back. He jerked around.

A swarthy man stood in the doorway, dark eyes flashing, hands clenched in hairy-knuckled fists.

A silent nod passed between the newcomer and Peig. If the swish of a blade through the air was any indication, their meeting was at an end.

CHAPTER FIFTEEN

....

The knife landed in the wall. It held a moment, suspended and vibrating, before falling to the ground with a clatter.

Seán's hand flew to his utility belt. No SIG. *Damn.* Now that he was demoted to uniform, a baton was his only weapon.

The dark-haired man strode past them, retrieved the knife, and began peeling an apple. It should have been an awkward task with a blade so big, but he had no difficulties.

"Blackie," Peig commanded. "Sit down and stop showing off."

Blackie glowered at Seán and Brian but lumbered toward the last remaining seat at Peig's small table. He lowered himself into it, large, threatening, and stinking of dog.

"My son," Peig said by way of introduction.

"What are the Guards doing here?" Blackie bit into his apple, spraying flesh all over his thick beard.

"They've come to ask about young Jimmy."

"Oh, aye?" An irritating sneer stretched across Blackie's face. "Found something out?"

Seán pinned the man in place with a hard stare. "Do you know who attacked him?"

Blackie shrugged. "No. Even if I did, I wouldn't tell you."

"Intending to take the law into your own hands?" Brian leaned closer. "If so, have a rethink. I don't care for having knives thrown at me." The words "especially not by a Tinker" hovered in the air—unspoken but implicit.

"All I did was show off my knife-throwing skills, officer." Blackie's tone was deceptively innocent. "I threw it at the wall, not you."

"Garda Glenn." Seán's voice held a note of warning.

Brian sat back down, a belligerent tilt to his jaw.

Blackie's grin grew wider, displaying tobacco-stained teeth. "Garda Glenn...the name is familiar. I do believe you arrested me once."

"I do believe I arrested you more than once, Mr. Murphy."

"Enough with the macho grandstanding," Seán said. "Let's focus on Jimmy's attack. How can no one at the caravan park have seen anything? Someone must know something. You're all adamant it was an outsider. You must have a reason for this suspicion."

Blackie poured himself a shot of whiskey, knocked it back in one, and slammed the glass onto the table. "No one saw anything because it's never wise to see anything, Garda Mackey."

"Sergeant Mackey." Murphy was winding him up deliberately. "It's never wise to take matters into your own hands. Tell us what we need to know, and we'll do our best to see justice is done."

Blackie sneered. "Sure, you don't believe that, man. Justice? What a bloody joke. You can't even stamp out corruption in your own ranks. If you're really interested in finding out who hurt a Traveller, you're the first Guard I've met to pay more than lip service to justice."

Seán rose to his feet. "We won't take up more of your time." He tossed his card on the table and looked from one to the other, ensuring he had their full attention. "If you think of anything relating to the attacks, anything at all, give me a call. Day or night."

Blackie drew snot up his nostrils. Peig's nose twitched. Neither made a move to pocket the card.

"That was a total waste of time," Brian muttered while they were trudging back through the mud to the police car.

"Not entirely." Seán's paused to collect his thoughts. "We suspected the Travellers were hiding something about the attacks. Now we *know* they know more than they're saying. The person behind the attacks has to be someone with clout."

Brian slid him a curious look. "How do you work that out? There are a lot of people in Ballybeg who'd prefer the Travellers gone."

Seán slid the car key from his pocket and rapped it against his knuckles thoughtfully. "If it was an eejit like my...like John-Joe Fitzgerald or Buck MacCarthy, the Travellers would take care of it themselves. Whoever's doing this has got them scared shitless. It takes a lot to intimidate the Travellers."

"Are you thinking a vigilante group?" Brian asked, opening the car door.

Their eyes met across the roof of the car. "That's exactly what I'm thinking."

Seán slid behind the wheel and started the ignition. He eased the vehicle off the halting site and down the bumpy track through the woods.

"If a vigilante group is responsible for the attacks," Brian said, furrowing his brow in thought, "then who's organizing it?"

Seán gave a wry laugh. "That, my friend, is the million-euro question."

They'd reached the main road when his phone started to buzz. He hit speakerphone.

"Seán?" The sound of the super's raspy voice echoed through the car speakers. "Where the hell are you?"

"We're driving back from the halting site."

His boss's dismissive harrumph grated on Seán's nerves. "I told you to escort Helen Havelin shopping this afternoon," the super snapped. "Why aren't you at Clonmore House?"

"Sir, after the attack last night, I judged questioning the Travellers to be the priority. I sent Reserve Garda Doyle round to Clonmore House."

The older man gave a derisive snort. "That fool? He never showed. Ms. Havelin is understandably upset."

"Understandably." Seán's voice dripped sarcasm.

"Get your arse over to Clonmore House right now."

His hands tensed around the steering wheel. "What about Jimmy Murphy?"

"Who?"

"The Traveller boy who was attacked," Seán said through gritted teeth.

"Oh, him. Never mind the Tinker. It was probably one of their own."

"That's not an attitude befitting a member of *An Garda Síochána*. Sir," he added belatedly. This being-demoted business was a pain.

Superintendent O'Riordan was not impressed. "Are you telling me how to do my job?"

"No, sir, I—"

"Then get your arse over to Clonmore House right now, Mackey. I decide which cases take priority, and I judge the threat to Helen Havelin's safety to be of paramount concern. Let young Garda Glenn deal with the Tinkers."

"Yes, sir." Seán exhaled through clenched teeth. "Flaming Helen Havelin," he said to Brian after the super had disconnected. He threw his phone up on the dashboard with force.

"What do you make of Helen's story?" Brian asked. "I'm inclined to think the deranged stalker is a load of bollocks."

"I don't know. She seems genuinely jumpy to me." He scowled. "Whatever the truth of the matter is, Helen is used to having her diva demands met. I resent her showing up here and commandeering police time when she could hire bodyguards, especially when we're stretched thin as it is."

"The super is smitten. Seems to think Helen is the greatest thing ever to grace the town of Ballybeg," his partner said with a grin. "What's that saying? No fool like an old fool? Ah, well. Let him have his fun."

"He should have his fun on his own time, and not at the expense of our meager police resources." Seán slapped the steering wheel. "This is insane. We have a serious assault on a member of a minority group, yet we're supposed to give precedence to the alleged stalker of an alleged celebrity? In what world is that fair?"

Brian sighed. "Look, I agree with you, but Helen is only in Ballybeg a couple of days a week. We have the rest of the time to concentrate on the Travellers case."

"What about everything else that needs to be done?" The road forked before him, and Seán swerved right toward the coast and Clonmore House. "McGarry's no slouch, but Reserve Garda Doyle is a disgrace. We can't leave this case to them."

Brian pinched the bridge of his nose. "I know you think I don't have the experience, and you're probably right, but you're going to have to trust me. I'll help you to track down whoever is responsible for the attack on Jimmy Murphy, even if it means working unofficial overtime. Deal?"

"I can't ask you to do that. It's against regulations, and you have your university coursework."

"I've handed in all my assignments, and my thesis is almost finished. I can juggle the time."

"How will Sharon feel about you spending extra time at work?"

The mention of his new girlfriend brought a wide smile to Brian's lips. "Sharon's cool. She'll understand this case is important."

"All right, then," Seán said reluctantly, "but take no unnecessary risks. We'll divide the unofficial investigation time between us and try to do as much together as possible."

"Fair enough."

Seán grimaced. "Now that we've sorted that out, I'd better go and play chauffeur to a diva."

CHAPTER SIXTEEN

....

"I'm offering to buy you new clothes. What possible objection can you have to the idea of a new wardrobe free of charge?"

Clio tensed her fingers around the handle of the duster. She placed a statuette of Venus back in its place on the display table. "Nothing's free of charge, Mother. Not with you."

Helen was reclining on the chaise longue, watching while Clio cleaned and adding what she referred to as "helpful criticism" at regular intervals. "Don't be cynical. You're my daughter. I simply want you to look your best."

"In other words, you don't want me to embarrass you."

"That's ridiculous. I don't want you to embarrass yourself. Your clothes are a disaster." Her mother gestured to Clio's worn jeans and frayed pullover. "How can any woman wish to walk around looking like a homeless person? As for your makeup..." Helen shuddered. "How can any daughter of mine not know how to apply eye shadow?"

"I don't *wear* eye shadow, therefore I don't need to know how to apply it." *Besides, how hard can it be, right?*

"If you knew how to apply eye shadow, you'd wear it."

Clio sighed. There was no arguing with Helen's logic, or lack thereof. She was determined to transform her daughter into her clone and seemed impervious to the fact that this was never going to happen.

"Don't you want to look your best?" Helen opened her cosmetics bag, extracted a powder compact from its depths, and flipped open her portable makeup mirror. "I always feel better when I make an effort with my appearance."

"Your idea of 'making an effort' and mine are a little different," Clio said in a dry tone. "I feel good with a swipe of mascara and comfortable shoes."

Her gaze dropped to her mother's feet. Helen had on her signature towering heels. Clio's toes were still recovering from those silly red stilettos. The idea of wearing shoes like that all day, every day, was horrifying.

Her mother slid the powder compact back into her makeup case, stretched, and stood. "You've done a good job with the unpacking," she said, trailing a fingertip over the freshly dusted mantelpiece. "The house is almost perfect."

Clio cupped her ear. "Is that praise I hear escaping your lips? Are you feeling unwell?"

"Don't be cheeky." A small frown threatened the smooth perfection of Helen's forehead. "Have I been such an ogre?"

Did her mother want the unvarnished truth or a bland platitude? "Put it this way," she began, searching for the diplomatic approach, "I'm pretty sure I'd find your picture next to the dictionary definition of 'perfectionist.'"

"I'm sorry, dear. I do like things to be just right." Her mother bit her lip. "I want the three of us living together to work out, especially come the summer."

The duster hovered over a selection of porcelain figurines. "Why? What's happening in the summer?"

Helen blinked, her lips parting in a small O of surprise. "My retirement, of course."

"What?" Clio felt as though the air was being forcibly removed from her lungs with suction force. "You're retiring? Why didn't you tell me?"

"I assumed you knew. It was all over the news. Everyone knows this is my last season doing the show."

"Clearly 'everyone' does not know. I certainly didn't." If Emma had heard about Helen's plans, she would have mentioned it before the move to Ballybeg.

Her mother sighed and tilted her head to one side. "That's what you get for watching British TV and international streaming services. If you paid more attention to Irish television and current affairs, you couldn't have missed the announcement."

A sinking suspicion weighed in Clio's stomach. "After you retire, where will you live?"

"Why, here, of course. That was the entire point of buying this house. I'd always planned to move back to Cork when I retired. Once I realized my days at the station were numbered, I began house hunting." Helen's slim shoulders stiffened, and her expression grew strained. "I assumed you were aware of this before you moved into Clonmore House. Is it going to be a problem?"

Yes! a voice in Clio's head screamed. "When I agreed to live here and act as your housekeeper, it was on the understanding that you'd be away during the week."

"I'll be away Monday to Friday. Until I retire."

She gripped the handle of the duster so tight she was sure it would snap. "I can't imagine you giving up work. How will you cope?" Without the limelight, Helen would wilt.

A curious expression settled over her mother's fine-boned features. If Clio didn't know better, she'd have identified it as insecurity. "I don't exactly have a choice. The TV station execs decided not to renew my talk show. They've commissioned episodes until June but not beyond. Over the past few seasons, ratings have fallen steadily." Her lips trembled briefly, then settled into a hard line. "Much as it pains me to admit, I'm not getting any younger. My shelf life for television is nearly up, and I was lucky to survive the last budget cuts."

Frankly, Clio was surprised her mother hadn't gotten the chop years ago. The views she espoused were old-fashioned by most people's standards and totally out of step with modern Ireland. "Don't you want to try to do something else? Perhaps behind-the-camera work?"

Helen gave a dry laugh. "Not where my talents lie, I'm afraid. Besides, I've spent years working. I missed much of your childhood and Tammy's. I'd like to spend quality time with my granddaughter before she's grown and gone. That was one of my hopes when you agreed to move down to Ballybeg."

"If you're planning on developing a relationship with Tammy, you might start by easing up on her. You harp on about her appearance and about how clumsy she is, just like you do with me. I can cope with you belittling me all the time, but I won't stand for it with Tammy."

Helen appeared to be genuinely shocked. "Is that what you think I do? Belittle you? All I want is the best for you. I happen to think that the best includes making the most of your appearance, regardless of what Mother Nature has seen fit to bestow on you."

Clio rolled her eyes. "Even that sounds like an insult."

"If I cared so little about you, I'd hardly have invited you and Tammy to live with me, not to mention accepting your sudden change of mind with good grace."

She stiffened. "How do you mean?"

"You made it very clear that hell would freeze over before you'd accept my offer. Then within a week, you were suddenly desperate to move to Ballybeg." Her mother gave a theatrical sigh. "I don't know what caused you to change your mind, but when you asked me for help, I gave it to you without question. All I want in return is a rapport with you and your daughter. Surely that's not expecting too much."

"You might have a rapport with me if you'd stop criticizing who I am and everything I do. Are you so perfect that you feel qualified to criticize everyone else?"

A small nagging voice in Clio's head—one with a nasty nasal tone reminiscent of Ray Greer—reminded her that the events of the last few weeks had erased all the hard work she'd put in over the previous several years to build a stable life for her and Tammy.

"I have high expectations of myself but I don't feel my expectations of you are unreasonable. At your age, I already had a successful advice column and was starting my television career. You're unmarried, unemployed, and a single parent."

"Technically, *you* were a single parent." A fact her mother preferred everyone to forget, especially her viewers.

"Only briefly. You were little when I married Larry. By marrying him, I ensured a comfortable lifestyle for both of us."

Clio laughed. "How romantic. I don't consider nannies and boarding school a substitute for an emotionally engaged parent."

"That isn't fair," Helen protested. "I did my best. I know I made mistakes—"

"You threw your pregnant seventeen-year-old daughter out of the house."

"—which I've regretted ever since. We've been over this before, Cliona. Had I known you'd end up on drugs, I would have come after you. As for your current predicament, I don't understand it. You appeared to have gotten your life together over the last few years."

The vein in Clio's temple throbbed. "You have no idea about my life."

"So *tell* me about it. I might not have kept in touch as much as I should have, but I'm trying to make up for lost time."

"Whenever I try to talk to you, your phone rings or there's a reason you need to run off." An idea formed, blurry at first, but sharpening with each millisecond. She'd arrange to cook dinner for her mother and tell her about the Ray situation. Just blurt out the whole mess and hope for the best. Coming clean to her mother and explaining the whole situation—warts and all—had to be better than this stomach-churning guilt, not to mention the nail-biting terror whenever Helen neared the safe in spite of the fact that she'd returned the money in full. "If you want us to build a relationship, we're not going to manage by sniping at one another."

"I do not snipe," Helen said, bristling.

"Mother, I'm trying, and you're not making it easy."

"Oh, all right. Why don't I cook dinner for us one evening? I can start with a light supper this evening, before you go to work." Helen returned her attention to her makeup and applied a lashing of inky black mascara.

Clio glanced at the clock on the mantelpiece. If they didn't leave soon, she'd be pressed for time later. "Are we taking your car or mine?" It was a rhetorical question. Helen wouldn't be seen dead in Clio's banger of a car.

"We'll take mine. Seeing as that fool of a reserve policeman has failed to show up, Superintendent O'Riordan will be along shortly to escort us."

Ah-ha. That explained the extra war paint. Clio gave a wide grin. "Got a thing for the superintendent? I suppose the silver hair is sort of dashing in its own way."

Helen packed her cosmetic case into her handbag and rose gracefully from her seat. "Don't be absurd. Superintendent O'Riordan is merely a friend. We were at school together many years ago."

"Is that so?" Well, well. Clio had dismissed Helen's flirtation with the older policeman as pure show. Perhaps she had a genuine interest in him.

Her mother peered through the window. "I see a police car coming up the drive. Will you entertain the superintendent while I fetch my handbag?"

"Won't that one do?" Clio asked, gesturing to the powder-blue suede bag clutched in Helen's hand.

Her mother gaped in horror. "Of course not. It doesn't match my outfit."

"My bad." Clio swallowed a laugh.

Tammy poked her head round the door. "When you two are done bickering, that policeman is waiting to give you a lift."

"I'll be ready in a moment," Helen said. "Cliona, go down and offer him a cup of coffee."

How long did it take to fetch a different handbag? Clio opened her mouth to object but caught Tammy's eye. A look of sympathy passed between them, the first one in months. It warmed her insides to see a small smile of understanding on her daughter's lips.

"Fine," she said. "I'll entertain the dashing superintendent while you finish tarting yourself up."

Helen went upstairs, and Clio headed toward the kitchen with Tammy. "Are you sure you won't come shopping with us?"

"I'm positive." The girl shuddered. "I'd rather tackle my chemistry homework than trail after Helen all afternoon. I can't imagine she'd darken the door of any of my favorite shops."

Clio laughed. "I feel your pain. You can think of me while you're getting to grips with the periodic table."

"Oh, it's much worse than that," Tammy dropped her voice to a dramatic whisper. "We've started organic chemistry."

"There's chocolate in the kitchen if you need some moral support." She linked arms with her daughter. "Apart from the horrors of organic chemistry, how's school? Have you made any friends yet?"

Tammy's cheerful expression faded. "School's okay. The teachers are nice. The kids...It's early days, I guess."

Clio gave her a hug. For the first time in forever, Tammy didn't pull away. "You'll settle in soon."

"I hope so, Mum."

Seeing her daughter hesitant and unsure of herself hurt like a thousand paper cuts. "It's getting harder to hug you now that you're so tall. Be glad you didn't inherit my height, or lack thereof."

The girl laughed and patted Clio on the head. "I like having such a little mother."

Clio drew back and pulled a face. "I suppose I'd better entertain our guest until your grandmother finds her bag."

"Have fun shopping. Said with complete sincerity, natch." Tammy grinned and headed in the direction of the library.

Still laughing, Clio trudged downstairs. At the foot of the stairs, she sucked in a breath. Seán stood in the entrance hall, devilishly handsome in his police blues. Her heart lurched at the sight of him in his uniform. He looked strong, heroic, and dependable. The kind of man she should want in her life. The kind of man she tended to scare away. "My mother is expecting your boss."

The corners of his mouth tugged into a smile. "Your mother will have to make do with me."

"How is the Traveller boy?"

His smile evaporated in an instant. "In a coma. The doctors don't know if he'll pull through."

Clio's fingers fluttered to her throat. "How awful. Do you have any idea who attacked him?"

"No. Not so much as a whispered rumor." He raked her outfit, pausing to peruse her figure-hugging skinny jeans. "It's good to see you, Clio. Or what name are you going by today?"

Heat crept up her cheeks. "Clio. Just Clio."

"You're never just Clio. Remember that."

A look passed between them, loaded with silent significance. She wanted to reach out to him, to kiss him, to blurt out the whole sordid tale. The words surged up her throat. She tasted them on her tongue, tantalizing, enticing. Unfortunately, she couldn't risk losing her nerve. Not now. Not when she was so close. And certainly not in front of a cop.

"I'm ready," Helen called from the top of the stairs. "Oh. It's Sergeant Mackey."

"Indeed." Seán's tone was stiff and borderline unfriendly.

Clio had noticed he wasn't Helen's greatest fan, but his hostility seemed odd.

"After you." He gestured for her to exit the house before him.

In her jacket pocket, her phone vibrated. Thank goodness. Emma had promised to send her a progress report this afternoon. She pulled the phone out and checked the display. The text message was from Ray. A spiral of panic coiled through her body. *Be ready on the 28th.*

....

CHAPTER SEVENTEEN

A shopping trip. Superintendent O'Riordan wanted him to accompany Helen Havelin on a flaming shopping trip. A Traveller boy was left in a coma, and his superiors didn't seem to give a damn. They'd decided a diva demanding a chauffeur-cum-pack mule should be given priority. Seán gripped the steering wheel so hard his hands hurt. Dublin transfer or no, this was bollocks.

From the passenger seat, Helen looked down her nose at him and arched a pencil-thin eyebrow. Over the past week, he'd grown to seriously hate that eyebrow.

"You needn't look like I'm sending you to the seventh circle of hell, Sergeant Mackey."

"Fourth," Clio said from the backseat.

Helen jerked around. "What?"

"I think you mean the fourth circle of hell, Mother. The seventh represents violence. The fourth is greed."

"Well, well," the older woman drawled. "So you did learn something at that frightfully expensive boarding school."

"Actually, I gleaned that info from reading Dante. In the original. I picked up a few languages during my time gallivanting around Europe."

A laugh escaped Seán's lips.

An ironic smile twisted Helen's mouth. "Touché, my dear. What a shame you didn't put that sharp mind of yours to good use and get a decent job."

"Nothing wrong with being a translator, Mother."

Seán's gaze met Clio's in the rearview mirror. He smiled at her, and a look of understanding passed between them.

One thing he'd learned over the past few days was that Helen Havelin wasted no opportunity to belittle her daughter, and Helen always had to have the last word. Whatever tied Clio to her mother, she wasn't in Ballybeg willingly.

Seán drummed his fingertips on the steering wheel and seethed. He had more than enough to do at work without this bullshit.

"Pull over here," the diva said. "I have an appointment at that boutique."

Was she out of her mind? "It's a bus lane, Ms. Havelin. I can't stop here."

"Why ever not?" Helen's tone was cold, clipped, and less than courteous. "My Dublin driver uses them all the time."

"I'm not your Dublin driver, Ms. Havelin. I'm a member of *An Garda Síochána*. I obey the rules of the road."

"I don't understand why you won't let me out here."

"Because it's a bus stop." *Jaysus.* It was like talking to a truculent toddler. "See the markings? The only vehicles permitted are buses and emergency vehicles."

"*You're* the police. Doesn't that entitle you to stop there?"

"Only when there's a legitimate reason for me to do so." Seán turned to face Helen, glowering at her. "Let's get one thing straight. I'll come along on this farce of an expedition, but I'm not your servant. I'm not bending the law to suit you."

"Sergeant Mackey—"

"Mother, leave it." Clio leaned forward in the backseat and placed a hand on Helen's shoulder. "He's just doing his job. More than his job, actually."

Helen stiffened under her daughter's touch and cast Seán a withering look. "Very well." She sniffed. "Find a spot as near to the boutique as possible. I suppose my umbrella will have to suffice. If I catch cold in this deluge, I'm holding you personally responsible."

Seán found a free space in the parking lot of a nearby shopping center.

Clio let herself out of the back, pulling up the hood of her worn raincoat. Helen waited for him to open the passenger door for her. He and Clio exchanged glances.

Accepting his chauffeur duties with a modicum of good grace, Seán reached for the handle.

Helen stepped out of the car daintily. Her spindly heels were ill equipped for the driving rain. Holding her umbrella aloft, she glared at Seán. "You could have at least let me out of the car in front of the boutique."

He bit back an acidic retort and counted to ten—first in English, then in Irish.

Clio cast him a look of sympathy. "Mother can be difficult," she murmured after Helen strode ahead. "She's used to getting her own way."

"I've noticed," he said grimly. "Doesn't anyone ever say no to her?"

Clio laughed. "Rarely. It's generally not worth the hassle."

Their first stop during Seán's Afternoon from Hell was Les Oiseaux, a French boutique specializing in obscenely expensive evening wear. This information Seán garnered from the doorbell at the entrance and the conspicuous lack of price tags inside. The shop door was opened by a man in a tailored three-piece suit.

"Madame Havelin. Welcome." He didn't spare Seán or Clio a glance.

A tiny woman materialized from behind a mass of puffy evening gowns, trailed by a pretty blond assistant. "Helen," the older woman said in a breathy French accent. "Always a pleasure."

Air kisses and hand gestures followed. Seán and Clio exchanged eye rolls—hers obvious, his discreet.

"What delights have you in store for me today, Claudette?" Helen asked, gesturing around the shop.

"We have wonderful new stock just in from Paris." She pronounced it *Paree*.

Clio caught Seán's eye and grinned.

"How long has she lived in Ireland?" he whispered. "I'm no expert, but her French accent sounds a tad... stagey?"

She leaned in close enough for him to smell her shampoo—something fruity and fresh. "I suspect she amps it up for the customers. According to Marcella at the pub, Claudette's lived in Ireland longer than Marcella's been alive."

Following her doorman's example, Claudette completely ignored Clio and Seán, focusing all her attention on the person with the platinum credit card.

Finally, after Helen had tried on a hundred outfits, she turned to her daughter. "Do you see anything you like?"

The expression of horror on Claudette's face was priceless.

Noticing her disdain, Clio stiffened. "These clothes aren't exactly my style."

"I'm offering to buy you a dress," Helen said. "Surely you can find a few you'd like to try on."

"Perhaps mademoiselle would feel more... comfortable...shopping elsewhere?" Claudette began hopefully. "I'm not sure—"

The sight of Helen's glacial expression froze her vocal chords midsentence.

"I would like *my daughter* to have a cocktail dress suitable for a casual but select gathering. Either you find her something to wear, or we will take our business to another boutique. I believe Janine's on Oliver Plunkett Street has an excellent reputation for quality clothing *and* customer service."

166

Claudette looked as though she'd swallowed her tongue. "*Non, non.* Janine's is not as good as my shop." The petite woman grabbed Clio's elbow. "Come with me, mademoiselle. I have the perfect dress for you."

Clio's resigned expression morphed into one of alarm. "What party? You never mentioned any party."

Helen flicked an invisible piece of fluff from her trousers. It was a habit of hers, Seán had observed, and generally came before she launched a grenade into the conversation. "Didn't I tell you? I'm hosting a little soirée. A sort of housewarming event."

Her daughter looked aghast. "When?"

"The Saturday after next."

Clio's eyebrows shot up and her eyes widened. "The weekend of the twenty-eighth? But you said you'd be away then."

"That was the original plan, but my filming schedule changed."

Clio's features tensed, then relaxed into a small grin. "The twenty-eighth is an excellent date for a party."

Her mother nodded. "As I'll be at a loose end, it's the perfect opportunity to invite some old friends down from Dublin to see the house and get to know some of our new neighbors."

Show off to them, more like. No doubt he and Brian would be expected to stand guard while she played hostess.

Helen regarded him with narrowed eyes. "Do you find my choice of cocktail dress amusing, Sergeant

Mackey? I wouldn't have thought *you* were an expert on women's fashion."

He hadn't paid attention to which dresses Helen had chosen. "Hardly. I was thinking of something else."

She eyed him suspiciously but turned back to Claudette, who'd sent her assistant scurrying upstairs in search of dresses for Clio. "I don't think red suits my daughter. A nice shade of green or blue to bring out the color of her eyes would be preferable."

Claudette rooted through the row of dresses her assistant had arranged neatly on a portable clothes rack. "*Alors...*" She extracted an emerald green beaded twenties-style dress and held it against a protesting Clio. "*Oui, c'est parfait.*"

Parfait indeed. Clio would look stunning in that dress.

"Try it on," Helen urged. "Claudette and I will look for matching shoes and accessories."

Clio's large eyes grew larger. "I don't accessorize."

"Nonsense. You can't wear a dress like that without the proper jewelry and handbag."

A few minutes later, a bashful Clio shuffled out of the changing room. As Seán's eyes trailed over her figure, his mouth grew dry. The green dress molded her slight curves to perfection, reminding him of what lay beneath the beaded fabric. She wore an emerald necklace wrapped around her slim neck a couple of times, leaving an oval of beads hanging between her cleavage.

Seán let out an involuntary whistle. To say she looked stunning would be an understatement. She looked...

enchanting? Beguiling? Simply fucking gorgeous? "It suits you. I can imagine you as a Twenties flapper."

That brought a smile to her lips. "I've spent too long growing out an ill-advised buzz cut to contemplate going for a bob."

"Buzz cut?" He eyed her face critically, examining her high cheekbones. "You know, you could probably pull that look off. You have the bone structure."

Helen glided across the shop floor, holding a pair of delicate beaded green shoes with dainty heels. "Given that you're not used to wearing high heels, I thought these would be suitable."

"Not red this time," he murmured beneath his breath. "A pity."

Helen gave him an odd look, but Clio laughed. "I think these heels are manageable," she said, flashing him an impish grin. "Even for me." She slipped on the shoes and took the handbag Claudette's nameless assistant had found to complete the outfit.

"Perfect," her mother said with a sigh of satisfaction. "You look beautiful, Cliona."

Given Clio's look of astonishment, Seán suspected compliments from her mother were a rarity.

Helen wore a self-satisfied expression on her face. "I booked the caterers this morning. Now that we've found dresses for the party, the last item left to arrange is the entertainment. I was thinking of hiring a local singer of note. Garda Glenn mentioned him when he was at the house last weekend. A fellow by the name of Fitzgerald. Have you heard of him, Sergeant Mackey?"

Seán struggled to maintain his composure. Behind that placid demeanor, Brian Glenn was a rascal. "Indeed I have, Ms. Havelin. John-Joe Fitzgerald is well-known in these parts." A vision of Helen's reaction to the sight of John-Joe cavorting in his swim trunks brought a gurgle of laughter surging up his throat.

"Do you think it's short notice to book him for the twenty-eighth?" she mused, checking her calendar. "I like the idea of hiring someone from Ballybeg."

Seán thought of his aunt and uncle's shabby house and the look of genuine tension on John-Joe's face when he'd spoken of his financial woes. He thought of the fine John-Joe would have to pay as a result of the bird shooting incident. "Why don't I give him a call and ask? Perhaps he's had a cancellation."

"Would you?" She beamed. "Thank you, Sergeant. That's one less thing to take care of before the party. I want to make it an event to remember."

Seán caught Clio's eye. She put a hand over her mouth to stifle a giggle. A wicked smile curved his lips. If John-Joe was involved, Helen's "event" would indeed prove to be memorable.

CHAPTER EIGHTEEN

....

When they returned to Clonmore House after the shopping trip, Clio retreated to her room, using the excuse of needing to change for work. Ruairí's efforts to get his staff to wear T-shirts with the pub's logo on them were halfhearted and respected only by Clio. The MacCarthy sisters ignored their brother, Sharon sticking to sequins and exposed cleavage, and Marcella to whatever outrageous T-shirt slogan caught her fancy. Clio, as the only nonfamily member on staff, couldn't play the sibling card.

After a quick shower, she changed into black jeans and one of the pub's long-sleeved T-shirts. Then she fired up her laptop and sent Emma an instant message.

Hey, Em. Do you have time for video call?

Within seconds, Emma's pretty face appeared on the screen. Her outfit was pure Forties glamour, right down to scarlet pout.

"Wow," Clio said with a laugh. "What job has you dolled up like a slightly-more-dressed version of Dita Von Teese?"

Her friend stuck out her tongue, revealing a very un-Forties-like tongue ring. "A suspected blackmailer. He's attending an Old Hollywood–themed party at the Irish Film Institute tonight. I wrangled an invitation." Emma took a sip of her ever-present energy drink and leaned closer to the screen.

"What's up? Have you heard from Ray again?"

"Yeah." Clio scowled. "The weasel sent me a text message to set the date for the break-in. He wants to do it on Saturday the 28th, but the date's a no-go. My mother is planning to host a housewarming party."

"That's good news, right? It gives you a legitimate excuse to stall him. And just as well." It was her friend's turn to pull a face. "I haven't discovered anything we didn't already know. Ray's a careful bastard, and his men are loyal. The sole reason he's in a position to hold the attack on O'Leary over your head is that the guys he sent to do the job aren't part of his core crew and have a reputation for being loose cannons. He's as happy to have something to use against them as he is to have dirt on you."

"Crap. You'll keep digging, won't you?"

"Of course. In the meantime, ask Helen to elaborate about her stalker. Perhaps there's a connection."

"It seems unlikely," Clio mused, "but it's an angle worth pursuing."

Emma glanced at her watch. "I'd better log off or I'll be late to this party."

"And I'd better get going to the pub. My new boss took me up on my suggestion of a cocktail hour. Tonight is the first one."

"Best of luck," her friend said, giving her the thumbs up. "Talk soon."

"Bye, Em. Go catch your blackmailer."

After she disconnected, Clio grabbed her phone from the nightstand and punched in Ray's number.

While the ringtone sounded in her ear, she focused on the hideous floral patterned wallpaper—the previous owners of Clonmore House had had a penchant for Victorian-style patterns. She was on the verge of disconnecting when he finally answered.

"Clio," he purred. "To what do I owe this pleasure?"

Taking a deep breath, she got straight to the point. "Saturday the twenty-eighth won't work."

An ominous silence echoed down the phone. She wiped sweaty palms on her jeans and swallowed hard.

"Why won't it work?" Ray's voice was sharp and clipped, not his usual high-pitched squawk. "I've given you plenty of notice to get rid of your mother and daughter."

"My mother is planning a housewarming party for that evening."

"Persuade her to cancel."

"I've tried, but she's invited half the country."

He fell silent for a while, each second dragging by like a tension-filled hour. "Half the country?" he asked finally. "Perhaps we can make this work in our favor. Tell you what. Why don't you nick the leopard aquamanile while the party's in progress?"

She almost jumped out of her skin. "Oh, no. Absolutely not. There's no way I can manage that."

"Try." Ray's tone turned glacial. "I'll send Tank to help you. I believe you've already made his acquaintance at MacCarthy's pub. He's been seen in the neighborhood. All you need to do is introduce him as a friend of yours."

"God, no." The notion of hanging out with that no-necked low-life made her skin crawl.

"Would you rather *I* went as your date?"

An image of Ray at her side, clutching her waist, turned her stomach inside out.

"Of course, I could send Delaney," Ray mused. "I believe you're *very* well acquainted with him."

Clio ran a shaking hand through her hair. *No fecking way.* Delaney at large in Ballybeg was the absolute last thing she needed to add to the mix of her train wreck of a life. "Don't send anyone. I can handle this myself. I'll check my mother's schedule and send you alternative dates." Alternative dates as far in the future as she could manage without being too obvious...either she or Emma had better come up with the goods on Ray fast.

"Good girl, Clio. You were always the best worker I had."

Hazy memories of the bad old years when she'd done jobs for Ray surfaced. "Stick to threats," she said coolly. "You're better at them than flattery. Besides, my time working for you ended years ago."

"There's a job opening for you whenever you change your mind. You have a particular gift for your line of work."

"Thanks, but no thanks." Over her dead body. Her days of safe-cracking and petty thefts ended the moment she'd received a suspended sentence on the condition she attended rehab.

His laughter echoed down the phone. "I thought not, but it was worth a try. I'll be in touch about the handover. I'll probably send Tank. One of the Ballybeg policeman knows me and several of my men from his previous posting, but Tank's new."

The Ballybeg policeman he was referring to had to be Seán Mackey. *Feck.* The pulse in Clio's neck throbbed painfully. She had to figure out a way to get out of Ray's clutches. Having Seán and Brian Glenn hanging around was bad enough. Knowing Seán had a connection to Ray was even worse.

"I asked you if the plan sounded good to you?"

"What?" In the fresh shock of discovering Seán had a connection to Ray, she'd tuned him out. "Why do you care what I think? What choice do I have but to go along with whatever diabolical plan you come up with?"

"Absolutely none," he said cheerfully. "I think this partnership is working out splendidly. Don't you?"

For him, perhaps. For her, not so much. Fortunately, he'd rung off before she could formulate a suitably cutting response.

A knock sounded, making her jump. Helen peered round the door. "I've made sandwiches. You said you'd like one before you headed to work."

"Uh, okay. Thanks." Her mother let loose in the kitchen was a frightening prospect, but surely even Helen couldn't screw up a sandwich. Plus it would be an opportunity to have a chat with Helen, sound out if telling her about Ray was a smart move.

When she entered the dining room, all plans to talk to her mother evaporated. Seán sat at the table, wearing a pained expression. In the seat next to him, Tammy regarded her sandwich with the trepidation one might feel when approaching a vicious animal.

Clio's heart thudded in her chest. "Hey, Seán. I thought you were leaving after you dropped us home."

A half smile played at one corner of his mouth. "My boss made it clear that I'm to stay for another couple of hours."

Helen struggled into the dining room with a platter of sandwiches. Jeez. How many did she expect them to eat? She'd made enough to feed an army. She dumped it on the table and said breathlessly, "Sergeant Mackey is keeping Tammy and me company until Superintendent O'Riordan arrives at seven o'clock."

Tammy, Seán, and Clio exchanged amused glances.

"That's...gallant...of the superintendent," Clio said tactfully, ignoring her daughter's choke of laughter.

"He's a gentleman," Helen said with prim dignity. "And I think he's lonely. Did you know he separated from his wife last year?"

Seán's expression turned to granite. "A man without strings must be a novelty," he said in a hard tone.

Clio stared at him. His delivery seemed...off. What did he care who his boss chose to date?

"At my age, single men are hard to come by," Helen replied, seemingly oblivious to the bitter undertone. "Help yourselves to sandwiches. Ham and pickle is on the left," she said, breathlessly. "Smoked salmon is on the right. Chicken salad is in the middle."

Clio opted for ham and pickle. One bite and a forced swallow later, her gut rebelled. Her mother had been liberal in the application of mustard. At this rate, her dormant ulcer would come out to play.

"Do I have to be at the housewarming party?" Tammy was making a show of picking up her salmon sandwich and putting it back on her plate but was careful to avoid consuming it.

"I'd appreciate it if you put in an appearance, Tamara. Why don't you invite some of your little friends from school?"

"I don't have friends, little or otherwise."

"Come, now. You've been at Glencoe College for a whole week. Surely there's someone you eat lunch with."

Tammy's silence echoed. Clio exchanged a sympathetic glance with her daughter. Helen was one of those irritatingly confident individuals who assumed everyone would like her and collected companions wherever she went. She refused to accept that navigating a new social environment was less straightforward for her granddaughter.

Helen took a bite of her chicken sandwich, gagged, and took a discreet gulp of water. "You're not eating, Sergeant Mackey. Would you prefer another flavor? Perhaps smoked salmon and cress?"

"I'm fine, thanks." Seán avoided meeting Clio's eye. "One sandwich is plenty. I've been invited to Garda Glenn's house for dinner after my shift. Don't want to spoil my appetite."

Abandoning all pretense of eating her culinary creation, Helen whipped a pencil and notepad out of her ever-present handbag. "Right," she said in a determined voice. "Let's start planning the menu for the party."

"Didn't you say you'd hired a caterer?" Clio asked in confusion.

"Yes, but I always come prepared with my own ideas. The caterer then makes suggestions, and we adjust the menu accordingly. Do you have no experience at hosting events?" Her mother wrinkled her nose. "No, I suppose not."

Clio recalled the impromptu get-togethers she'd hosted in Barcelona. Not exactly on the same scale as her mother's parties.

Helen spent the next quarter of an hour chattering about hors d'oeuvres and suitable wines. Clio nodded at what she hopped were appropriate intervals and zoned out. Seán made civil-but-disinterested responses when required. Tammy was visibly restless, playing with the string bracelet around her thin wrists.

The mention of food reminded Clio how thin her daughter looked. She'd lost even more weight. The sooner she had her first appointment with the new therapist, the better. After her worrying weight loss earlier in the year, Tammy had gone from puppy fat to gaunt. It didn't suit her. Clio hoped it was a temporary circumstance and not the start of an eating disorder, but every time she broached the subject, Tammy clammed up. Yet another taboo topic between them. At this rate, the only safe subject for conversations would be the weather.

"Would a dessert buffet be too gauche, do you think?" her mother asked.

Clio shrugged. "I have no idea how people entertain in West Cork."

"I doubt the locals would know the difference between pâté and *foie gras*, but my Dublin friends certainly do."

"*Foie gras* is inhumane," Clio said with quiet determination. "I'd rather you left it off the menu."

For a moment, it looked as though Helen would argue the point. Then she gave a haughty sniff. "Very well. I suppose we can come up with a suitable alternative."

Seán was manfully nibbling on his inedible sandwich. "What are your plans for the weekend, Ms. Havelin?" he asked between bites. "I'll be with you tomorrow, and Garda Glenn will be here on Sunday. If possible, I'd like to put in an appearance at the Valentine's Day fair at the town hall. Things don't usually get raucous, but it's smart to show a police presence."

Helen raised an eyebrow. "In other words, it would suit you if I went to that fair."

A thin smile appeared on Seán's lips. "Precisely."

"All right," her mother said with a nod. "I can manage that. I know you've been pulled off your regular duties to guard me. Besides, Tamara will be there with her school class. Won't you, dear?"

"For my sins." The girl looked morose. "They're making us sing. I hate singing."

"Nonsense," her grandmother said with forced cheer. "You'll have a lovely time. It'll give you a chance to get to know your new friends better."

Tammy glanced in Clio's direction and rolled her eyes. The gesture, the girl looked so like her grandmother that Clio almost laughed.

She wiped her mouth with her napkin and stood. "Thanks for the sandwich. I have to get going to the pub."

Helen's expression dripped disdain. "I can't believe you took a job at a *pub*."

"It's honest work, Mother, and it pays weekly. I've sent applications for translation jobs and taken out a couple of ads, but it will take time to build my clientele."

"Good luck with the cocktail hour," Seán cut in, deftly steering the conversation before Helen could utter any more critical comments. "I saw the posters you made. You're a talented artist."

Clio smiled. "Thank you. It's a fun hobby."

"Mum's helping me paint a mural on my bedroom wall," Tammy added. "We're starting work on it this weekend."

Clio dropped a kiss onto her daughter's cheek. For once, the girl didn't flinch. "I'll pop in to check on you when I get home from work."

"Bye, Clio," Seán said, holding her gaze a little longer than strictly necessary. "See you tomorrow."

CHAPTER NINETEEN

....

The first cocktail evening at MacCarthy's pub was a roaring success. Marcella and Clio had brainstormed a trial menu featuring six basic cocktail recipes that utilized the liquor the pub always had in stock. The only extra expense was for a few fruit juices and cocktail glass decorations.

Clio put her artistic talent to good use and created a beautiful poster in addition to prettifying the chalkboard outside the pub's entrance. By nine o'clock, the cocktail hour was officially over, but customers were still clamoring for fancy drinks.

Olivia, the red-haired woman Clio had met in the bookshop on Monday, ordered her second mai tai of the evening. "These are excellent. Well done, Clio."

"Thank you. I'm sorry I had to cancel our night out. I didn't know I'd get a job working here when we arranged it."

"Don't worry about it. I'm sure we'll get another opportunity." Olivia gave Marcella a wink. "If this slave driver ever gives you a break, come on over to our table."

"Trying to lure away my staff, Olivia?" Marcella sidled up to Clio with a tray full of freshly washed cocktail glasses. "All right. I can take a hint. Clio's due a break in any case."

"Are you sure you can manage on your own?" Clio asked, eyeing the queue of customers.

"Not a problem. Máire, my girlfriend, just walked through the door. She can help me out while you take your break."

"Follow me," Olivia said. "I'll introduce you round."

Olivia led the way to the neat little snug in the corner of the main lounge. Three steps descended to a little room that had been wallpapered with vintage newspaper highlighting events from Irish history—some serious, some inane. Olivia's friends were seated at a table in the corner. She indicated a handsome dark-haired man Clio recognized from TV interviews. "This is Jonas, my husband."

"Hi." Clio shook his hand. "I stayed up late last night finishing the first of your DI Brady mysteries. Very well done."

The man gave a slow smile. "I hear Bridie put in a good word for me."

"It paid off. Now I want to read the rest in the series."

"Have you met Gavin and Fiona yet?" Jonas nodded to the couple seated across from him. "Fiona is Bridie's niece."

"Welcome to Ballybeg." Fiona was a pretty, slightly plump woman with long, curly dark hair and a warm smile. "Are you settling into Clonmore House?"

"We're still unpacking," Clio said, taking a seat next to Olivia. "My plans to be finished by the weekend were scuppered by getting this job."

Gavin, Fiona's husband, was tall and blond with an athletic build. He looked vaguely familiar. "Didn't we pass one another jogging the other day?" he asked. "Out on the promenade?"

"Probably. I'm trying to get back in shape in time for the Cork City Marathon. I ran marathons when I lived in Spain and kept up my training when I moved back to Dublin. Since we arrived in Ballybeg, I've barely managed a quick jog."

"Marathons?" Gavin perked up visibly. "Say, you don't want to train with us, do you?"

"Oh, no." Fiona wagged a finger. "You suggested we get in shape for the Ballybeg Sports Day. You never mentioned us running *marathons*."

"Sports day, marathon." Gavin shrugged. "If we keep at it, who knows what we might achieve?"

Fiona rolled her eyes. "Gavin is always trying to recruit people to train for the annual Ballybeg Sports Day. As you can see"—she grabbed a little excess flesh around her midriff—"he hasn't been successful with me."

Her husband flashed her a wicked grin. "New Year, new goals, Fee. Why don't we all arrange to go for a morning jog a couple of times a week?"

Clio gave her schedule a mental check. Getting back into a running routine would be wonderful. Squeezing a run into the days she worked at the pub would be tough, but she could manage it on the other days. It would be good for her asthma and good for her head. "I can do a run on the days I'm not working here. My current schedule has me working Tuesdays, Thursdays, and Fridays."

"How about next Wednesday morning?" Gavin beamed at the assembled company. "I'm sure Jonas would love to join us, and Olivia will be free then too."

"I run my own café," Olivia explained. "Wednesday is my morning off."

"Okay," Clio said. "Sounds like a plan. When and where do you usually meet?"

"Seven a.m. at the carousel on the promenade." Gavin knocked back the remainder of his whiskey sour. "Do you know where that is?"

"I think so. Just off the main square and toward the seafront?"

"That's the place."

"In that case, I'll see you then." Clio glanced at her watch. "I'd better get back to work. Enjoy your evening." She strode back to the bar with a spring in her step, whistling a tune under her breath. Finally, something was going right. While working at MacCarthy's was a temporary solution, she liked the other staff, and a job in a pub was an excellent opportunity to get to know her new neighbors. The tune she was whistling faltered when her phone buzzed with an incoming message. With a sinking heart, she scanned the display: *March 14.*

CHAPTER TWENTY

eán stood in line at the drinks stand and suppressed a groan. The people of Ballybeg used any event as an excuse to party, and Valentine's Day was no exception. The town hall was full of people with forced cheer and jollity, overindulging in cheap sweet wine and even sweeter treats. The walls were festooned with cheesy red hearts, cupids, and streamers. Liberating a few coins from his pocket, he paid for three drinks and then began to navigate the crowd.

Ballybeg's town hall was located in a building dating from the mid-nineteenth century. He recalled the hall from his childhood, especially from attending the annual Christmas bazaar with his family. In those days, the high ceilings seemed to stretch to impossible heights, and the rich polished wood floors were a wide expanse. When he'd seen the hall again for the first time in over twenty-five years, he'd been shocked to observe how much smaller it was than in his memories.

To the left of the entrance, Clio and Helen Havelin stood waiting for him, the former wearing a bored expression, and the latter surprisingly on edge for one used to public attention.

"Not your scene?" he asked, handing them their drinks.

"Not exactly." Clio took a sip of her sweet drink and winced. "You're one to talk. You were regarding the crowd with all the enthusiasm of a man faced with babysitting sextuplets. *Incontinent* sextuplets."

He smiled down at her. "No," he said wryly. "This is definitely not my idea of a fun Saturday excursion. I'm here in my professional capacity. I'm due to take over from Brian in a few minutes. He'll drive you home after the fair."

Helen was clutching her drink in one hand and her handbag in the other. Her eyes grew wide as she scanned the crowd. "Some of the visitors seem on the rough side. Do fights often break out at these events?"

Clio's gaze met his and her nose twitched in that adorable gesture she made when she was fighting back laughter.

"Where the drink flows freely," he said, straight-faced, "fists have been known to fly."

"How undignified." The older woman sniffed. "I only came to lend Tammy moral support."

"Didn't they hold these fairs when you were a child?" Clio asked her mother. "Surely you came to a few with your family."

"My father didn't believe in parties of any kind." Her mother's mouth hardened. "He was rather strict. Speaking of people I used to know, I think I see a girl I went to school with over by the potted plants. My, hasn't she aged?" With this parting remark, Helen swanned across the hall toward her hapless former classmate.

This time, Clio's nose twitch gave way to a hearty laugh—deep, dirty, and oh so sexy. His trousers felt tight at the sound. It brought back very pleasant memories of their night at the hotel.

"How's Tammy settling in at her new school?" He nodded toward a group of uniformed singers, keen to distract himself from X-rated visions of Clio mid orgasm.

Her gaze flitted to her daughter. "She's finding it difficult to make friends, but it's early days. Like my mother, I'm here for Tammy's sake. She has a lovely singing voice but she loathes performing in public. I promised I'd come along if she was forced to attend."

"The Reluctant Revelers," he said with a grin. "We should form a band."

"No chance. Tammy's the one with the musical talent, and she certainly didn't get that from me."

"From her dad, then?" He was curious to know more about Clio's past. She was always careful to steer the conversation away from any mention of her life before Ballybeg.

Her lips parted as if to answer. His gaze lingered on their soft pink surface, recalling the soft heat of her mouth on his. As if reading his thoughts, she licked them, and a searing jolt of awareness turned the tightness in his trousers into a full-blown hard-on. Not appropriate under the present circumstances. And yet he couldn't look away.

"Yes. She gets her musical talent from her father."

Taking a step back, she put an arm's worth of distance between them, effectively ending both that particular conversation thread and the charged vibe between them in one movement. Seán exhaled the breath he hadn't noticed he'd been holding.

The plump and cheery face of Mrs. Coombs bobbed before him, beaming from ear to ear, sliding unsubtle glances from him to Clio and back again. "Want to buy your girlfriend a Valentine's Day rose, Sergeant Mackey?"

"I'm not—" Clio said at the same moment he said, "We're not—"

Mrs. Coombs's smile didn't falter. "It's for a good cause. All proceeds go to the breast cancer foundation."

Seán slid a hand into his uniform pocket and retrieved his wallet. "I'll take three," he said, handing her a twenty-euro note.

"Oh, that's very good of you, Sergeant." The older woman turned to Clio. "I don't think I've seen our Sergeant Mackey out with a girlfriend since he moved to Ballybeg. You're a lucky woman."

Clio's every gesture brimmed with mirth. "He's a lucky man."

"Tut-tut," he said once the woman was out of earshot. "By the time she's finished spreading rumors, half Ballybeg will be planning our nuptials. That said"—he handed her one of the roses—"this is for you."

"Why, thank you." She buried her nose in the delicate bloom. "Mmm...at least I can say I got one Valentine this year." She observed the other roses with curiosity. "Who are you planning to give those to?"

"They're for Tammy and your mother." He hesitated briefly, recalling her outburst in the Book Mark. "That is, if you don't mind me giving one to Tammy. A flower might cheer her up."

"No, that's fine. It's sweet of you, actually." A frown line appeared between her brows. "I'm surprised you want to give one to my mother. I've gotten the distinct impression that she's not your favorite person on the planet."

He shrugged. "Maybe not. I could hardly give you and Tammy roses and have none for her."

"You're a gentleman," she teased. "Your mother must be very proud of you."

He sucked in a breath, blinked rapidly. "My mother is dead."

Shite. She hadn't expected that response. "I'm sorry. I didn't know."

"No reason you should have." His Adam's apple bobbed, and he blinked a couple of times. "The vinyl collection Brian was teasing me about used to be my mother's. That's why I keep it. Playing her records reminds me of her swaying to her favorite songs."

"That's a lovely way to remember her, Seán," she said softly, touching his arm and sending a frisson of awareness skittering over his skin.

He cleared his throat. "I'd better check in with Brian. Also look for potential stalkers in your mother's vicinity."

Clio laughed and tossed her empty cup into a nearby rubbish bin. "She hasn't even mentioned the stalker again. I'm convinced it was a figment of her imagination."

"Well, we have to take these reports seriously. Wouldn't do to have Ireland's favorite agony aunt clipped before our very eyes."

"Seán!" she said in faux outrage before dissolving into giggles.

"Sorry. Gallows humor. A job prerequisite."

She scrunched her brow. "My mother has a few overzealous admirers, but I can't imagine anyone wanting to harm her. At this point, her conservative views on family life are treated more as a joke than a threat."

"Don't let her hear you saying that. I get the impression Helen is as particular about her professional reputation as she is about her appearance."

"The understatement of the year." Clio's laugh sounded hollow. "As you can imagine, I'm a bitter disappointment."

Taking this as an excellent excuse to check out her assets, he allowed his gaze to roam over her tight-fitting pullover and skinny jeans. "Don't be daft. You're a good-looking woman."

She jabbed him in the chest with a finger. "And you, Sergeant Mackey, are a shameless flatterer."

"No flattery needed," he said softly. "I'd take you over polished perfection any day." On impulse, he reached out to smooth back a stray strand of red hair that had escaped her messy ponytail. His fingers lingered on her silky soft hair, brushing the tip of her ear.

"You'd better go and find Garda Glenn." Her voice had dropped to a husky whisper that set his blood humming through his veins. "We Havelins are commandeering far too much of your time as it is."

"Time spent with you is no hardship at all," he murmured, mesmerized by her aura. In his mind, he shoved her against the wall, ripped off her clothes, and had mind-altering sex with her right there in the town hall, spectators be damned.

"Cliona!" A sharp voice cut through the electrically charged moment. Helen shoved her way through the crowd, clutching her handbag to her chest as though it were in imminent danger from thieves. "I'd like you to meet some of the people I've invited to the housewarming party."

Seán dropped his hand to his side, the feel of her skin lingering on his fingertips.

"Coming, Mother." Clio shifted awkwardly. "See you later, Seán. Thanks for the lift."

"My pleasure." He caught her arm as she moved to leave. Those full pink lips begged to be kissed. For a moment, he was tempted to throw caution to the wind and give in to the impulse. Her breath was warm and smelled sweetly of mulled wine and cloves. They stood there for a moment, caught in a weird electricity, the sparks between them dancing, ready to ignite.

"Cliona," Helen demanded. "Are you coming?"

She was breathing heavily, her breasts rising and falling with each breath. "I really had better go. See you soon."

Motionless, he watched her disappear into the crowd. He'd come close to kissing her in public. Too close. So long as he was supposed to keep an eye on Helen, her daughter was off limits. But once he was no longer Helen's unofficial bodyguard...

The sound of raucous laughter made him spin round. "Oh, no," he groaned when he registered the source of the laughter.

John-Joe Fitzgerald was holding court behind the hot whiskey stand. If his unsteady hands were a reliable indicator, he'd imbibed at least as much of the alcohol-laced beverage as he'd served. Much to a gathering throng's amusement, he was having difficulty pouring the hot liquid into mugs. It splashed over the side, burning his hand.

"Who the hell put that eejit in charge of serving drink?" he said, thinking aloud. "In what universe did anyone think that was a good idea?"

Aunt Nora sidled up to him, wafting cheap perfume and lingering cigarette fumes. "He volunteered," she said, pursing her lips. "It was either that or have him play Cupid. But after he got drunk at last year's fair and had to be fished out of the fountain, he was banned from coming in costume."

Cupid? Jaysus. "I'm glad I was spared that sight."

"As if his Elvis getup isn't bad enough." Nora shook her head and fiddled with her cigarette packet.

"Sorry, ma'am," a pimply-faced usher said. "There's no smoking in here."

"Bugger off." Nora lit her cigarette and inhaled deeply, spidery lines snaking out around her puckered lips.

"Come on." Seán took his aunt's arm and steered her toward the exit. "Let's chat outside."

"It's bloody freezing outside," she muttered but allowed him to propel her through the crowd.

"I'll get you one of John-Joe's hot whiskies to warm you up. I can't be seen tolerating someone flouting the smoking laws."

"Wankers, the lot of them," snapped Nora. "I hope they get hemorrhoids. We're all going to die of something, aren't we?"

"I suppose we are," Seán said, stifling a grin.

Nora eyed him through the smoke. "You'll be over for my birthday, I hope?"

"Over? You mean at your house?"

"Of course," she said. "You're family, and both our boys are working in Australia. I'd like to have someone to celebrate with other than my fool of a husband."

"I—"

"It falls on a Sunday this year," she continued. "I always serve Sunday dinner at two o'clock sharp. Whether or not John-Joe can rouse his fat arse out of his armchair to join us at the dining room table is another matter. He was snoring by noon last year." Nora patted Seán on the arm. "At least I'll have you for company this year."

His shirt collar felt tight all of a sudden. "I might be on duty."

"Nonsense. It's not for another couple of weeks. Plenty of time to get that cheeky young nipper Brian Glenn to fill in for you."

"Speaking of John-Joe, Helen Havelin wants to hire him to perform at her house party."

Nora threw back her head and let out a hoot of laughter. "Does she know what she's letting herself in for?"

"No, and I'm not going to enlighten her. If he wants the job, here's her phone number." After scribbling the number on the notepad he always kept in the front pocket of his shirt, he tore it off and handed it to his aunt.

"Thanks, J—Seán." She gave a rueful smile. "Sorry, love. I keep forgetting your new name." His aunt dropped her cigarette on the pavement and ground it out with her heel. After glancing at her watch, she said, "I'd better get going. Don't want to miss my daily soap opera fix. My eejit of a husband can walk home. The air will do him good. With a bit of luck, it'll piss rain on him."

The picture of domestic bliss, Seán thought when his aunt climbed into her car and drove off. Had he really been roped into Sunday lunch with the outlaws? He rubbed a hand over his jaw. Nora had always been a ruthless manipulator, hence his determination to avoid her. Much easier said than done in a place the size of Ballybeg. Ah, well. It was just dinner. No promises of future happy family get-togethers. Perhaps it was time to confront his past and move on.

CHAPTER TWENTY-ONE

....

The next few days passed without incident. Clio didn't hear anything more from Ray. Garda Glenn was assigned to watch over her mother on Sunday, thus sparing Clio a confrontation with her conflicted feelings over Seán Mackey. There was no denying that the chemistry between them was on an oh-my-effing-God scale. Why, of all the men she'd ever met, did *he* have to be the one to get under her skin?

On Wednesday morning, she went to meet Olivia and her friends on the promenade as arranged. Finding a parking space this early was easy. Outside the car, Clio clipped her water bottle into its holder on her little backpack and completed stretches before jogging over to the carousel. The weather was cold and crisp with a biting wind. The idea of a run to clear her head and get her blood pumping put a broad beam on her face. A beam that wavered when she saw *who* was waiting for her.

Seán stood beside Olivia, laughing at something she'd said. He wore running gear that accentuated his muscular legs. Shame she couldn't catch a glimpse of his chest muscles through his zip-up shell jacket. The memory of his strong torso and washboard abs brought heat to her cheeks.

He glanced up when Clio jogged over to join them, his eyes widening perceptively and a smile curving his lips. "I didn't know you were joining us." His gaze darted behind her and an expression of relief settled over his handsome features.

She gave him a wry smile. "Don't worry. Mother isn't coming. She prefers to work out in her home gym or with a personal trainer. She hates people to see her sweat."

"Speaking of your mother," Olivia said, "did you know she's hired me to cater her party next Saturday?"

"No, I didn't. You said you run a café, right?"

"Yes. You must stop by for a coffee. We're on Curzon Street." Olivia pointed to a small side street that led off from the promenade. "In addition to the café, I also do the odd catering job for parties. Bridie put in a good word for me."

Clio laughed. "It sounds like Bridie takes care of her family."

"Very much so. She's married to my grandfather but she always looks out for the people she likes. Apparently, she likes you."

"She went to school with your mother," Seán said in a deceptively casual tone. "Did you know that?"

"No. Really?" The bookshop owner appeared to be several years older than her mother, but then Clio couldn't recall the last time she'd seen Helen without a carefully applied mask of cosmetics. "I know my mother knows your boss from years ago too."

"I gathered that," Seán said in a dry tone. "He seems to hold her in great affection."

"Right, troops." Gavin tapped his watch. "Let's get moving. I need to start work in an hour. I suggest we head out as far as Craggy Point and double back by the dunes."

They took the stone steps down to the beach, careful not to slip on the icy patches. The tide was out, leaving a wide stretch of sand hardened by the cold temperatures. Gavin lead them in the direction of the caves Clio had spied briefly on her previous run. Even though she had to slow her usual pace to accommodate the others, the joy was glorious.

About fifteen minutes into the run, Fiona stopped to catch her breath and clutch her sides. "Feck, I'm unfit. And my bad leg hurts. Whose idea was this, anyway?"

"Your husband's," Olivia said dryly. She was wearing designer jogging gear and cute runners, her hair pulled up in a high ponytail that swung from side to side as she jogged on the spot. "He seems to think we can all go as fast as him and Seán."

Clio laughed. "You call this pace fast?"

"Oh, I can see how this will go." Olivia tapped the side of her nose. "Fiona and I will be stuck dragging behind while you three speed on ahead."

"Speaking of numbers, where's Jonas? Didn't he want to join us today?"

Olivia nodded. "That was the original plan. Luca, his —our—son, has come down with a cold. We didn't want to pack him off to his grandmother's house when he's not feeling well."

"I can understand that. It's that time of year, isn't it? My daughter woke up with a sore throat. I'm expecting her to share the love with me at any moment."

"Is your mother looking after her this morning?" Olivia asked.

"No, she went to school. Even if she'd stayed home, there would be no need for a babysitter. Tammy is fifteen."

"Fifteen?" Fiona examined her face closely. "Surely you're not old enough to have a kid that age."

Clio was used to this reaction. Thankfully, Fiona's remark was devoid of the poorly disguised censure she usually encountered. "I'm a few years older than I look but, yes, I had Tammy just before my eighteenth birthday."

"Wow. By the time I get around to contemplating babies, yours will be grown and gone."

"I hope not. I'm not ready to let go of her yet." Particularly not when she and Tammy were finally starting to talk again after months of tension-taut silence.

"Come on ladies," Gavin yelled. "Move your ar— beautiful behinds."

"Slave driver," Fiona shouted after him. "Go on ahead, Clio. I can see you're itching to pick up speed."

She was, actually. Being out here, flying along the beach, she felt free. "Are you sure you don't mind?"

"Not at all." Fiona took a swallow from the water bottle Olivia proffered. "Let's get together another time for a proper chat."

"Why don't you both come round to the café one evening after closing?" Olivia suggested. "I can put some food by for us and we'll be away from our respective families."

"That's a great idea," Clio said. "I'll discuss my schedule with Ruairí and send you a text message when I know which evenings I'm not working."

"Most evenings work for me," Fiona said. "Check when you're free and square it with Olivia. I'll roll with whatever you two decide."

Olivia nodded. "Sounds perfect."

"Okay. Enjoy the rest of your day and let's talk soon." Clio waved good-bye and picked up pace.

She soon caught up with Gavin and Seán. They'd only run for a few minutes when Gavin's phone began to ring. He slowed to a slow jog. "Sorry, guys. I have to take this. It's a client."

While Gavin spoke to his caller, Clio took the opportunity to take a swig from her water bottle. A minute later, Gavin slipped his phone back into his pocket, irritation writ on his handsome face. "I'm going to have to cut our run short. There's a problem with a building project I'm involved in. I need to get to the site."

"No problem," Seán said. "Given the numbers of times I've had to cut and run on you—no pun intended

—I understand. Clio and I can keep going for a while, then turn back. Okay by you, Clio?"

"Yeah, that's fine." Even if it meant being alone with Seán, she was reluctant to cut short a run she was enjoying.

After Gavin left, she turned to Seán. "Are you training for this Ballybeg Sports Day event?"

He gave her a crinkly-eyed grin that warmed her to the core. "The Ballybeg Sports Day is a disgrace. The highlight is the three-legged race, and that's usually won by John-Joe and his pal, Buck MacCarthy."

She laughed out loud. "Sounds like a classy event. John-Joe's swimming Elvis act notwithstanding, neither he nor Buck strikes me as particularly athletic."

"I don't know about Buck, but John-Joe used to be athletic. I remember him training for hours when I was a k—" He broke off, cleared his throat, and picked up speed.

"You knew John-Joe when you were a kid?" Clio asked when they paused for a water break. "How? Don't you come from Dublin?"

Seán stared out to sea, his face a blank mask. The waves rose and crashed against the rocks in a violent maelstrom of foam. Finally, he capped his water bottle and turned to meet her questioning gaze. "I lived in Ballybeg until I was ten. John-Joe is my uncle."

"Oh," she said, even more confused than she'd been before. "What's the big deal? Why are you reluctant to mention it?"

The smile was back, this time self-deprecating. "Would you want to admit to being related to John-Joe Fitzgerald?"

"If I was related to him, I wouldn't care if anyone knew. Why would I? Why should you? I have a slew of relatives I'm not supposed to mention on my biological father's side of the family. I honestly don't give a toss what people think."

"It's a little more complicated than me being ashamed of John-Joe. It's not John-Joe's fault that I feel this way."

"Care to elaborate?"

"Not particularly." He averted his gaze, his voice rough with emotion. "I'm not good on sharing. Suffice it to say I left Ballybeg for what I hoped was forever and ended up being sent here to work just under a year ago."

"What did you do in Dublin to get sent to this backwater?" she asked, curious to know more.

"A mistake I didn't make." He clipped the water bottle onto his belt and flashed her the killer smile that never failed to set her pulse racing. "Come on. Let's get moving or we'll never keep our heart rates elevated."

No fear of that when she was in his vicinity. The man had a similar effect to an adrenalin shot.

They ran for another thirty minutes, past the rocky protrusion of Craggy Point, then circling back and retracing their steps toward the town. Clio's feet skipped over the rocks and the sand, giving her the impression of flying. Both she and Seán were pushing themselves hard enough that conversation was out of the question.

Finally, they reached the side street where she'd parked, and she collapsed against her car.

"That felt good," she said, draining her water bottle. "The shower after will feel even better."

"I know a way to make a shower feel very good indeed." His cheeky smile made her ache in all the right places. Even dripping with sweat and panting, Seán Mackey was drop-dead gorgeous.

She gave him a playful swat. "I'm sure you do, Sergeant Mackey, but don't you have a job to go to? Some stray sheep to round up, or a speeding ticket to write?"

"Alas, yes." He smile faded. "This morning's task isn't going to be pleasant. I need to question the local Travellers again about a series of attacks against their community. The boy who was attacked is out of his coma but not fit to talk to us yet."

She nodded sympathetically. "Good luck. I need to get home and finish cleaning the house before I start my shift at the pub."

He leaned closer. The musky scent of sweat and sexy male made her breath catch and her loins ache. His gaze was fixed on her mouth. For a moment, she was certain he was going to kiss her, but he changed course at the last millisecond and planted a soft kiss on her cheek. The sensation of not-yet-shaven male jaw brushing against her skin sent a shiver of anticipation through her.

Then he drew back, flashed her one last smile, and was gone.

CHAPTER TWENTY-TWO

....

Seán took a bite of fruit bread and washed it down with black coffee. The tiny café at the Book Mark was packed with giggling schoolgirls. He tuned them out and ran over his day. And what a day it had been.

After spending as much time as he dared under the shower fantasizing about Clio Havelin, he'd received an emergency callout from the florist's on Patrick Street. One of Danny Hegarty's sheep had made a run for it the previous day and had finally deigned to put in an appearance at Mamie Driscoll's flower shop. By the time Seán and Reserve Garda Doyle showed up at the scene of the crime, Dolly the Sheep had munched her way through half Mamie's wares.

The inanity of that encounter was sobered by a fruitless last-ditch attempt at squeezing information out of Jimmy Murphy's relatives. The good news on that front was that the boy's health continued to improve and his prognosis was no longer as bleak as it had been in the initial hours after the attack.

By four o'clock in the afternoon, Seán was bone tired and in need of a jolt of caffeine before facing the tower of paperwork that awaited him back at the station.

At the table nearest the door, Tammy Havelin sat with a couple of other schoolgirls. She seemed nervous, ill at ease. After some whispered conversation with her companions, she got up from the table and moved toward the old comic section. If the girl's hunched shoulders and furtive looks in his direction and in Bridie's were a reliable indicator, she was about to do something stupid. He exhaled a sigh. Dealing with teenage shenanigans was the last thing he wanted to add to his agenda.

The two girls at Tammy's table giggled when he caught their eye. With her liberal application of eye makeup, the dark-haired one looked like a raccoon. She smirked at him. Seán took an instant and perhaps irrational dislike to the child. The girl's spotty-faced companion had made a valiant attempt to hide her blemishes under a mask of foundation. Unfortunately, the poorly applied makeup served to draw attention to her uneven complexion.

His attention shifted to Tammy. She was pretending to peruse the selection of vintage comics preserved in plastic covers. Her hand hovered over one particular comic, and her side-glance at Bridie had him on his feet in an instant.

He moved with the stealth of a panther and sidled up to her at the comic stand. "Do you like comics, Tammy?" he asked in a voice low enough that only they could hear.

"I...um...I guess so," the girl stammered, suddenly finding her shiny black school shoes fascinating.

He examined the comic she was holding through its shiny wrapper. "Spider-Man. My favorite when I was a kid."

The girl flushed from her jaw to her cheekbones.

"Why don't you pay for this, Tammy, and then I'll give you a lift back to Clonmore House?"

Her throat convulsed, but she nodded, keeping her eyes downcast.

When they were outside the shop, Seán pressed his car key to unlock the doors. He waited until he'd eased the vehicle into the sparse traffic of Patrick Street before confronting her. "What was that about?"

Tammy shrank against the back of the passenger seat. "I'd rather not talk about it."

"Because it seemed to me as though those two little madams were daring you to steal that comic. Am I right?"

She was fidgeting with her rings now, twisting them back and forth on her slim fingers. "Can we forget it?"

"No, Tammy, we can't forget it. If you'd stolen that comic, I would have come after you and made you face the consequences." He indicated right and turned onto the winding country road that led from the town down the coast toward Clonmore House.

The girl continued to stare at her hands.

"Was it a hazing ritual?" he probed. "Was that why there were so many girls from your school in the Book Mark this afternoon?"

She chose to ignore his first question, focusing on the second. "Ballybeg doesn't exactly have a lot of choice when it comes to cafés. The Chew and Chat might be cheap, but it's a total dive. The Cottage Café is out of my price range. That leaves the café in the Book Mark."

Seán had a feeling he'd found the culprits behind the stolen money from the Book Mark's tip jar. "Did those girls put you under pressure to steal the comic?"

She shrugged, gave one of her rings a final twist, and shoved her hands into the pockets of her school blazer. "I can't rat them out. If I do, my life at that school is over before it's begun."

"Bullying is a serious offense. If you're being harassed, please tell your teachers."

The girl gave a derisive snort. "It doesn't work that way, Sergeant. If I tell tales, I'll be an outcast until I leave school. The first couple of weeks are crucial. If I f...screw up now, my life will be miserable. Believe me, I know how the game works. I've changed schools frequently enough over the years."

The kid had a point. However, he wasn't willing to let her off the hook that easily. "Will you at least tell your mother if you're having problems at school?"

Tammy's laugh was laced with hysteria. "After what happened the last time I confided in her? Hell no." She crossed her arms over her chest and turned to stare out the passenger window. "I suppose she's blabbed to you about that. With you being a policeman and all."

Curiosity piqued, he stole a glance at the girl. This had to be in reference to whatever it was that had Clio freaked about men and her daughter. Speaking of which...*damn.* Would she be upset that he'd given Tammy a lift home without calling her first? He drummed his fingers on the steering wheel. *Stupid, stupid.* He'd acted on instinct, made the offer he'd have made to any kid he'd found in that situation. "Clio hasn't mentioned anything about your last school to me," he said carefully, hoping to sound her out a bit.

The girl tugged the sleeves of her blazer down. It was something she did a lot. He'd noticed it before, but the potential significance hadn't hit him until now. Suicide attempt? Cutting? Or just a nervous repetitive gesture?

"That's a surprise." Tammy's tone was bitter. "Mum couldn't wait to run to the police in Dublin."

"Is there something I should know?" he asked gravely. "Something you're hiding?"

She turned to face him. Her expressions were as vivid and mercurial as her mother's, every emotion and mood change displayed for all the world to see. "The girls in the café are called Jenny Cotter and Roisin Quirke. They pull stunts like that all the time. I believe my 'task' was mild in comparison to others'."

This was a deflection, of that he was certain. The real reason she was upset had little to do with two bitches and their power games. On the other hand, the information was valuable. He'd heard the girls' names before, when Bridie had mentioned the stolen money.

Love and Shamrocks

He had a feeling he'd be having a word with them before too long.

His mobile phone began to vibrate to the tune of "Bat Out of Hell." This elicited a reluctant laugh from Tammy. Seán switched on his Bluetooth headset. "Sir?"

"Hey, Seán." The super's cheerful voice boomed into his ear. "Good news for a change. Police in Galway have arrested a man they suspect of sending Helen Havelin the threatening letter."

This information was a melody to Seán's ears. "Oh, aye? Does that mean we'll be wrapping up the bodyguard duty?"

"If the suspect is charged, yes." The super chuckled. "I bet you're pleased."

Conflicted, actually. He turned onto the winding tree-lined drive that led to Clonmore House. "What about the car she thought was following her?"

"Nothing's shown up so far. My guess is that the threatening letters have made her paranoid."

He certainly hoped so. Once he'd put his dislike of Helen aside and concentrated on the stalker angle, something had niggled. It was a nagging sensation they were missing something, some tiny detail that hovered like vapor but never coalesced into anything concrete.

"I've been in touch with Helen," the super said. "We've agreed to continue to keep an eye on her until the Galway Guards confirm they've got the right man. She's already offered a generous donation to the force's widows and orphans fund in return for a police presence on the night of her housewarming party. Once that duty is fulfilled, we can leave the Havelins in peace."

The note of regret in his boss's tone made Seán chortle. "Would I be right in guessing there's a part of you that's disappointed by this turn of events?"

"Best leave the matchmaking in Ballybeg to Bridie Byrne, lad."

Seán was still grinning when he disconnected. Despite his misgivings about potential loose ends, the end of surveillance on Helen meant there was no professional impediment to him asking Clio out on a date. A proper date this time, complete with dinner and music better than the shite they'd been subjected to at the Sheldon Hotel bar. If it led to a repeat performance of what had happened in his hotel room...well, he had zero objections on that score.

CHAPTER TWENTY-THREE

·······························

When the police car drove into the gravel courtyard of Clonmore House, Clio was busy polishing the brass knocker on the front door. Although she rarely wasted time worrying about her appearance, the sight of Seán Mackey climbing out of his car made her acutely aware of her messy bun, raggedy long-sleeved T-shirt, and the smudge of dirt on her nose that the by-now gleaming knocker took perverse delight in reflecting. Given her past experience with policemen, the realization that she found his uniform a turn-on was as uncomfortable as the unsatisfied ache of longing in her loins.

She blinked in surprise to see Tammy get out of the passenger side. "Isn't the Ballybeg police force only obliged to chauffeur my mother?"

Tammy's stance was hunched, defensive. *Uh, oh.* This didn't bode well.

"I hope you don't mind me giving her a lift, but"—Seán's grin displayed his dimples and sent her limbs aquiver—"the mobile phone number I have for you isn't exactly accurate."

Feck. She'd gone and given him a fake number the night at the hotel, hadn't she? Heat warmed her cheeks. "No, it's fine. What happened?"

He nudged the girl forward. "Would you like to tell her, Tammy?"

"I tried to steal a comic from the Book Mark." Her daughter dropped her gaze to the ground.

"What?" Clio's jaw dropped. "Why would you do that? You don't even like comics."

Tammy darted a glance at Seán, then focused on toeing some gravel. "A couple of girls from school dared me. But I didn't actually steal it. Sergeant Mackey made me pay for it."

"Thank goodness for that." Clio gave him a grateful smile before refocusing on her daughter. "Why would you, of all people, let a couple of classmates persuade you to steal? You don't usually care what other kids say."

"Jenny Cotter is a cow and her sidekick, Rosin Quirke, isn't much better. I don't know why they wanted me to nick a tatty old comic. They said it was a test." Tammy snorted. "More like a hazing ritual designed to torture new students."

"Why didn't you tell them to get stuffed?" Clio demanded.

Tammy's fingers rubbed the wrists of her blazer. "For once, I want to belong. I don't want to stand out in any way. After changing schools four times over the past five years, I know the best way to survive is to get the support of the so-called popular crowd, even if I end up being absorbed into their band of satellites."

Clio could understand wanting to become someone so devoid of personality that no one at school would ever think to notice her, let alone pick on her. She'd been in a similar situation in her last couple of years at secondary school—before she'd discovered she was pregnant and had gotten expelled. The idea of her own daughter feeling that low made her heart ache. "Why don't you go upstairs to your room and start your homework? I'll come up with hot chocolate in a few minutes and we'll have a chat."

Tammy's head shot up. "You're not going to bawl me out?"

"Given that you didn't get as far as stealing the comic"—she shot a grateful look at Seán—"I'm more concerned about the motivation behind it. That said, you're not getting off scot-free. You're grounded for the next two weeks."

Her daughter opened her mouth as if to protest, then obviously thought better of it. "Fair enough. I can deal with grounded. Especially if you use the fancy Swiss chocolate powder to make my hot chocolate."

"Cheeky," Clio said, suppressing a laugh. "Don't push your luck."

After Tammy left, she turned her attention to Seán. "Thanks for bringing her home. I can't believe she'd do something like this, yet on the other hand, I'm shocked I'm even surprised."

"Has she been acting up since you moved to Ballybeg?" His gaze was direct and probing, searching her face for clues.

ZARA KEANE

She released a sigh. "Yes, but the move wasn't the start of the problems. Look, I'd rather not get into the details, but I don't intend to make excuses for Tammy's behavior. She's been through a tough time these last few months. I'd hoped Ballybeg and a new school would give her a fresh start. Clearly, I was being overly optimistic. So where do we go from here? Will the shop's owner press charges?"

"No. Bridie was busy serving customers, and I don't think she noticed Tammy was contemplating taking the comic. Fact is, she didn't steal it."

"But she would have, had you not intervened," she said softly. "I can't help but feel it's my fault."

"Why do you say that?" he asked, his intelligent eyes shrewd.

She bit her lip and weighed her next words carefully. "I haven't always lived an exemplary life."

That brought forth a deep chuckle that sent a shot of unfiltered lust straight to her nipples. "Which of us has?"

"Now, now, Sergeant Mackey. Surely a member of the police force has no questionable past?"

He threw back his head in a guffaw. "I was a teenage boy once upon a time. I'm hardly a saint."

Somehow, she doubted any of Seán Mackey's youthful exploits could rival her stint working for Ray Greer and scrounging for her next fix. She was certain *he* didn't have a criminal record.

"If Tammy is troubled," Seán said, suddenly serious again, "is she seeing anyone? A counselor, I mean. I

216

realize this is none of my business, but we have a few contact numbers for youth psychologists back at the station. I can pass them on to you."

"Thanks, but we've made an appointment with a woman in Cork City. I'm hoping Tammy is more cooperative with this counselor than she was with the one in Dublin."

His eyes slid past the house toward the sea. "It can take a while to find the right therapist, and the counseling route isn't for everyone."

The gravity of his tone and gestures made her wonder if he spoke from experience. "I know," she said. "I'm not keen on the idea of baring myself to a stranger with a pen, either. In Tammy's case, I think it's necessary. I'm out of my depth."

"You underestimate yourself, Clio." His gaze was focused on her again, searching her face with a charged intensity. "You're doing the best you can with the cards life's dealt you."

Clio let out a bitter laugh. "Some of those cards are the result of my own poor life choices."

His lips curved into a smile. "Not all your life choices were bad. You had Tammy."

"Having her was the one smart move I made," she said, returning his smile.

Seán closed the space between them and cupped her chin in his hands. The way he searched her face with such concentration seared her soul. He rubbed her forehead with his thumb, eliciting a small groan from the back of her throat.

"A smudge of brass cleaner," he murmured, close enough that his breath warmed her neck. She was dizzy, falling, heady with anticipation. *Kiss me, please.* The words danced on the tip of her tongue.

"You've heard your mother's stalker may have been caught?" The words tickled her ear.

"Yes," she said, breathlessly.

"Which means there'll soon be no reason we can't see each other." He nipped her earlobe playfully, making her ache in all the right places. "Would you like to go out with me some time, Clio?"

No, the sensible part of her screamed. "Yes," she murmured seconds before he dipped his head and claimed her mouth with his.

Surrendering to the moment, she responded with such intensity that her knees grew weak. When he broke the kiss, it was like an invisible rope held them in place.

"I have to get back to the station," he said, touching his fingertip to her nose. "Before I go, can you give me your number?" A wicked grin. "Your *real* number this time."

She giggled and slid her phone from her back pocket. "Do I get a personalized ringtone?"

His grin stretched from ear to ear. "Everybody I talk to regularly gets a personalized ringtone."

"What's mine?" she asked after he'd keyed her number into his phone.

His dirty laugh made her acutely aware of the wetness between her legs, and of the aching need in her groin. This man slayed her, slashing through her barbed-wire defenses with alarming ease. He hit a button on his display and 'Blitzkrieg' by the Ramones started to play. "Reminds me of your outfit the night we met."

"You remembered the logo on my ratty old T-shirt?" She was oddly touched by the admission.

"How could I not?"

He dropped a last kiss on her forehead, climbed back into his car, waved, and drove off.

Still shaking from the intensity of his kiss, she watched the police car wind its way into the distance. Was she crazy to go on a date with him? Her mind told her that getting closer to Seán Mackey was a lousy idea, but her body screamed the opposite.

She was slipping her phone back into her pocket when it vibrated with an incoming message. It was an e-mail from Emma. Heart thudding wildly, Clio scanned the display.

Hey, Clio,

I *finally* turned up something potentially useful on Greer. He was a silent investor in a shopping center development near Ballybeg. The project went bust last year. One of the partners— the former owner of your new home!!!—skedaddled to Marbella. Another partner wound up dead, but that doesn't seem to be directly connected to the bust project. In the aftermath of the murder inquiry, Greer was investigated for money laundering and art smuggling, but he wriggled off the hook with his usual finesse. No clue if any of this relates to his interest in your mother and her aquawhatsit. Give me a call for the full deets.

Love ya,

Emma x x

CHAPTER TWENTY-FOUR

....

Seán spent the week following the arrest of Helen Havelin's stalker buried in work but feeling like he was chasing his own tail. The investigation into the attack on the young Traveller boy, Jimmy Murphy, had reached a dead end. No one was talking, no one knew anything, and apart from him and Brian, no one seemed to give a damn. Meanwhile, he was facing another evening at Helen's beck and call, but at least it would be his last. The consolation was having an excellent excuse to see Clio again.

The memory of their kiss lingered on his lips. His feelings for her were a jumble of raw sexual attraction and conflicted emotions he'd rather not explore. For whatever crazy reason, he found himself seeking emotional intimacy from her—the sort of intimacy he'd spent years avoiding. Whenever he was near her, his resolve to keep their connection to one of his no-strings flings took another battering. Still, what harm would a date do? They'd already had sex, after all.

"Penny for your thoughts?" Brian's voice jerked him back to the present. It was the Friday before Helen's party. They were in the Cottage Café, eating a spot of lunch and drowning it with hot tea and coffee respectively.

"Just thinking about the weekend." Seán shoved another forkful of Olivia's divine chicken lasagna into his mouth.

Across the table, Brian scrunched up his freckled nose. "Are you sure you don't mind covering the housewarming party on your own?"

"Nah," he lied. "I'll have the reserves to help me, and the super will be there as a guest. Enjoy your weekend away with Sharon."

"I'm not sure that 'enjoy' is the appropriate word." Brian stirred a second sugar cube into his tea, as if forgetting he'd already added one. "This will be the first time Sharon meets my parents, and it'll be on my mum's territory. I don't know how it'll go. I think she'll get along fine with my dad and my sisters, but frankly I don't see Mum and Sharon hitting it off."

"Families, eh?" Seán's experience of family was of ill-fitting jigsaw pieces—supposed to fit together to form a whole but somehow never managing to do so. And speaking of families, he needed to resurrect the half-written e-mail to his brother from his drafts folder and hit send. Last he'd heard, Dex was exploring a shipwreck off the coast of North Queensland, Australia. Although his brother was officially attached to the Irish National Monuments Service's Underwater Archaeology Unit, he was frequently sent abroad for work. When had they last seen each other? Last year? The year before?

They'd been close as kids but their relationship had suffered once their parents died and they'd been sent to live in separate households. Their maternal grandmother couldn't cope with raising more than one lively boy, so Seán had stayed with her and Dex had been sent to live with an aunt and uncle on the other side of Dublin. While he still cared about his brother, the bond they'd had as children had never recovered. All the same, he was proud of his little brother and his achievements.

In the corner of his eye, he registered a movement that triggered his policeman's inner red alert system. A man clad in a biker jacket and boots strode into the café. He'd removed his helmet to reveal a shaved head with tattoos creeping up his neck. Due to the scarf the man had wrapped around the bottom part of his face, Seán couldn't pinpoint who the guy was or where he'd seen him before, but he definitely knew him from somewhere. Memories whirred in the computer center of his brain.

The man took a seat by the window, finally shrugging off his leather jacket and unwinding the scarf.

Seán banged the table in a subconscious gesture. Of course he knew the guy. It was Laurence "Lar" Delaney, a notorious Dublin wide boy with connections to everyone from the Real IRA to organized crime within the Traveller community to slippery fuckers like Ray Greer. Seán hadn't seen Delaney in the flesh since the summer. And he wasn't happy to see him now.

He nudged Brian. "Word to the wise. Dude sitting by the window? That's Lar Delaney. You might remember the name from the Gant murder investigation and then the money-laundering-business inquiry."

"Eh?" Brian cast a surreptitious glance over his shoulder.

Delaney didn't move a muscle nor give any indication he'd noticed them. All bollocks in Seán's opinion. A man like Delaney didn't walk into a random café and fail to register the presence of two uniformed policemen.

"What's he doing in Ballybeg?" Brian asked.

"I don't know, but I intend to find out." Seán abandoned his half-eaten lunch and approached Delaney's table. Abandoning his undrinkable tea, Brian scrambled after him.

The waitress Olivia employed part-time had taken the man's order and now set a mug of steaming black coffee in front of him.

The biker saw them approach but he deliberately waited until the waitress retreated and they'd slid onto the bench opposite him before making eye contact. "Afternoon, lads," he said. "To what do I owe the pleasure?"

Delaney's accent was an odd mix of working class North Dublin and American twang. He'd spent time on the other side of the Atlantic, that was for sure.

"Don't play dumb, Delaney. We know who you are. We worked the Gant case last summer."

Delaney's smile revealed unexpected dimples on his unseasonably tanned cheeks. The man didn't strike Seán as the solarium type, so he'd recently spent time in sunnier climes than their Irish winter. "So you did, Detective Inspector Mackey."

Seán felt his cheeks grow warm. "Sergeant Mackey."

The smile didn't falter. "Ah, yes. I heard about your demotion."

Seán was sure he had. It had come about as the result of a takedown gone wrong. The raid in question was supposed to catch Ray Greer's gang red-handed with stolen museum pieces. Had the plan succeeded, Seán would have been well on his way to securing a transfer within the National Bureau of Criminal Investigation from arts and antiques thefts to homicide. Instead, the evening had ended with a dead rookie detective and Seán's disgrace, demotion, and transfer to Ballybeg. Someone had ratted them out to Greer. Seán's hands formed fists under the table. If he ever found out *who* that someone was, he'd make them pay.

Delaney quirked a pierced eyebrow. "What crime am I breaking by having a coffee in a public café?"

"None," Seán replied smoothly, "but this café belongs to Aidan Gant's former wife. We just want to make sure you're not here to harass her."

Delaney's surprised expression was too convincing to be feigned. "I didn't know she owned this place. My only agenda is coffee and food."

"Well, you've found it. Drink up and leave."

"I haven't paid for it yet. And I haven't had a chance to order my lunch."

Seán tossed a few coins on the table. "Courtesy of Ballybeg Garda Station. Now be on your way."

Delaney settled back in his seat and raised his palms in a placating gesture. "No can do. I'm meeting someone for lunch."

"Whether or not you were directly involved in the business over the summer, we don't want your sort in Ballybeg. Finish your coffee, get on your bike, and leave."

The door to the café swung open, letting in a gust of icy wind and Tammy Havelin. She was wearing her Glencoe College uniform, and a school bag was slung over one shoulder.

To Seán's astonishment, Tammy made a beeline for Delaney's table. She dropped a kiss onto Delaney's cheek and rubbed his shaved head affectionately. "Hey, Dad. Did I keep you waiting?"

CHAPTER TWENTY-FIVE

···

Seán looked from Delaney to Tammy, then back again. Blinking away the fog of surprise, he could see the resemblance. Truth be told, Tammy looked more like her father than her mother. She'd inherited his height and striking blue eyes. Recalling Clio's panicked reaction to Seán having a cup of coffee with Tammy, he decided he was going absolutely nowhere until he was certain Delaney posed no threat to the girl.

"Does your mother know you're here?" he asked, eyes narrowing in suspicion.

"Of course." The girl's wide-eyed innocence oozed insincerity.

"Okay." He pulled his phone from his pocket. "In that case, I'll just give her a call to make sure."

"What?" She reached out to put a hand on his arm. "No, don't do that. She's working at the pub. She'll be busy."

"Clio texted me to say it would be okay for me to meet Tammy today." Delaney flipped open his phone and showed Seán the message.

"That wasn't sent from Clio's number."

Delaney frowned then turned to his daughter. "Did you fake a text from your mother to me?"

Tammy slumped into her seat and crossed her arms over her chest. "So?"

Her father sighed. "I don't have custody, Tammy. I can't see you without your mother's permission. You know that."

"She's been jumpy lately. Totally paranoid after—" She cast a furtive glance at Seán and Brian.

"After what? What happened?" Delaney's brow creased in concern. And unless he was a world-class actor, he wasn't faking.

"Nothing," the girl said quickly. Far too quickly to convince any of them that she was telling the truth. "Let's just forget it and order lunch. I'm starving."

Delaney's gaze met Seán's. A moment of reluctant understanding passed between them. "Can you give Clio a call, Sergeant? Or give me her number and I'll call?"

"Dad," Tammy protested. "Please don't. Mum will make me go home. I haven't seen you in ages."

Her father ran an agitated hand over his shaved head. "I have to tell her, Tammy. You know the rules."

Seeing Lar Delaney, suspected Real IRA hit man and convicted bank robber, acting the role of responsible parent was a turn-up for the books. Well, well. Perhaps the man had a couple of redeeming features to display alongside his mug shot gallery.

Seán hit dial. Clio answered on the second ring. "What's up? I hope you're not calling to say your uncle can't perform at the party." Her tone was bone-dry. "My mother would be devastated."

"Nothing to do with the party. I'm at Olivia's place—
the Cottage Café on Curzon Street. Tammy is here with
her father. It seems she didn't have your permission to
meet him."

"What? What the hell is *he* doing in Ballybeg?"

Crazy as it might sound, Seán was relieved to hear
the irritation in her voice. From Clio's reaction, the idea
of her ex being at large in her new hometown was a
source of irritation rather than fear. Whoever had hurt
Tammy, it wasn't Lar Delaney.

"Do you want me to drive her back to Clonmore
House? I need to check in with your mother this
afternoon anyway. The super wants to make sure the
security plans for tomorrow are in place."

"Would you? I'd be very grateful. My shift at the pub
doesn't finish until six o'clock."

"Can't I at least eat lunch with Dad?" Tammy pleaded.
"She'll never let me see him after this."

"I'm guessing you heard that," Seán said into the
phone.

"Depends on your schedule, Seán. If it won't
inconvenience you to wait, she can have lunch with him,
but then she's to go straight home." Clio released a sigh.
"I just don't want her getting any daft ideas about
moving in with her father. Not that I think he'd offer,"
she added with a rough laugh. "Unreliable is Lar's
middle name, but Tammy doesn't see it. He swans into
her life when it suits him and is nowhere to be found
when he might prove useful."

"Okay. Unless all hell breaks loose in Ballybeg over the next half hour, Brian and I were going to order dessert and brainstorm our schedule for next week. Tammy can hang with her father, and I'll escort her home when I'm leaving. Sound good?"

"Sounds perfect. Thank you so much." She dropped her voice to a husky whisper. "I promise to make it up to you. My mother will be home this evening. Want to meet after work? I could come round to your place."

Aware of the audience around him, he kept his voice neutral. "An excellent idea. I'll text you the details."

Her husky laugh sent a tingle down in his spine. "You do that. I'm looking forward to meeting your famous vinyl collection."

"I'll play a record for you later." Smiling, he rang off and slipped the phone back into his pocket.

Lar Delaney was eyeing him in detached amusement, beefy arms crossed, and sweater sleeves pushed up to his elbows to display the intricate sleeve tattoos on each muscled arm. "You seem to know Clio well."

"Ballybeg is a small town. I know a lot of people." Seán met the big man's gaze, but the brief period of frankness between them was at an end. Delaney was back in wary mode, defensive shields in place.

An idea nagged at the back of Seán's mind, a loose thread floating in the winds of memory that he instinctually knew was significant but couldn't link up to the whole. *Clio...Lar Delaney...the Gant murder case...money laundering...*

And then it hit him. The man he'd suspected of taking something from Clio's handbag that evening at the Sheldon hotel had seemed familiar. *Of course he bloody well had.* Even if Seán couldn't fix a name to the guy, he'd seen his mug shot. And where had he seen it? Among the mountain of files dedicated to Ray Greer, one of the slimiest bastards to disgrace the Dublin crime scene. Greer's shenanigans had set in train the course of events that had led to Seán losing his job and young Alan Brennan losing his life.

What the hell was Clio Havelin mixed up in?

***

Clio clutched the wine bottle with stiff fingers and coaxed her lips into a smile. The bravado from earlier had dissolved, leaving her a mass of nervous energy.

A date. Seán had asked her out on an official date. When was the last time she'd had dinner with a guy? Probably not since Juan, an ex-boyfriend from her time in Barcelona. And when was the last time a man had offered to cook said dinner? That would be never.

Taking a deep breath, she pressed the bell on the door of Seán's apartment building. A moment later, the intercom crackled into life.

"Hey, Clio. I'll buzz you in. My apartment is on the top floor. I'll meet you on the landing." Even through the static, his deep voice had the power to weaken her knees.

The buzzer sounded and she entered the small lobby. Seán's apartment was located in a three-floor modern new-build on the outskirts of town. The house was a blocky, cubic structure with a slanted metal roof. In deference to the Ballybeg tradition of brightly colored facades, it was painted a warm shade of red-orange. All the buildings in close proximity to Seán's were no older than five or ten years. If Clio's guess was correct, the area had been farmland until relatively recently.

True to his word, he was waiting on the top landing, the door to his apartment ajar. A wide grin split his face when he saw her. His gaze roved over her black trousers and lacy blue top. "You look lovely."

Her cheeks grew warm. She'd made more of an effort than she usually did, even adding a light coating of mascara and a touch of lip gloss. "You don't look too bad yourself, Sergeant Mackey," she said, taking in his dark shirt and denim jeans.

Seán ushered her into his home. The slate-gray tiles and white walls gave the place a sleekly modern appearance, and tasteful posters and paintings added a splash of color. With the exception of two closed doors that Clio took to conceal the bathroom and the bedroom respectively, the apartment was open plan. Dramatic floor-to-ceiling windows overlooked farmland and gave the room the illusion of extra space.

In one corner of the living room, Marvin Gaye's "Midnight Love" was spinning on the record player. After handing him the wine bottle, she flipped through a stack of vinyl records. "I see you like Motown music."

"My mother was a huge fan. I grew up listening to the Supremes and other Motown artists. My record collection belonged to her."

"You're lucky. My mother pretends to like opera. That's what I was subjected to as a child."

Seán laughed and held the bottle of wine she'd brought aloft. "Want a glass? I also have white in the fridge, or beer if you'd prefer."

"If it's already chilled, a small glass of white would be perfect."

While Seán was pouring wine, Clio moved toward the kitchen and peeked into a pot on the stove. "Mmm... This smells heavenly."

"It's nothing fancy," he said, handing her a glass. "Just a chicken tarragon casserole."

"Just?" she teased. "Admit it. You've been slaving over a hot stove for hours."

"Maybe a couple." His dirty grin made her veins hum.

Taking a clean spoon from the drawer, he tasted the sauce. "Pretty good, if I do say so myself. Want to try?"

He held the spoon out and she closed the space between them. This close, their electrically charged sexual attraction fairly crackled. She put her lips round the spoon, licking the yellow sauce from it suggestively. "Delicious."

Seán's eyes darkened, and his gaze dropped to her mouth. Clio's nipples hardened under her lacy blue top. A vision of shoving cooking utensils to the side and having sex on the kitchen counter loomed large...and then her treacherous stomach grumbled. Loudly.

That got a low rumble of a laugh. "I'd better dish this out," he said in a thick voice.

"I think you'd better."

The chicken tarragon casserole lived up to the promise of its tantalizing aroma. "This was seriously good," Clio said after she'd eaten her fill. "Why hasn't some smart woman snapped you up already and chained you to the kitchen?"

Seán's eyes twinkled with amusement. "Do you like the idea of chaining me up?"

"I like the idea of you cooking for me, with or without chains." *And with or without clothes...*

As if reading her thoughts, he grinned and refilled her wine glass. "So, Miss Clio. Are you going to fill me in on the Lar Delaney story, or will I have to drag it out of you?"

She made an exaggerated grimace. "I figured you'd recognize him."

"Kind of hard not to. He was the youngest person on Ireland's Most Wanted list when I was a junior policeman. I'd love to know how he managed to persuade the judge to give him an eight-year sentence and walk free after five."

Clio gave a noncommittal shrug. She wasn't stupid enough to divulge any information on her ex to a policeman, even one who was off duty. Truth be told, she didn't know anything concrete to share. If Ray Greer was a slippery bastard, then Lar Delaney was opaque. And despite their shared child, Clio was wary of Lar, and even warier of his family.

She took a sip of her Pinot Gris and eyed Seán over the rim of the glass. "You're curious to know how a wealthy private school girl got knocked up by the son of a shady paramilitary leader."

That made him laugh. "I'm assuming the conception occurred in the usual way. But yeah, I'd like to know how you hooked up."

"Lar worked part-time in his uncle's betting shop. It was next door to a chipper that my friends and I sometimes went to after school. He was big, bad, and handsome and I fell for him. Plus he was the first guy to ask me out, and I was flattered. Within three months, I was pregnant."

"And your mother hit the roof." His smile was gone now.

"To put it mildly." The memories of their explosive reactions were as fresh in her mind as though it had all happened yesterday. "My stepfather was still alive then. I believe he was the driving force behind the decision to throw me out."

"Did Delaney dump you?" His voice hardened and his mouth formed a grim line of condemnation.

"Our situation was more complicated than that." She sighed and angled her chair toward the window, staring out over the snow-speckled fields. "I'd assumed—and Lar had allowed me to believe—that he was nearly nineteen.

He was tall and broad and had the swagger to pull it off. When my parents found out I was pregnant, they freaked out and hauled me round to the housing estate where Lar's family lived. And we all got a shock. Turned out Lar was two months shy of his fifteenth birthday. Far from me being seduced by an older bad boy, I was nearly three years *his* senior."

"Jaysus." Seán blinked. "He got you pregnant when he was *fourteen?*"

"Yes. He was fifteen by the time Tammy was born and I was eighteen. So you see, he was never in a position to support us. Despite the streetwise attitude, he was still just a kid."

"Where did you go after your parents kicked you out?"

"Lar's aunt's spare room. By the time Tammy was born, Lar and I weren't even pretending to be a couple. He made an appearance at the hospital, then scarpered."

Seán cleared their plates and fixed coffee. He set an espresso cup before her and reclaimed his seat. "Truth be told, I don't know that I'd have been any more reliable when I was fifteen."

"To be fair to Lar, he did come round to visit us regularly during the first few months of Tammy's life, but he played with her like she was one of his younger siblings and not his daughter. I knew I couldn't rely on him for support, and I'd been obliged to leave school before my Leaving Cert. Without a school certificate, I had no chance of getting a decent job. And once Lar was sent to a juvenile detention center, he was out of the picture for several years."

"Right." He nodded, a thoughtful expression on his face. "At what point did you move to Spain?"

She blushed and toyed with the handle of her coffee cup. "I guess you know all about my run-in with the law."

He nodded, his gaze solemn. "I read your file when we were asked to look into your mother's stalker. You got a suspended sentence for petty theft and possession of crystal meth."

"Lar's aunt...Lar's family...well, you know who they are. Drugs were easy to come by, and I'd hit rock bottom." An abridged version of events for sure, but she was keen to avoid elaborating upon what, precisely, the Delaneys got up to when the police weren't looking. In comparison, Ray Greer was a candidate for sainthood. She'd met Ray through Lar's aunt, Siobhan. Crazy as it sounded, taking a job with Ray was a smarter move than continuing to live with the Delaneys.

"One of the conditions for your suspended sentence was rehab," Seán said quietly. The look of understanding in his eyes brought her to the brink of her self-control.

"Yes. After my sentencing, I went to rehab and Tammy was sent to live with a foster family."

He took her hand in his, stroking the skin between thumb and index finger. "That must have been tough."

"It was awful, but it was the best thing that could have happened. I got myself straightened out, and

Tammy was cared for by a lovely family. I can't say enough positive things about the Reillys. Despite having five kids of their own, they started fostering when their youngest was two. Tammy was their twenty-sixth foster child."

"Wow. That's impressive."

"Despite my conviction and drug problem, they treated me with compassion. Officially, I was allowed one visit with Tammy each week, but Mrs. Reilly made sure I saw her more often than that. The only reason I regained custody as quickly as I did was due to the Reillys putting in a good word for me with social services."

"They sound like decent folk." He flipped her hand over and ran his thumb over her pulse. It beat wildly under his touch.

"I'm still in touch with the Reilly family. Actually, one of their daughters ended up becoming my closest friend. Funny how life turns out."

"Yes," he murmured, dropping a kiss onto her wrist. "The man upstairs has an odd sense of humor."

The irony in his voice gave her pause. "What about your family? Are you close?"

He dropped her hand back onto her lap. "No." The haunted look she'd noticed when he'd mentioned his mother's death was back. "We're not close. After my parents died when I was ten, my brother and I were sent to live with family in Dublin. My grandmother took me in, but because she didn't feel able to look after two boys, my little brother was sent to live with an aunt and uncle."

"After your *parents* died?" Clio blinked in surprise. "You mentioned your mother was dead, but I didn't realize your father was too." How horrible to lose both parents at such a young age.

An expression of raw pain froze Seán's features. "It was a murder-suicide," he said finally. "My mother discovered my father was having an affair and snapped."

"Oh my God," she gasped. "That's awful."

"They didn't even own a gun." His voice broke on the last word. "My father had borrowed one from a local farmer to get rid of a couple of foxes that kept wreaking havoc on our land. If my mother hadn't had easy access to a loaded weapon, she'd probably have come to her senses and they'd still be alive."

"I am so sorry that happened to you, Seán. It makes anything I've gone through pale in comparison."

He gave a wobbly smile. "So you see why being back in Ballybeg isn't easy. I went to all the trouble of changing my name and trying to bury memories only to end up being transferred to the very police station where my father used to work. The only saving grace is that both the building and the staff of Ballybeg Garda Station has changed since my father's day."

"You changed your name?" She reached for his hand and squeezed it. "Seán Mackey isn't your birth name?"

He shook his head. "Mackey was my mother's maiden name. Until I turned eighteen, I was Jonathan Fitzgerald.

I started to go by Seán when I was in my early teens. Legally changing my name was a dramatic step, but I was young and dumb enough to think it would help erase the past."

"It didn't make a difference?"

"Not enough of a one," he said grimly. "I'm sorry the conversation has taken a morbid turn."

He stood abruptly and strode to the record player. A moment later, the Ramones started singing "Sheena is a Punk Rocker." He turned and held a hand out to her. "Will you dance with me, Clio?"

"With pleasure." And it truly was a pleasure. The sensation of his arms around her felt oh so right. Snuggling against his warm body, she traced a finger down the front of his shirt. She inhaled the twin scents of fabric softener and aftershave and leaned her head against his chest.

He was a good dancer. Way better than she was. After a couple of songs from the *Rocket to Russia* album, he switched from vintage punk back to seventies soul. After swinging her around to James Brown's "Get Up (I Feel Like Being a) Sex Machine," Seán slow danced with her to "Neither One of Us" by Gladys Knight & the Pips.

"Do you want to go to my bedroom?" he whispered into her ear.

The ache of longing that had been building since the moment she'd seen him standing outside his apartment door became a throb. She ran her hands through his short dark hair and murmured, "Yes."

Tugging her by the hand, Seán led the way into his bedroom. Like the rest of the apartment, it was neat and tidy with colorful posters on the walls. "You're a neat freak, aren't you?" she asked with a laugh.

"I've been accused of being a tad excessive in my tidiness, yes. But right now, I have more interesting things on my mind than my housekeeping abilities." He ran his hands over her shoulders and down her back, making her tremble. He tugged at the hem of her top. "How easy is this to remove?"

"Not as easy as your shirt." She toyed with his collar and unfastened a button. "I see you opted for snap fasteners this evening."

His laughter reverberated against her neck, sending her pulse into overdrive. "After our last encounter, I figured snap fasteners were a safer bet than buttons."

He bent to kiss her, banishing all thoughts of buttons, snappers, and other fasteners from her mind. Not breaking the kiss, Seán pushed her top upward, finding her bra. They broke apart and she pulled her top off, discarding it onto the floor.

The sight of a light smattering of chest hair where his shirt was open sent her wild. Yanking the rest of the snappers open, she pulled his shirt off.

Her trousers were the next to go, quickly followed by his jeans. Not bothering with the niceties of a slow strip tease, they discarded their underwear and hit the bed.

Trailing kisses down her torso and over her abdomen, he located her clit with ease. Pushing her thighs apart, he teased it with his tongue. The twin sensations of his mouth on her clit coupled with his stubble grazing the tender flesh of her inner thighs had an electric effect.

She squirmed in pleasure, her breath coming in short, sharp gasps. He maintained the pressure, kneading her buttocks, massaging the small of her back, tugging her nipples. "Don't. Stop."

He didn't.

Clio ceased to think of anything but the wave surging inside her, finally cresting in a tsunami of pleasure. When it subsided, she collapsed against her pillow and gave a sigh of intense satisfaction. "Wow. That was even better than the last time."

Seán danced his fingertips around her navel, and trailed them upward. "That, my dear," he murmured into the base of her throat, "was merely the appetizer."

CHAPTER TWENTY-SIX

....

C lio heaved the last tray of champagne glasses onto the table and wiped sweat from her brow. "Did my mother's guest list reproduce? This seems like a lot of glasses for eighty guests."

"Eighty?" Olivia blinked in surprise. "She told me to prepare food for one hundred people."

"Oh, no." Phoebe, Helen's mousy and long-suffering PA, whipped out her smart phone. "I have one hundred and fifteen people on the guest list."

Olivia swore beneath her breath, caught Clio's eye, and laughed. "How do you think your mother's Dublin guests will react to being served store-bought bread sticks if I run out of food?"

Clio thought of the overnight guests already causing mayhem and issuing orders upstairs. "Not well. Judge and Mrs. Carroll are very particular about their food."

The corners of Olivia's eyes crinkled in amusement. "Are they the snotty-nosed pair who waltzed in a few minutes ago?"

"Shh." Phoebe pressed a finger to her thin lips and looked about in alarm as if the Carrolls—or Helen—would pop out of the wallpaper at any second. "Judge Carroll is a very important man," she said in a stage whisper. "He was appointed to the High Court a couple of years ago."

"Judge Carroll is a pompous git," Clio said, placing a display bottle of champagne in a bucket of ice. "And if we have to serve him bread sticks because my mother was too scatty to keep track of all the people she invited, then he'll just have to deal."

Olivia grinned. "I can't believe Helen asked John-Joe Fitzgerald to perform at the party. Does she know what she's letting herself in for?"

Phoebe dragged her attention away from her phone. "Is that the entertainer? Helen said she'd hired a local singer of note."

Clio struggled to keep a straight face. "I haven't seen his act, but I've heard it's...original."

Phoebe beamed. "Excellent. Helen loves crooners like Tom Jones and Daniel O'Donnell. I'm sure she'll be delighted." The PA's phone beeped a reminder. "I need to check on the drinks delivery. See you both later."

After Phoebe left, Olivia met Clio's eye and they both dissolved into a fit of undignified giggles.

"A local singer of note?" Olivia asked between heaves. "Does your mother know what sort of entertainment John-Joe provides?"

"I doubt it. Seán Mackey booked him for her."

"Did he now?" A curious expression settled over the woman's pretty features. "I get the impression that Seán isn't your mother's greatest fan."

"I get that vibe too. She's very bossy with him." Her eyes crinkled with mirth. "Mind you, she's bossy with everyone."

"And..." Olivia paused for dramatic effect. "I also get the impression that Seán is *very* fond of you."

"What? I don't know what you're talking about." The butterflies in Clio's stomach performed a little dance, erotic memories of last night flashing through her mind. True to his word, Seán had kept her busy—and satisfied —all night long. Leaving in the early hours of the morning had been a wrench.

"Oh, don't give me that." Olivia's mouth curved into an amused smile. "Every time you look at Seán Mackey, or he looks at you, I think I'm in imminent danger of witnessing spontaneous combustion."

Clio felt a fiery flush crawl up her cheeks. "Nothing as dramatic as that." And yet it was—at least between the sheets. Or on the sofa. *Or in the shower...*

"Oh, I don't think so. I think I've hit the target. I'm right, aren't I?" The edges of Olivia's eyes crinkled with mirth. "There *is* something going on between you and the sexy Sergeant Mackey."

She laughed out loud. "You think he's sexy? Does Jonas know?"

"The women of Ballybeg—and some of the men, I dare say—have been mooning over Seán since he moved here last February. He could be on the screen with those features. You agree, don't you? Go on. Admit it."

"You're very nosy."

"Only about people I like. Besides, Bridie thinks you and Seán would be perfect together, and she's had some success matchmaking couples in the past."

"I think Bridie's matchmaking skills would be stretched finding the perfect man for me." A sexual partner was one thing. A permanent companion wasn't for her, at least not until she'd ironed out the wrinkles in her life. "Hey, can I ask you something?" Clio plunged on with the question she'd been angling to ask since Olivia had arrived earlier. The same questions she'd intended to ask Seán last night but hadn't felt comfortable doing so once he'd confided in her about his parents' murder-suicide. "I heard a rumor that the former owner of Clonmore House was involved in some dodgy dealings and that one of his partners ended up dead. What was that all about?"

Under her perfectly applied makeup, Olivia paled. She blinked several times before answering, and when she did so, her voice held a wobble of emotion that was far from the poised and confident woman Clio had grown to know over the past couple of weeks. "The man who died was my former husband."

Clio's hand flew to her mouth. "Oh, God. I'm so sorry. I had no idea."

"No, it's fine." The other woman's chest rose and fell at a rapid pace, then she seemed to pull herself together. "You'd have heard about it eventually. Might as well be from me. As it happens, Aidan's murder had nothing to do the dodgy dealings he and Bernard Byrne—Clonmore House's former owner—were mixed up in." With a wobbly smile, Olivia glanced at her watch. "I'd better get back to the kitchen and check on the food. Hope you enjoy the party."

Clio doubted that "enjoy" was the accurate adjective under the circumstances, but she managed a nod. "My mother said she'd invited Jonas."

Olivia's serious expression gave way to a proper grin. "I think she wants to persuade him to be interviewed on her show before it goes off the air."

"Yeah, that sounds like Helen," she said in a tone dry as sandpaper. "She never lets an opportunity pass her by. Hey, if you and your staff need any help, just let me know."

After Olivia went downstairs to the kitchen, Clio reflected on what she'd learned. She could scratch the dead partner off her list of subjects to discover more about. Next move was to approach Bridie and glean what she could about this Bernard Byrne dude. All she knew about him so far was that he was rich, a suspected crook, and Bridie's brother. Perhaps she could persuade the older woman to divulge more details. She could only hope that this angle of inquiry would shed some light on whatever it was that attracted Ray to Ballybeg.

In the ballroom, the party was in full swing. Helen was in her element. The moment she spotted Clio, she beckoned her over, eyes sweeping over her outfit. "That dress looks lovely on you."

Clio fingered the beads of her gown. Despite her reservations in the boutique, she had to admit the dress suited her. "Thanks for buying it for me."

"Well, you couldn't wear your usual jeans and T-shirt to an event like this." Helen waved an imperious hand. "Now come and mingle with the guests. There are a couple of eligible single men present."

Clearly, their brief moment of mother-daughter bonding was at an end. Clio suppressed a smile. "I'm not exactly a mingler, and I'm definitely *not* in the market for a husband."

"Nonsense. You just haven't met the right man." Her mother slipped an arm through hers and dragged her across the room. "Judge and Mrs. Carroll have a son your age. Pity he couldn't make it down to the party."

The notion of being forced to talk to the Carrolls again had Clio looking wildly around the room in search of salvation. Her mother propelled them toward the table where the judge and his wife were seated. Both husband and wife wore matching expressions of haughty boredom.

"How did you enjoy your afternoon golfing at the Clonmore Castle Hotel?" Helen asked. With a snap of her fingers, she indicated to a hovering waitress that she should refill the judge's glass.

"Splendid. Simply marvelous. Wonderful golf course, don't you know," the judge replied in his ponderous monotone. If a person could speak in beige, this was what he or she would sound like.

Helen's tinkling laugh grated on Clio's nerves. "Why don't I introduce you to Major Johnson? The Earl of Clonmore, actually, although he insists on not using his title. He's a keen golfer and a wonderful bridge player. I think you'd have a lot in common."

"Well, I—" Judge Carroll demurred, but Helen hauled him to his feet and dragged him off toward the table where Bridie and her husband were sitting with Jonas.

After flashing an apologetic smile at Mrs. Carroll, who seemed utterly disinterested in pursuing a conversation with Helen Havelin's irrelevant daughter, Clio dashed off in pursuit of her mother. This was her opportunity to chat with Bridie and do her best to ferret out information that might give her a clue as to what Ray was really after.

Her path through the crowd was intercepted by a morose-looking Tammy. The girl was pale and drawn, an impression not alleviated by the long black velvet dress she was wearing.

Clio put a hand on her daughter's arm. "Are you okay, pet? You're chalky white."

"Period cramps. Can I go up to my room and read? I swear the sight of Gran air kissing people is making them worse."

Clio laughed. "Go on. I'll cover for you. Besides, you've put in an appearance. I think that was all she wanted you to do."

"Thanks, Mum. I'll nick a couple of painkillers from your bathroom cupboard and head to bed."

After Tammy melted into the crowd, Clio continued toward Bridie's table. Raised voices on the other side of the room made her spin round to see who was causing the commotion.

Over by one of the indoor trees Helen's gardener had bought to decorate the ballroom, an older man she didn't recognize was in a police uniform, jabbing a chubby finger into Seán Mackey's chest. Seán, in turn, was holding what looked like a hip flask and sniffing its contents suspiciously.

Clio strained to hear what the old man was yelling about, moving closer to the scene of the argument.

"That's enough, O'Shaughnessy. If you've been imbibing this concoction"—he raised the hip flask—"I'm not surprised you're off your head. That said, Helen is our hostess. Show some respect while you're under her roof."

"Show respect?" The older man spat on the floor. "Fuck that. She's nothing but a Tinker-loving whore."

Silence fell over the assembled company. At Bridie's table, Helen's perfectly made-up cheeks paled under the rouge.

Seán's expression turned grim, his stance defensive.

Without pausing to consider the wisdom of her actions, Clio marched over to the soon-to-be ex-guest. "Shut your gob before I chuck you out on your arse. No one speaks about my mother like that. Who the hell do you think you are?"

The old man's gray-stubbled jaw jutted. "We don't like Tinkers around these parts, and we like Tinker-lovers even less. I'm just saying what other people are thinking. I believe in calling a spade a spade. Colm MacCarthy has the right idea. Drive the feckers out of town."

"I have no time for obnoxious bigots." She placed her hands on her hips and stared him down until his defiant gaze dropped to the floor. "Given your disdain for the Travelling community, I'm surprised you accepted my mother's invitation. Or did the promise of free booze make you temporarily forget your prejudice?"

"Cliona, that's enough." Her mother stepped forward. She held her champagne glass so tightly that Clio was sure the stem would snap. "Sergeant Mackey, would you escort Inspector O'Shaughnessy from the premises? Please make sure he doesn't drink and drive."

"With pleasure, Ms. Havelin." Seán took hold of O'Shaughnessy's arm. "And I intend to learn more about Colm MacCarthy and the Travellers while we're waiting for his ride. Not to mention"—he took a sniff of the older man's hip flask and recoiled—"where you got this vile concoction."

The retired inspector wrenched his arm free, breathing heavily. "I don't need a police escort, for fuck's sake. I can find my own way to the door."

"You're not driving after drinking *poitín* and goodness knows whatever else." Punching a number into his phone, Seán turned to Helen. "I'll call him a taxi and make sure he leaves."

After Seán followed the old man out of the ballroom, Helen smoothed down her dress. "Let's put that unpleasantness behind us and enjoy the evening. Waiters, can you make sure everyone's champagne glass is topped up? We'll be going down to the pool area soon for the performance."

A few minutes later, Seán returned. "The man's a prick," he said, catching Clio's strained expression. "Ignore him. Do you want to tell me what that was about?"

"You know my biological father came from a Traveller family, right?"

Seán started visibly. "No. I had no idea."

"It's not relevant to my life. He came from a Traveller community but left the life to take up acting in Dublin. That's how my mother met him. She did some stage acting before her television career took off. Anyway, they married and had me, but my father died when I was still a baby. I don't remember him, and I've never had anything to do with his family. Larry Havelin was the only father figure I had. All the same, it pisses me off when idiots make racist comments about Travellers. As long as they're not harming anyone, let them live their lives."

"I agree." Seán rubbed his jaw, where the barest hint of stubble shadowed his skin. She longed to reach out and stroke it, yearned to rub her nose against his bristly cheek and inhale his scent.

His eyes met hers, held her gaze. The intensity of his look seemed to strip her of all inhibitions. The ballroom and its occupants receded into nothingness. All that remained was him, her, and their red-hot connection.

The gong sounded, sending Clio's heart straight to her throat.

"Jaysus," Seán said. "Helen has a gong?"

"An affectation left by the previous owners, apparently."

"Ladies and gentleman, may I have your attention?" Phoebe, Helen's hapless assistant, squeaked into a microphone, looking as though she wanted the marble floor to split open and swallow her whole. "Please proceed to the pool area downstairs, where a well-known local singer will perform for us."

"Ugh," Seán groaned. "Why did I let my inner imp take over? I never should have suggested my uncle to your mother. His act is going to be a flaming disaster."

"It's a cross between the Chippendales and an Elvis tribute, right?"

"That's right." He sighed. "Thankfully, he stops at his swim trunks. Unless he gets drunk. In which case I'll have to arrest him for indecent exposure."

"My mother is expecting some sort of Tom Jones—style act. This sounds a lot more interesting."

Seán laughed. "Oh, it's interesting, all right. Helen will be livid."

"I almost hope he does go for the full monty," Clio murmured, linking her arm through his and following him down the stairs to the pool. "It would certainly liven this shindig up. With the notable exception of Bridie and a couple of others, I've rarely seen so many pompous gits in one place."

"Olivia's cooking is a redeeming feature," he said, snatching a savory pastry from a tray before they exited the ballroom.

"The food is delicious. I'm hoping I can persuade my mother to ask Olivia to cook a takeaway meal for Tammy's birthday." She dropped her voice to a whisper. "She's threatening to cook dinner herself."

He pulled a face. "I take it your mother's cooking isn't an improvement on her sandwiches?"

"Gosh, no. Unless she's planning on casting a magic spell, it's bound to be disgusting."

"Come on, everyone," Helen trilled. "Time to go downstairs and enjoy the show."

Seán and Clio exchanged glances and dissolved into laughter.

CHAPTER TWENTY-SEVEN

....

Taking Clio's arm, Seán escorted her down to the swimming pool area. The beaded tassels on her dress swished as they descended the stairs. The outfit looked even better on her tonight than it had in the boutique. The green material clung to her figure, accentuating her delicate curves. A long necklace wound about her throat, and dangled down to brush against the hint of exposed cleavage. Seán's mouth grew dry and his trousers tight. Memories of last night loomed large. He'd far rather drag her upstairs to find a bed than watch his uncle disgrace himself.

The swimming pool was located in the basement of Clonmore House. The area surrounding the swimming pool reminded him of a Roman bathhouse. A makeshift stage had been erected near the exit to the showers. John-Joe, clad in his Elvis costume, was already strutting his stuff. He'd managed to get himself tangled in wires from the speakers, but appeared to be oblivious to his predicament. A bottle of water stood at the side of the stage. Somehow, he doubted water was all it contained. Feck. If O'Shaughnessy's drunken rant while waiting for the taxi was accurate, he'd need to question his uncle again, but that could wait for another day.

"Oh, dear," Clio said. "I'd better disentangle John-Joe from those wires before he lands on his face." She strode toward the stage, dress swishing sexily.

Seán's aunt Nora spotted him through the crowd and made a beeline for him. Wafting cheap perfume, she leaned close and squeezed his arm. "Thanks so much for putting in a good word for your uncle, Johnny. He hasn't had a gig in ages."

He resisted the urge to ask her, once again, not to call him by that name. "No problem, Nora. Although I don't think Helen knows what she's letting herself in for."

His aunt laughed hard enough to set off her rasping smoker's cough. "I'm looking forward to seeing the look on her face when John-Joe starts undoing the Velcro of his costume. Helen was a couple of years ahead of me in school. She was always a prig. That's why we were all so shocked when she married that Tinker boy."

"Clio says he died when she was a baby."

"That's the story Helen told. Killed in a bar fight, supposedly. I guess it must be true. She couldn't have married Larry Havelin without a death certificate back in those days. Divorce wasn't legal in Ireland until ninety-six." Nora leaned in, treating Seán to a generous view of crinkly cleavage turned orangey brown by tanning solution. "Rumor has it that Helen was involved with Larry Havelin before her husband died. When Larry gave her a job working for his TV production company, she kicked her husband out. Helen always had a thing for married men."

Seán stiffened beside her and yanked his arm free. Breathing hard, he turned away from his aunt.

"Feck," Nora said in an earnest tone. "I'm sorry, Johnny. It just slipped out."

"Forget about it," he said roughly. "What else do you know about Clio's father?"

"Not much. He had the good grace to get himself knifed to death in a bar fight, leaving Helen free to marry Larry Havelin and preach conservative family values with a straight face."

"Given that Clio uses his surname, I'm assuming Havelin adopted her."

Nora nodded. "That was one of Helen's stipulations when she married him, but I don't think he ever liked the child."

Which would explain the man's callous treatment of Clio when she got pregnant. Seán felt an irrational urge to punch the dead man.

Clio hopped down from the stage and strode back toward him. The subtle sway of her hips and the way her beads jangled made him hard. Thoughts of throwing her against the wall and screwing her senseless were dashed with the efficacy of a bucket of ice water to the groin when Helen materialized at her daughter's side, dragging Mrs. Carroll in her wake.

Mrs. Carroll clutched the sleeve of Helen's cocktail dress. "Why are we going to listen to music beside your pool? Why not in the ballroom?"

Helen, already on her fourth glass of champagne, waved a hand and sent a tray of bruschetta flying out of a horrified waiter's arms. "I have no idea, my dear. Apparently, the musician prefers to play near water. Who knows why? Perhaps it has something to do with the acoustics. Oh, look. There's Superintendent O'Riordan. I must go and say hello."

Clio met Seán's eyes and covered her mouth to hide her smile.

"Your mother is in for a nasty shock," he said wryly.

"I think we all are," she whispered. "John-Joe is so inebriated he can barely stand, hence the microphone problems. I'm not sure he'll make it through the first song, let alone an entire show."

Helen's guests continued to troop into the room. Seán recognized Judge Carroll from giving evidence at the Dublin courts. The man was a pompous prick, but good at his job. Several television celebrities of Helen's vintage were also present. Clio pointed out a few producers, actors, and other Dublin luminaries. There were a couple of photographers hanging about, taking snaps of the more famous guests.

Familiar faces from Ballybeg included Bridie Byrne and her husband, the Major. Jonas O'Mahony stood near the exit chatting to a man Seán had seen around the town but couldn't put a name to. Helen stood at the front of the stage, clutching Superintendent O'Riordan's arm in a possessive manner. Judging by the expression on the man's face, he had no objection to being claimed.

"Where's Tammy?" Seán asked, searching the crowd in vain.

"Reading in her bedroom. She only lasted a few minutes at the party. I can't blame her. If I could have done a runner, I'd have been off like a shot."

The next quarter of an hour passed quickly. The beginning of John-Joe's act went surprisingly well at first. Despite Clio's claims to the contrary, the man appeared sober and made the most of his belter of a singing voice. There was a slight hiccup when John-Joe's hips got stuck doing a dance move, but he made a rapid comeback. Helen and her friends started to dance to the music, their steps faltering at the first rip of Velcro.

Lulled into a false sense of security by John-Joe's surprisingly good rendition of "Jailhouse Rock," Seán had almost forgotten the stripping part of his uncle's Swimming Elvis routine. Up until the moment his shirt came off, John-Joe's routine had consisted of surprisingly good singing, gyrating, and dancing around the microphone. As the performance progressed, however, it became clear that Elvis had had a few too many drinks. By the time he peeled off his snow-white shirt to reveal a very hairy chest, medallions, and an impressive beer belly, his uncle's singing was so slurred that the lyrics were impossible to decipher.

Most of the guests were none too sober themselves, and many were busy dancing when the first items of clothing were discarded on the stage, but the sight of

John-Joe Fitzgerald topless and gyrating in a tight pair of swimming trunks stunned everyone into instant silence.

"What is he doing?" cried Helen. "Where are his clothes?"

Superintendent O'Riordan patted her arm. "Don't worry. He usually leaves his pants on."

Helen wrenched her arm from his grasp, sobering by the millisecond. "What do you mean by 'He usually leaves his pants on'? What sort of act is this?"

"Well..." The super stared beseechingly at Seán for moral support. "He's not like the Chippendales, exactly, but—"

"Are you telling me I've hired a *male stripper* to perform at my party?" Helen's voice rose to a screech. "Did policemen from a station over which *you* have jurisdiction recommend a lewd performer for my housewarming event?"

The super, slowly but surely recognizing the peril of his situation, blinked owllike and opened his mouth to respond. But before he could utter a word, John-Joe tripped over his microphone stand and flew off the stage and into the throng below.

His fall was broken by a couple of party guests. He was then passed along from one person to the next like a crowd surfer. The guests screamed. Whether it was caused by the weight of a half-naked, sweating Elvis impersonator or with delight at his performance was hard to tell.

Helen stood ramrod straight and slack-jawed. Clio gasped and clutched Seán's arm. Aunt Nora raised her wine glass in the air and clapped.

Overcome by paroxysms of laughter, Clio leaned into Seán's chest. She smelled delicious—a mix of champagne, sugary treats, and the flowery scent she always wore. Despite the absurdity of the situation, he longed to take her in his arms and kiss her.

"Oh my goodness," she gasped. "I figured the show would be bad, but I didn't think it would end like this."

"Help," Nora shouted. "John-Joe has fallen into the pool."

"Don't worry," the super said with confidence. "He calls himself the Swimming Elvis. I'm sure it's all part of the act."

Seán peered into the chlorine blue water. "Feck. He's not moving." He pulled his shoes off, running through water rescue procedure in fast forward.

"Get him out, for heaven's sake," Helen shouted. "I don't want a corpse defiling my pool. Particularly not the corpse of a half-naked, half-witted Elvis impersonator. My reputation will be ruined."

Seán dove into the water. Ignoring the flash of the photographer's cameras, he swam to his uncle and dragged the man to the side of the pool. By the time John-Joe was hauled onto the tiles surrounding the pool, he was hacking and spluttering.

"I suppose we had to save him," the super said with a regretful sigh. "We are supposed to be the keepers of the peace, after all."

"My poor darling." Nora threw herself down beside her husband and squeezed his hand. "I thought I'd lost you."

"No fear of that, Nora my love," he said between coughs, "I'm hard to kill."

"Not if I get my hands on you." Helen's petite form loomed above them. "You've ruined my party."

"Calm down, woman. Sure haven't I livened things up?"

"Back in the days when I was at school with your wife, you were a champion swimmer. So when Garda Glenn and Sergeant Mackey mentioned your act, I assumed it would be a respectable show." Helen danced a furious heel against the tile flooring. "How was I to know you'd turned into *a male stripper*?"

When Helen rounded on Seán, sparks were in her eyes. "That creature is an absolute disgrace. I want him arrested."

"He's committed no crime, Ms. Havelin. You hired him."

"On *your* recommendation." Her screech was nearing Banshee status.

"Actually," he said, straight-faced, "Garda Glenn suggested him first."

"And I backed up the recommendation." Superintendent O'Riordan tried to take Helen's arm, but she slapped him away. "I thought you knew the kind of act he performed and wanted to give your guests a laugh."

"I wasn't intending my party to be the comedy act of the year. I wanted to make a good impression, mingle with the sort of people I'd like to spend time with when I'm down in Ballybeg, and show off my new house to my Dublin friends. I did not expect the 'local singer of note' to be that drunken buffoon. He belongs behind bars."

"To be fair," Seán said, "he frequently is behind bars."

Rage spent, Helen dissolved into tears. "I need a drink."

Seán whisked a glass of champagne off a nearby tray and handed it to her.

She drank it in one unladylike gulp and thrust it back at him. "I have been humiliated in front of all my friends and my new neighbors. I won't be able to leave the house."

"Ah, come on," he said. "They all had a good laugh, no matter what they'll say. Anyone who's a true friend isn't going to care. As for the rest...feck them. They've no sense of humor."

The super nodded sympathetically to Seán. "I'll take Helen upstairs and let you get dry."

Clio strode over, armed with a warm towel. "Get this around you. You're welcome to use the shower area. There's shampoo and soap in each cubicle. In the meantime, I can try to dry your uniform, or borrow clothes from one of my mother's guests."

"Thanks. Dry would be nice."

She stepped closer. "Ignore my mother. You're not responsible for your uncle's antics. How does your aunt put up with him? She seems a nice woman, in an odd sort of way."

"I've given up asking myself that question. For whatever crazy reason, they're still together. I don't know why. Codependency? Can't live together peacefully, but would be lost without one another? I think they thrive on the drama. And for all Nora's bitching, John-Joe amuses her. Why else stay with him after all these years now that their sons are grown and gone?"

Any response Clio might have made was cut short by pandemonium. Helen's assistant, Phoebe, burst into the room wild-eyed, her mousy brown hair escaping from its severe bun. She looked about frantically, then made a beeline for Seán. "Come quick, Sergeant. Ms. Havelin has been burgled."

CHAPTER TWENTY-EIGHT

································

What the feck had Ray gone and done? That he was behind the robbery, Clio was in no doubt. *The low down, double-crossing weasel...* She shoved Seán's clothes into the dryer and contemplated shoving Ray in with them. After she'd switched the machine on, she sprinted upstairs to her mother's office.

Seán was already there, clad in a long white bathrobe. Were it not for the seriousness of the circumstances, Clio would have laughed and then fantasized about undoing the fluffy white belt.

Tonight, however, her gaze was riveted by the gaping safe. As she knew from her previous rummage through the safe, her mother stored few items in there. The majority of her valuables were in a bank vault. The couple of jewelry boxes the safe did contain were empty, as was the envelope in which Clio had replaced the money she'd taken a couple of weeks ago.

Helen's hands fluttered to her throat. "Thank goodness I wore my diamonds, but the money is gone."

Seán peered into the empty envelope. "How much cash did you have in here?"

"About two thousand euros, give or take."

Clio's heart skipped a beat and her eyes rolled back in terror. She'd have to 'fess up. This had to have been Ray or one of his people. *Oh, God.* Had they taken the leopard aquamanile, too? She was almost too scared to check.

"Is there anything else missing from the safe?" Superintendent O'Riordan asked. "I suppose we'll have to do a thorough search of the house too."

"Just a few old keys for the cellar, but they're of no use to anyone." Helen clutched her diamond necklace with both hands, as if warding off a potential attack. "I haven't been down in the cellar since I toured the house. I know we haven't put anything down there. My wine collection is kept in a separate area off the kitchen, and Olivia's crew have that key." Helen sighed. "At least my bank manager can supply us with the bank notes' serial numbers. Perhaps that will help you catch the thief."

Clio's stomach lurched. "Serial numbers?"

"Well, yes." Helen was regarding her as though she were a complete fool. "I picked up sequential notes in person when I transferred my valuables to a safe deposit box at my new bank in Cork City."

Feck. Now she was well and truly screwed.

"Mother—"

"Please, Cliona. Let the police do their jobs." Her mother sagged against the superintendent. "God, Dermot, I can't think straight."

He put an arm around her shoulders manfully. "Don't worry. We'll get to the bottom of this."

"Mother, you need to listen to me. It's about the cash."

Everyone fell silent and turned to stare at her.

Clio took a deep breath and plunged on with her story. "Your bank manager won't know what serial numbers were on the stolen notes. I withdrew that cash from an ATM in Ballybeg to replace money I'd borrowed from the safe."

Helen's features froze, then crumpled. "You took money from my safe?"

"Yes." She swallowed past the lump in her throat. "I replaced it four days later."

Disbelief hovered in the air like a communal held breath.

"But why?" her mother demanded. "Why did you need so much cash?"

Clio looked from Seán to the superintendent. "Can't we discuss that later?"

"No." Her mother's tone was brittle. "I want to discuss it now. Are you back on drugs, Cliona? Is that why you needed so much money?"

"What?" Her jaw dropped in horror. "No, of course not. I haven't touched anything stronger than alcohol in over twelve years. Honestly."

"Then why did you take the money?" Helen pressed. "Why didn't you ask me if you needed cash?"

A vision of a small metal object flashed before Clio's eyes. "The antiques," she breathed. "Oh, God. We'll have to check if they're all still here."

"Unless you want to press charges because Clio took the original bank notes," Seán said in a brittle voice, "we'd better search the house."

Her mother's stare hardened, her voice ice cold. "I can only hope nothing else is missing."

"You know better than anyone what antiques you own," Seán continued. "Will you help us search?"

"Cliona unpacked most of the delicate stuff when we moved. I didn't want to leave those boxes to the movers. She should have a fair idea of what should be there."

Clio cleared her throat. "Okay. Let's start in the reception room. My mother has a lot of paintings and antiques in that room."

"Sounds like a plan." Seán led the way into the reception room.

Helen glanced around. "I think everything is here."

Clio's gaze sought the display case that contained the leopard aquamanile. She felt like she'd been punched in the gut. "The little metal leopard," she whispered. "It's gone."

The room spun around her. She'd screwed everything up. Ray must have double-crossed her, the lying rat. And if he hadn't, if someone else had robbed the house before he could get there, Clio would be in even bigger trouble. It was all going to come out now. The fragile relationship she was building with her mother would snap, and Seán would hate her.

Helen leaned over the display case and shrugged. "Oh, dear. She's correct. The leopard aquamanile is missing."

"I think my mother is in shock," Clio said. "Phoebe, can you bring her a glass of brandy?"

"Certainly." Phoebe scurried off in search of a drinks cabinet.

Helen raised an eyebrow. "I'm not in shock, dear. I'm not pleased to have cash stolen out of my safe, and I don't like the thought of a thief roaming about my house."

"But how can you be so calm about the leopard aquamanile being stolen?" Clio turned to Superintendent O'Riordan. "You'll have to call in the antiquities thefts squad or whatever they're called."

Her mother laughed. "They'll have to be informed, yes, but don't get into a panic. It's not worth much. Frankly, they got more value out of the cash from the safe."

Clio's tongue felt leaden in her mouth. "What?" she mumbled. "But I thought it was worth a quarter of a million euros."

"The original is, certainly." Helen's neatly tweezed brows formed two perfect arches. "Darling, surely you don't think I keep the original in the house?"

"You don't?" Clio croaked.

"Of course not. It's far too valuable a piece to keep at home. At the moment, it's in a bank vault. I'm in negotiations with the national museum to allow them to display it. They have the security to keep it safe, and there's no point in leaving it to languish where no one can see it."

Clio exhaled in a whoosh. If Ray had taken the piece and later discovered it was a fake, he was going to go mad. And if he hadn't taken it and learned that the original was secure in a bank, he'd go ballistic. Either way, that would be a very unpleasant telephone conversation.

She bit her lower lip so hard she tasted blood. It was all going wrong. Her life had always been on the chaotic side. Her mother was right when she said she had a touch of the nomad in her. But since moving back to Ireland, everything had begun to unravel.

For feck's sake. She was supposed to be an adult. She was supposed to know how to manage her life. And yet these days, she woke to a weight on her shoulders and a feeling of utter helplessness and despair.

"I'll contact my former partner from National Bureau of Criminal Investigation and let him know to keep an eye out for someone attempting to sell a fake." Seán was careful to avoid meeting Clio's eye. From the grim set of his jaw, she could tell he was furious.

Damn. She'd blown it. Any trust they'd established that night at his house had snapped. And for the first time in forever, the thought of having messed up a potential relationship hurt with the vicious intensity of alcohol on an open wound.

Phoebe appeared in the doorway. "Most of the party guests have left, Ms. Havelin. I took the liberty of booking the Carrolls and your friends from the TV station into Clonmore Castle Hotel for the night. I didn't think having overnight guests would be desirable under the circumstances. The hotel is sending cars to collect them."

Helen nodded, distracted. "Thank you, Phoebe."

Reserve Garda McGarry's ruddy complexion hovered at Phoebe's shoulder. He addressed the superintendent. "I've taken everyone's contact details, sir. A couple of the ladies are very distressed."

Superintendent O'Riordan scrunched his face up and blew out a harrumph. "I'll go down and soothe ruffled feathers until the transport arrives."

When the super and Phoebe had left, Helen walked to the drinks cabinet and poured herself another brandy. She downed it in one, and poured a second. "Do either of you want a drink?"

Clio shook her head. "No, thanks."

"And I'm still very much on duty." Seán's gaze bore into Clio like pinpricks, making her squirm. "Why did you take the money?"

She swallowed and considered her options. They were nonexistent. "Long story short, I needed to pay a guy off. I tried calling you before I took it, Mother, but I couldn't get hold of you. With the clock ticking, I removed the cash and replaced it a few days later with money I borrowed from Emma Reilly."

"You owed someone two thousand euros?" Helen played with the necklace around her throat, twisting the beads around her fingers. "Whatever for?"

"I didn't *owe* him the money, exactly." She rubbed her aching temples. "It's a long story."

Silence permeated the kitchen, suspended like icicles. Seán shifted in his seat, eyes still trained on her. His expression was mild and deceptively blank. "We have all night, Clio. Enlighten us."

"I want the truth." Helen's voice broke on a sob. "Are you on drugs again?"

"No, of course not."

"If so, I'll get you into a rehab program. Residential is best, I think."

Clio's hands tightened around the arms of her chair. "I don't need rehab."

"That's what all addicts say." Her mother's voice rose to a crescendo.

"For the last time, I am *not* on drugs."

Helen raised her eyebrow.

"Mother! Not the thing with your eyebrow."

"What thing?" Helen looked genuinely perplexed.

Clio's eyes met Seán's. For a millisecond, she saw the old humor reflected in them. And then the shutters slammed down.

"Who asked you for the money?" Seán's deep voice was even deeper than usual.

She bit her lip. "A guy who's blackmailing me."

Helen's mouth gaped open. "What did you do to be blackmailed?"

Here goes. She tasted bile in her mouth and swallowed. "After the police told me they wouldn't be charging Trevor O'Leary with molesting Tammy, I sort of lost it. I didn't want the man hurt. Not really. I just wanted to make sure he never went near Tammy again."

"Molesting Tammy?" Seán's tone was sharp, alert. "What the hell?"

She took a deep breath. "Long story short, Tammy's music teacher seduced her. When I found out about it, I went straight to the police. To be fair to them and the school, they did take me seriously. After a few weeks of digging, they had nothing concrete with which to charge the man. Tammy refused to cooperate and denied he'd ever touched her. In private, she admitted he had. In fact, she thinks she's in love with him. No other girls came forward to say he'd behaved inappropriately with them. Basically, the police had nothing to persuade a judge to take the case to trial."

"You must have been furious." Seán's tone was gentler than before.

"Furious?" She ground her teeth to stop them chattering. "I was livid."

"So what happened next?" He'd removed a pen from his shirt pocket, but hadn't yet started taking notes.. "You obviously didn't let it drop."

"No, I didn't." She sighed. "Perhaps I should have. After the police told me O'Leary would get off scot-free, I freaked. I knew if I called Tammy's father, he'd have made sure O'Leary was six feet under before midnight, but I didn't want violence. Instead, I called a guy I used to work for. When Tammy was a baby and I was skint, this man employed me to do jobs of, shall we say, dubious legality. Anyway, he still owed me money for a job I'd done years ago, and I figured I could try to persuade him to do me a favor." She gave a bitter laugh. "Some favor it turned out to be. I asked him to get some of his men to scare O'Leary off. Give him a warning. I did *not* ask him to have the man beaten into a coma."

Her mother spoke. "I knew there had to be a reason you changed your mind about moving to Ballybeg."

"Yes. After O'Leary was attacked, I was keen to escape Dublin. But now the man behind the attack is putting the screws into me, wanting me to give him money and steal stuff."

"This man wouldn't happen to go by the name of Ray Greer, would he?" Seán asked in a dry tone.

Her heart leaped in her chest. "What?" Slowly, her heat rate began to return to normal. "Of course, you'd know Ray from the Dublin crime scene."

"Indeed." He leaned forward. "I also know that Lar Delaney works for him."

"That's not exactly accurate." Far from accurate, actually, but Clio had more sense than to invoke the wrath of the Delaney clan by discussing their business with the police. "Lar's kind of his own man. He'll do jobs for people if the money is right, but he's not part of Ray's usual gang of goons." This, at least, was true.

Seán tapped the table, forehead creased in thought. "I'll make a few phone calls to colleagues in Dublin. See what I can ferret out about Ray."

"There's more," Clio said, looking from one to the other. "I think Ray is behind tonight's robbery."

"Do you mean to tell me," Helen said in a quavering voice, "that a notorious Dublin gangster was roaming my house?"

"I doubt that. Ray doesn't like to get his hands dirty. He'll have sent one of his lackeys to do the job for him."

"Let's focus on the robbery angle." Seán scribbled something into his notebook, brow furrowed. "Why do you think Ray was behind it?"

She twisted the rings on her fingers, finally putting her trembling hands on her lap. "Because he was very interested in my mother's leopard aquamanile. He wanted me to locate it and arrange for his people to have access to the house."

"What?" Helen spluttered. "You're responsible for tonight's robbery as well as stealing the money?"

"The break-in wasn't supposed to happen until March 14. That was the date Ray gave me when I told him you were hosting a party tonight." Her head spun and it was difficult to keep her thoughts clear with panic clawing its way from her stomach to her throat. "This is all coming out wrong. I wasn't going to go *through* with the robbery. I had Emma on the case, looking for dirt on Ray that I could use to stall him."

"Emma?" Seán's eyebrows formed a question mark.

"I mentioned her to you before. Emma Reilly. She's the friend who's a private investigator."

"Ah. The woman whose parents fostered Tammy for a couple of years."

"That's right. In addition to translation work for the Dublin tourist board, I worked part-time as Emma's office assistant when I moved back to Dublin."

"And has your friend turned up anything useful?"

She shrugged. "I'm not sure. She discovered that Ray, through a guy on his payroll, was a silent partner in a shopping center development near Ballybeg. Apparently, the project went bust, and one of the partners did a runner to Spain."

"Bernard Byrne, the former owner of Clonmore House." Seán nodded. "I investigated the case."

"Exactly. But I'm not sure how this fits in with Ray's interest in my mother's aquamanile. I was never convinced that was all he was after. If he coveted a particular antique, he could have asked me to steal it for him. Instead, he wanted his people to have access to the house to take it. It didn't smell right."

"You don't say." Helen's tone dripped sarcasm. "Frankly, none of this smells right, Cliona. In fact, the whole situation reeks."

Clio focused on Seán. "Where do we go from here?"

"Unless your mother wants to press charges against you—"

"I don't," Helen said firmly. "We can sort this out between ourselves."

"—I suggest we keep quiet about it for now. We've been looking for something to pin on Ray for a long time. I don't want anything to screw this up. I'll contact my colleagues in the NBCI and see what I can find out about his interest in Clonmore House and what he might be expecting to find here. In the meantime, I suggest you change all the locks for the keys that were stolen."

Helen waved a hand dismissively. "Oh, all right. The burglars probably took them along with everything else. I doubt they're of significance. As I said earlier, there's nothing in the cellar to steal."

"All the same, it's best to be cautious." Seán got to his feet.

Clio jumped up. "I'll see you to the door."

"No need. I can see myself out." His smile was hard, his eyes granite. "I'll be in touch."
Watching his broad, blue-uniformed back descend the stairs, Clio's stomach cramped. She bit her lip and ran a hand through her by-now disheveled hair. She'd blown it with Seán. Whatever might have developed between them—no-strings sex, friends with benefits, or something deeper—she'd blown it into oblivion.

CHAPTER TWENTY-NINE

....

B y late Monday morning, Seán had been in touch
with a colleague from his old division in the
National Bureau of Criminal Investigation
regarding the robbery.

Frank was out sick, finally struck down by the flu that
had flattened his kids a couple of weeks previously.
Instead, Seán spoke with his friend's new partner. The
man promised to look into the matter and to call Seán
back when he had information to share. Paranoid about
information leaks after last year's fiasco, Seán
deliberately failed to mention a potential connection
with Ray Greer.

After hanging up the phone, he shoved his chair back
from the desk and stretched his stiff back. He'd won this
morning's toss for the portable heater. Being able to sit
in his office without a coat and scarf made for a pleasant
change. Less pleasant was the raw sensation he
experienced whenever his thoughts strayed to Clio. Why
hadn't she told him the whole story the night he'd
cooked her dinner? She'd opened up about Lar. Why not
tell him the truth about Ray? But he knew the answer to
that question, and it chafed at his conscience. Clio felt
let down by the police, and didn't trust them to take her
side over O'Leary's beating. Truth be told, he wasn't sure

he'd believe her side of the story if he hadn't spent so much time with her over the past couple of weeks.

A knock made him glance up. Brian peeked his freckled face around the door, clutching a fluorescent pink sticky note. "Got a sec, Seán?"

"Yeah. Come on in and pull up a seat by the heater."

After closing the door, Brian unwound the hand knit scarf his mother had made him for Christmas and plopped onto a chair. He stared at the pink note and scrunched up his nose. "Before I get to this, there's something I'd like to mention."

Sean eyed his partner with unease. "What?"

Brian's cheeks were stained with red. "The other day, Colm—Sharon's father—made a remark about your past. And, well, the story of what happened to your parents tumbled out."

"Too many people in Ballybeg know or suspect for it to stay a secret forever." He gave a weary sigh. "Frankly, I'm surprised it didn't get out before now."

His partner coughed and cleared his throat. "I just wanted you to know that you can talk to me."

Brian's concern touched Sean more than he'd expected. "Why don't we go out for a drink when the Greer business is over? I'll tell you the whole story, minus Colm Senior's embellishments."

"Sounds like a plan." Brian gave him a quick smile, then returned his attention to the pink note. "So...I've finished looking through the surveillance tapes from the Havelin's security system. The only people seen entering and leaving the house on the night of the robbery were party guests or police officers."

"Unfortunately, that doesn't mean much in terms of narrowing down the list of

suspects," Seán said, leaning back in his chair. "Given the size of Clonmore House, the security system is seriously lacking. There are only three cameras placed around the outside and one at the main gate. There are no cameras inside the house. Given the fuss Helen made about the stalker, I'm surprised she didn't have a new security system installed."

"Hopefully, she will now."

"Oh, yeah. On the super's recommendation, she hired his nephew's security business to install a new one. I believe they're due to come next week." Seán drummed his fingers on the desk. "I still think this was an inside job. Someone at that party stole the money and the copy of the leopard antique. The only fingerprints on the safe were Helen's and Clio's, and all that tells us about the robber is that they were smart enough to wear gloves."

His partner shifted in his chair, angling himself nearer to the heater. "I'm inclined to agree with you on the inside job. Have you and the super come up with a plan for the fourteenth?"

"We're still working out the details. My suggestion is that we get Clio to arrange for Ray's men to access the house. Arrange for Helen and Tammy to be away and try to catch them in the act. The super is going to talk to the higher-ups in the hope of forming a task force for the fourteenth."

Brian's auburn eyebrows arched. "How do you feel about arranging another sting operation?"

Lousy. "It's my job." In other words, he'd make damn sure nothing went wrong this time. "In other news, Clio spoke to Emma Reilly, her private investigator friend. Emma e-mailed me all the info she dug up on Ray Greer over the past couple of weeks. Impressive though her work is for the short timescale, she hasn't discovered anything I don't already know." The only oddity in Emma's e-mail was her failure to answer his question about Lar Delaney's connection to Ray, but that might be out of loyalty to Clio rather than an indication that she was hiding something.

"What's next on the agenda?" Brian asked. "Dare I hope it's lunch?"

Seán smiled but shook his head. "Sorry, mate. We'll have to grab a sandwich later. We have two imbeciles to question."

***

When Seán and Brian marched into MacCarthy's, heads turned. Everyone seemed to recognize instantly that the police were not there to eat a spot of lunch. Propped up at the bar in their usual spot sat Uncle John-Joe and his partner in crime, Buck MacCarthy. John-Joe's jeans had seen better days, but his Elvis hair was freshly gelled and sprayed. Buck was wearing sailor pants and a Right Said Fred T-shirt.

"Well, Ruairí," Seán said when he reached the bar, "We have a pair of eejits as uncles."

Ruairí raised his dark eyes heavenward. "What have Buck and John-Joe done this time?"

"We've done nothing." John-Joe bristled with indignation. Whiskey fumes rolled off him in pungent waves. "Why do you always blame us for everything that goes wrong in Ballybeg? Why not the fecking Tinkers?"

"The Travelling community hasn't been dealing in this." Seán pulled a bottle of clear liquid out of the carrier bag he was holding. "The pair of you know anything about this?"

"Ah, Buck," Ruairí said in disgust. "Have you been making *poitín* again? Did blowing up your garden shed over Christmas teach you nothing?"

Buck's one good eye swiveled. "I don't know anything about that there bottle."

"What about you, John-Joe?"

"Ah, no. It's nothing to do with me."

"Funny, because Inspector O'Shaughnessy says he bought it from you. But if you know nothing about it, you'll have no problem opening up *your* shed for us, will you?"

John-Joe didn't do subtle body language, and his relief was palpable. "Go right ahead. I've got nothing to hide."

"What about Buck's boat shed? Anything to hide there?"

John-Joe's Adam's apple bobbed. *Bull's-eye.* "Why do you want to go doing that, Johnny?" his uncle asked. "A man's entitled to earn a few bob where he can."

Ruairí tossed the cloth he'd been using to polish glasses onto the counter. "Do you have a search warrant for my uncle's boat shed?".

"Oh, yeah." Seán produced the document from his coat pocket.

"Looks like you're screwed, lads," Ruairí said nonchalantly and returned to polishing glasses behind the bar.

"Right, Brian. Let's get this freak show on the road."

They hauled their prey out of the pub and into the police car. Buck and John-Joe bitched and moaned the entire way to Buck's falling-down cottage by the sea.

"Put a sock in it, lads," Seán snapped from the driver's seat. "The only words I want to hear out of your gobs are answers to our questions."

The boat shed leaned against the house in a way that made it look like it would collapse at the smallest breeze.

"Right, Buck. Open up."

"Ah, Seán. Sure it was only a bit of fun."

"It's our cultural heritage," shouted John-Joe. "This is an outrage."

"*You're* the outrage." He felt his cheeks heat with anger and embarrassment. "Open this damn shed before I kick the door down."

Buck cursed and swore but finally persuaded the rusty lock to open. The door creaked on its hinges.

Inside the shed, distilling paraphernalia were plain to see, as were crates of bottles containing *poitín*. To add to the ambience was a mangy-looking basket containing an equally-mangy-looking puppy. The dog, thrilled to see company, bounded out of its bed and danced around Seán's ankles.

Seán scooped the little creature up into his arms and stroked its matted fur. "Well, boys, what do you have to say for yourselves?"

Buck jerked a thumb at his partner in crime. "It was him."

"No, it was *his* daft idea," John-Joe retorted. "I never wanted to go along with it, not in that damn boat."

"Boat? What are you on about?" Seán asked. "Is that how you've been distributing the stuff?"

Buck's sole working eye swiveled toward John-Joe. "Ah, you eejit. What did you go telling him that for?"

"Who are you calling an eejit?" John-Joe jabbed a finger into his friend's chest. "What sort of sailor can't even swim? That's the only reason you wanted me to come along."

"Come along where?" Seán demanded. "Jaysus, lads. Tell me you weren't transporting this shite to all the way to Britain?"

Furtive glances passed between the two culprits.

Seán exhaled a sigh. "Seriously, the pair of you are total fuckwits."

"We tried to sail to Britain, but we didn't make it farther than Cobh," John-Joe admitted.

Seán blinked. "Run that by me again? You loaded Buck's boat up with bottles to export and only got as far as *Cobh*?"

His uncle's beady eyes darted to the side. "We might have put a few too many crates in the boat. We were starting to sink, so we headed back to shore."

The puppy gave Seán's nose a lick. "Where does the dog come into the story?"

Buck did a slack-jawed shuffle, and rubbed his unshaven jaw. "A pal gave me a litter of puppies. I sold all but the runt."

"What were you planning to do with him?"

The older man shrugged. "Offload him somewhere. I got no time for a dog, and he's too ugly to appeal."

The dog whimpered against Seán's neck and gave him another lick to seal the deal. Clever little creature knew a sucker when he saw one. "I don't like the sound of 'offload.' This little guy's coming with me."

"Take a look at this," Brian called from the back the shed. He held up what looked at first glance to be a semiautomatic pistol.

"What the hell?" Seán swiveled toward Buck.

"I can explain," the older man said, his one good eye darting from side to side. "They're not mine. I swear."

Seán sighed. "They never are, are they?"

"They're all fake," Buck insisted. "My nephew gave them to me for Christmas."

Brian fingered the weapon with caution. "This one doesn't look like a fake to me."

Seán examined the gun. "That's because it isn't."

"What?" Buck's jaw dropped.

He pinned the man in place with his glare. "Which nephew gave you the guns?"

The man swallowed. "Young Colm," he muttered, staring at the filthy floor.

Seán rubbed his jaw with his free hand. "Bring Colm MacCarthy Junior in for questioning, Brian."

"Right-o. I'll step outside and make a few calls. The smell in here is killing me." Brian paused, his hand on the door. "Poor old Ruairí. He's always having to bail Colm out."

"It's them drugs," said John-Joe when the door closed after Brian. "Addled Colm Junior's mind. I might have a drop too much every now and again, but I don't go in for that shite. Sure you don't know what you're putting into yourself."

"So says the man knocking back lethal home brew," Seán said dryly.

"Colm MacCarthy was always a bad lot," John-Joe insisted, warming to his theme. "I told Buck not to store any of his stuff. Didn't I, Buck? Didn't I tell ye not to listen to that fecker's lies? And now look where we are."

"You're here because of illegal *poitín*, John-Joe. You can't fob that off on Colm." Seán held open the door. "After you, lads. We'll need to take a statement from you down at the station."

Outside the boat shed, Brian was leaning against the police car, mobile phone in hand. When he saw Seán, he opened the back door and helped shove John-Joe and Buck inside.

"I take it from your expression that you had no luck in locating MacCarthy."

Brian shook his head. "His missus says she kicked him out the day he got out of prison. Can't say I blame her."

"I doubt Colm's exactly a prince amongst husbands. But be that as it may, we need to find him and haul him in for questioning. I suspect he knows who's attacking the Travellers."

"How's that?"

"I never bought Buck's story about buying the air rifle on the Internet. Did you see his house? I found no sign of a computer or a laptop. And Buck's barely literate. I doubt he knows how to operate a computer, never mind order off the Internet. He has no credit card. How did he pay? Not saying it can't be done, but most people use a credit card or a service like PayPal."

"Yeah, that is odd. All right, then. I'll get back to searching for Colm, tracking down his pals, and so on. He's rumored to be linked to a Dublin gang, you know, but I never found anything concrete to support the claim."

"Dublin, eh? Hmm…he must go somewhere on his frequent disappearing acts. Easier to disappear in a big city like Dublin than elsewhere. I'll ring a mate of mine in the Dublin force and see what he has on Colm, if anything."

At least, thought Seán, this was one case the super couldn't shoot down as less important than playing bodyguard to a pampered television host. "Once we book the two eejits in the car, you track down Colm Junior and I'll go pay a visit to Colm Senior."

"What are planning to do with the puppy?" Brian asked.

Seán patted the wriggly canine and buried his nose in his smelly fur. "I think I know of a good home for this little creature."

....

CHAPTER THIRTY

The MaccCarthy farm was even more decrepit than the last time Seán had had the misfortune to visit it. He pressed the doorbell.

A stout man with a grizzly beard and unruly gray hair opened the door.

"Good morning, Mr. MacCarthy."

"Sergeant Mackey. Or Johnny Fitzgerald. Whatever name you're going by today." Colm MacCarthy Senior loomed in the doorframe, teeth bared in a snarl. "What the fuck are you doing here?"

"I'd like to have a word with you. Can I come in?"

Colm Senior's combative stance didn't falter. "Do I have a choice?"

Seán shrugged. "I can come back with a warrant. Or I can haul you down the station right now for questioning. I'd prefer a more civilized approach. What say you, Colm?"

The older man hesitated a moment, then stood aside with a show of reluctance. "Go through to the kitchen. I've just put the kettle on."

If Colm was willing to offer him tea, he definitely had something to hide. Either that or he intended to seize the opportunity to poison a member of the local police force.

Standards in the MacCarthy household had never been high, but since Molly MacCarthy's death last year and Sharon's decision to move in with Brian, the place had turned into a dump.

In the grimy kitchen, Colm Senior dumped two mugs of tea on the stained table and slumped into a chair across from Seán. "So what are you wanting me for this time?"

"I'm looking for Colm Junior. Any idea where he can be found?"

"So what are you wanting *him* for? Sure the poor lad's only just out of prison. Can't you leave him in peace for a bit?"

The pertinent point was whether or not Colm Junior would leave Ballybeg in peace.

"I just need to ask him a few questions." Seán took a sip of tea. It was vile. Overbrewed and thick with unfiltered tea leaves.

"Yeah?" Colm bared his nicotine-stained teeth. "Whenever a Guard wants to ask a man a few questions, it signals trouble. What do you think he's done this time?"

"I found crates of *poitín* out at your brother Buck's place. Not to mention distilling equipment and several semiautomatic pistols. Don't suppose you'd know anything about that?"

Colm put his mug down on the table and leaned forward, wafting body odor and stale cigarette smoke. "Don't suppose I would."

"Any idea where I can find your son?"

"No idea at all." The older man never broke his belligerent stare.

Seán put his mug down on the table. "Never mind," he said and pushed his chair back. "I'm sure I'll track him down eventually. I believe his wife kicked him out, and I presume he's staying here at the moment. Mind if I take a look at his room?"

"I bloody well do mind, you cheeky pup! Do you have a search warrant?"

"No, but I'm sure I can get one."

"Bollocks. You're not poking around my boy's belongings, not for no reason."

"Possession of semiautomatic pistols without a license is hardly no reason."

"You only got Buck's word they belong to Colm. Buck would sell his soul to the devil if he thought it'd save his own skin."

"I've no doubt Buck would do that, but he's also a lousy liar. He was telling the truth when he said Colm gave the guns to him."

"So what you going to do about it? Search my home without a warrant, and I'll have an official complaint made before your next shite."

"You've a way with words, Colm. Pity you never took to poetry."

"You're the smart-arse, aren't you?"

"Takes one to know one."

Colm stood up, fists clenched. "Get out of my house."

"Gladly...once you've told me where to find Colm."

"I don't know where he is, I tell you. He doesn't report in, and I don't keep tabs. He's a grown man now." Colm Senior marched behind him to the front door. If he could have gotten away with pushing him out the door, he would have done so, but not even he wasn't stupid enough to assault a Guard.

"Good-bye, Mr. MacCarthy," said Seán as he stepped out the door. "No doubt we'll meet again soon."

Colm's only response was to slam the door in Seán's face.

He whistled to himself as he walked back to his car. That had gone well. Not. Judging by the elder MacCarthy's body language, he knew far more than he was saying, and it definitely involved Colm Junior's dodgy dealings. Dared he hope he'd get the Travellers case wrapped up after all?

His phone beeped with an incoming text message. When he glanced at the display, he noticed there were two messages. He checked the latest one first.

Don't forget my birthday dinner next Sunday. Even if you did cause my fool of a husband to be up in court again, you're still family. Aunt Nora xxx P.S.: Can you bring a bottle of something? Money's scarce, seeing as Helen Havelin refused to pay your uncle the full price for his performance. She was always a tightwad.

His reluctance to dine chez John-Joe and Nora was slightly mitigated by his amusement at Helen's horrified expression when John-Joe had bodysurfed over her guests.

He clicked on the second message. It had been sent from an unknown number.

I hear you want a word with me about a mutual acquaintance. Might have better luck questioning some of your old colleagues. Ever find it strange that you got shunted off to Cork, yet certain members of your old unit got promoted? L.D.

An icy chill froze Seán in place. What the hell? And yet the sneaking suspicion that his former boss's promotion hadn't been on merit alone had nagged him for over a year. He'd had the misfortune to tangle with the odious Detective Inspector Connolly last summer during the Gant murder investigation. The entire time Seán had worked for him in the organized crime unit, Connolly had been angling for a transfer to murder. Within six months of the debacle at the Clondalkin warehouse, Connolly's wish had been granted.

But how much weight could he lend the word of Lar Delaney? The man was all smoke and mirrors, mystery and deflection. Seán had never been sure just how much power the guy wielded in the Dublin underworld. On the surface, he was an odd-job man—someone known to associate with less-than-salubrious characters, but not a person against whom any serious allegations had been levied.

Delaney's only conviction to date was a juvenile sentence for armed robbery during which a security guard was killed. After his release from prison, he'd vanished for a few years. Rumor had it that he'd gone to work as a hit man for his uncle in Boston. Whether or not that rumor was accurate was anyone's guess. After fifteen years on the force, little would surprise Seán, but he was prepared to keep an open mind.

In the meantime, he'd better call the local vet and get his new protégé checked out.

CHAPTER THIRTY-ONE

....

Clio pulled into the car park of Glencoe College. She wanted to scream. She wanted to put her head on the steering wheel and sob. But she had no time for hysterics. In five minutes' time, she was due in the school hall with a hundred other parents, and she'd be expected to play the part of the responsible mother attending her daughter's parent-teacher meeting.

The week since the robbery had been hell. By the time Helen left for Dublin on Monday morning, they weren't on speaking terms. Honestly, Clio couldn't blame her mother for being pissed, but she hadn't felt able to confide in her about the Ray Greer mess. That didn't justify taking the cash, regardless of how quickly she'd replaced it, but Helen was quick to paint the situation black and white when there was an entire spectrum of colors between.

After years of estrangement, it was disconcerting to suddenly see her mother every weekend. Clio couldn't force an intimacy that wasn't there any more than she could bring herself to forget the aftermath of the last time she'd confided in Helen. What sort of parent threw their pregnant seventeen-year-old out of the house, leaving her with no home, no money, and no school certificate? Little wonder she'd hit rock bottom. Clio might not win a Mother of the Year award, but she was a damn sight more maternal than her own mother had been.

After checking her reflection in the rearview mirror—wan with shadows smudged beneath her eyes—Clio grabbed her handbag from the passenger seat and climbed out of the car.

Inside the main school building, she received a nametag and list of teachers and table numbers to visit at the reception table. Clutching the list, she entered the main hall. It was abuzz with chatter. Designer-clad parents hobnobbed with one another, wafting expensive scent and hauteur in equal measure. Some ignored her when she walked by. Others stared at her nametag and eyed her nondesigner clothing with disapproval.

A lady with a sleek bob blocked her path. "Hello, Mrs. Havelin."

"Ms.," said Clio, suddenly self-conscious. Surely she couldn't be the only single parent present.

"I'm Eileen Quirke." The woman's sneer set her teeth on edge. Did she think Clio couldn't read the nametag attached to her enormous bosom? "My daughter, Roisin, is in Tammy's class. She says she's a bit rowdy."

Of all the adjectives that could be used to describe Tammy, "rowdy" was not among them.

Eileen's plastered-on smile looked as synthetic as her cloying perfume smelled. Clio opened her mouth to deliver a cutting set-down, but before she could formulate the first word, someone grabbed her arm and yanked her to the side.

It was Olivia, impeccably dressed as always and wearing a determined expression on her face. "Sorry, Eileen," she said, sounding not the least contrite, "I need to talk to Clio."

Eileen pursed her artificially plump lips. "I should have known you two would be friends."

"Like attracts like. Speaking of which, I see your good pal, Marjorie Jobson, is flirting with your husband again. You might want to intervene." Olivia nodded in the direction of a short man of fiftyish whose florid face was practically stuck into a blond woman's cleavage.

Eileen's bee-stung lips parted in horror. An angry flush stained her cheeks. Without uttering another word, she sallied forth to fight for her man.

Clio allowed herself to be dragged out of range.

"My brother told me that Roisin and her venomous pal, Jenny, are harassing your daughter," Olivia offered by way of explanation. "In comparison to her mother, Roisin's bitch-level ranking is merely a five. I didn't think you needed to deal with Eileen."

"I was about to give her a blistering response."

Olivia's smile was knowing. "That's why I intervened. Eileen Quirke is on the school board. She's not a person it's wise to antagonize."

Olivia grabbed two glasses of wine from a side table and handed one to Clio.

"Thanks," she said, taking the glass. "You didn't heed your own advice."

Olivia grinned over the rim of her glass. "I have enough ammunition against Eileen to ward off several attacks."

"What brings you to the Glencoe College parent-teacher evening? I thought you said your stepson was in primary school."

"My younger brothers are pupils here. Our parents aren't the most reliable, so tonight's event fell to me. My youngest brother, Ronan, is in Tammy's year."

"She's mentioned the name. They had lunch together, I think."

Olivia's grin widened. "I believe he's rather fond of Tammy. She could do a lot worse."

"Of that, I am quite certain," Clio said dryly, recalling Trevor O'Leary's smug smirk.

"I'm glad I ran into you," Olivia said. "We still haven't set a date for dinner."

"I'm sorry about that. My work schedule keeps changing. Ruairí's wife isn't well, and he keeps needing to go home at short notice."

"No worries. I'd heard Jayme was having a difficult pregnancy. Why don't we do something spontaneously? Text me when you're free. If I can swing it, we can meet up."

"Sounds like a plan. It's Tammy's birthday this weekend, but I should have time for a coffee next week." Clio glanced at the list in her hand and groaned aloud. "I'd better start working my way through Tammy's teachers. I'll get the worst over first. Where's her math teacher?"

***

On the afternoon of Tammy's birthday, the smell of burning alerted Clio that all was not well in the kitchen.

Helen's hair hung limp around her ears. She was red-faced and clasping a spatula tightly in one hand. "I don't understand. The cookery book made it sound so simple. What did I do wrong?"

Clio inspected the batter. Stray specks of eggshell warred with an unidentifiable glutinous lump for Clio's attention.

Helen sobbed. "I wanted Tammy's cake to be perfect. It's the first birthday I've spent with her in years."

Actually, it was the first birthday she'd *ever* spent with Tammy. Clio bit her tongue to stem the acid retort, aware she'd been on tenuous ground with Helen since the night of the robbery. "Don't sweat. Let's see if any of this is salvageable." She took the bowl from her mother and made a show of examining its contents. This was one batter that should *never* make it to the oven. "Okay. I'll check what we have in the fridge. I'm sure we can whip up an alternative."

"What about the beef bourguignon?" Helen's voice rose to a helium squeak. "Is it supposed to have that funny smell?"

Clio pulled the lid off the large pot on the stove and recoiled. "What in the bejaysus did you put in it?"

299

Helen blinked. "I can't remember. There were so many ingredients lying about on the counter. I got a bit panicked."

She replaced the lid and turned to her mother. "When was the last time you cooked a meal from scratch?"

Her mother considered the question, then shook her head. "I can't remember. It must have been after your father left. He'd always taken care of the cooking. Thank goodness I married Larry and his cook."

"You make it sound like a polygamous relationship," Clio said, laughing.

"Oh, you know what I mean." Helen slumped onto a kitchen chair and uncorked a wine bottle. "I did everything that damn recipe book said. Even idiots can cook. How can I not figure out how to follow a recipe correctly? I wanted to make Tammy's birthday dinner perfect."

As if on cue, her granddaughter slouched into the kitchen, even moodier than usual. "What's that awful smell?"

"Tammy," Clio said in a warning tone.

The girl leaned over to sniff at the pot. "Oh my God. I am so not eating that mess. It smells gross."

"Tammy, that's enough." Clio handed her daughter a knife and a chopping board. "Help me chop vegetables, would you?"

"If it's the only way I'll get something edible, I don't suppose I have much choice."

"Your grandmother worked hard to create this...um... meal. Show some appreciation."

"Appreciation for what? The worst birthday dinner ever?"

Helen was looking uncharacteristically frazzled. Her hair had slipped free of its ponytail, and was curling wildly around her ears. She sloshed more wine into her glass. "If you have a problem with my cooking, Tamara, *you* try to produce a five-course meal."

Tammy, giving the prospect serious consideration, glanced at the new watch Clio had given her for her birthday. "It's too late now. It's already after five o'clock. If I start now, we'll be eating at midnight."

"We don't need a fancy meal." Clio tossed burnt green beans from a frying pan into the rubbish bin. She examined the remaining options in the fridge and the larder. It appeared Helen had used almost every item they'd had in stock to whip up the meal of the decade. Clio grabbed a package of dried spaghetti and put water on to boil. "We have eggs, cream, and bacon. I can make us spaghetti carbonara and garlic bread. How does that sound? We're low on vegetables, but I think we'll survive an evening without our greens."

"And I don't need a cake," Tammy said. "Emma sent some marshmallows in my birthday package. They're up in my room. Why don't I fetch the box, and we can use them to make Mum's killer hot chocolate?"

"That sounds like an excellent idea." Clio exchanged a significant glance with her daughter and lowered her voice. "Thanks for being a good sport about this, pet."

A small smile played on Tammy's lips. "No worries. It's kind of fun to watch Gran try to cook."

"I heard that!" Helen said, hands on hips. "Cheeky madam."

Tammy laughed and left to fetch the marshmallows.

Watching Clio chuck the disgusting remains of the beef dish into the bin, Helen began to sob. "I'm sorry. I wanted this evening to be perfect."

Clio glanced up at her mother. Helen was taking the birthday celebrations way more seriously than she'd anticipated. "I appreciate the sentiment, Mother. I'm truly sorry about taking that cash."

Helen's smile was wobbly. To Clio's astonishment, her mother stepped forward and treated her to a stiff hug. "Don't worry about it. You did it because you were desperate, and you replaced it soon after. For what it's worth, I'm not sorry Trevor O'Leary got beaten up, even if that's not what you intended to happen."

Clio's responding smile was equally wobbly. Her mother getting visibly emotional? A rarity, indeed.

"I want us to talk like normal mother, daughter, and granddaughter. I want us to get along," Helen said. "Tonight's dinner was supposed to be the first step."

"Define normal. I don't think there's a truly normal family out there."

"You know what I mean." Her mother shook her head, sending stray strands of hair flying. "I never should have listened to Larry when you got pregnant. I should have been more supportive. He said I'd ruin my career if I let you stay. I regretted my decision soon after you left, but by then it was too late."

Clio's stomach clenched. Yes, her mother *should* have been more supportive, but then Clio had tried to be supportive of Tammy last year and look at the mess she'd caused. Perfect parenting didn't exist. Or if it did, Clio certainly couldn't claim to have mastered it. "If I've realized anything in the weeks since I moved in with you," she said softly, "it's that we're going to have to let the past go. Whatever relationship we establish has to be based on the here and now with an eye to the future. And I'm sorry for bringing the Ray Greer mess to your doorstep."

Helen tucked a stray strand of hair behind her ear. "You were trying to protect your daughter. You did what I should have done for you—stood up for your child. I can appreciate that, even if your methods were... interesting."

Clio let out a laugh. "'Interesting' is one way of putting it. And I'm grateful to you for giving Tammy and me a home, especially at short notice."

Her mother patted her on the back. "I'm glad you're here, no matter the circumstances."

Tammy returned to the kitchen, bright pink marshmallows in tow. "More hugging? For a family that doesn't go in for displays of physical affection, we're going all out today."

"Come here." Clio dragged her daughter into a group hug.

"Next year, I'll hire caterers. I promise," Helen said between sobs. "I don't think I'll ever learn to cook something edible."

"When you're done crushing my ribs," Tammy said in a sardonic tone, "we have a visitor. Did you two not hear the doorbell?"

Clio looked over her daughter's shoulder to see Seán leaning in the doorframe.

He nodded to her and gave the crinkly-eyed smile that indicated everything between them would be okay.

She exhaled sharply and went to him. "Seán."

"Clio." His voice deepened a notch when he said her name, making her heart leap. "Hope you don't mind me interrupting. I know you're busy cooking for Tammy's birthday."

She winked at him. "Actually, my mother cooked."

"Tried to cook," Helen corrected with a sigh. "Cliona and Tammy are coming to my rescue. It seems I'll have to scratch cooking off my list of potential talents."

"I have a gift for Tammy," Seán murmured in a low voice into Clio's ear. "I need to run it by you first though."

"What is it?" she whispered, inhaling his scent greedily.

"A stray puppy."

Taking her hand, he led her out into the hallway, where he'd deposited a small basket. Inside was the ugliest dog Clio had ever seen.

"Oh my gosh. Poor little guy is so thin."

"Believe it or not, he's in better shape than he was on Monday, but he'll need feeding up."

Helen and Tammy appeared in the doorway that separated the kitchen from the hall.

The girl gasped. "Is that a puppy?"

Seán met Clio's eye. Clio looked at her mother.

A wry smile twisted Helen's lips. She nodded. "As long as I don't have to walk him, it's fine by me."

Tammy kneeled by the basket in raptures. She picked up the little dog and stroked him tenderly. "He's adorable. Thank you so much, Sergeant."

"I have his papers here." He handed an envelope to Clio. "I took him to Dr. Mulligan, the Ballybeg vet. She gave him the first set of shots. The details are in the envelope."

"Thank you, Seán. That was really thoughtful of you."

"Would you like to stay for food, Sergeant Mackey?" Tammy asked, still cradling the puppy. "We were about to make Mum's super hot chocolate."

"I'd love to but I'm still on duty. I have to get back to the station in a sec."

"Maybe another time," Clio said, giving him a significant look.

A small smile teased the corners of his mouth. "I'll take you up on that offer. For now, I'd better get going. Bye, ladies. Enjoy your birthday, Tammy."

After Seán left, they returned to the kitchen with the puppy. Helen eyed her daughter curiously. "Sergeant Mackey seems very fond of you."

Clio felt her cheeks grow warm. "He's a good man."

"The pair of you are unbelievable," Tammy said with a grin. "Mum and her sergeant and Gran and her superintendent."

It was Helen's turn to blush. "How ever did you discover that? I thought we were being discreet."

"Yeah," Tammy drawled, "so discreet that you made arrangements outside my bedroom door."

"When was this?" Clio asked with a smile.

"On the night of the robbery," her mother said primly. "The superintendent was merely offering me a shoulder to cry on."

Tammy's grin was wide and mischievous. "Is that what they're calling it these days?"

Helen opened her mouth, presumably to give her granddaughter a lecture about giving cheek to her elders.

"More wine?" Clio asked hastily, sloshing a generous serving of liquid into Helen's glass.

"I don't usually drink more than one glass of wine," Helen lied with perfect sincerity. "But as it's a special occasion, I suppose I can let my hair down a little."

Clio and Tammy exchanged amused glances.

It wasn't long before Helen was flushed and merry. She even made a risqué joke or two. It wasn't enough to mend the damage done to their relationship, thought Clio, but it was a start. Now if only she could pull off a similar feat with Tammy. They were making tentative steps in the right direction.

"Mum?"

"Hmm?" Tammy's voice jerked her back to the present.

"Will you help me clear the table? Gran's...not up to the task."

Helen was singing a song off key, a party hat perched precariously on her frazzled hair. She looked a far cry from her usual groomed, sleek self. "Have we any more wine?" Her voice was slurred, her eyes not properly focused.

"Run out," Tammy said promptly.

"What sort of establishment is this? How can we run out of wine at a birthday party? Well, never mind. Bring out the gin, Cliona."

"I'm not sure that's wise, Mother."

"Why wouldn't it be? It's my idea, and my ideas are always excellent." Helen staggered to her feet and weaved her way to the drinks cabinet.

"Watch out for the dog."

The newly christened Travis leaped out of the way just in time to avoid being trampled by five-inch stilettos.

Helen had some difficulty unscrewing the gin.

"Here. Let me." Clio opened the bottle and poured a modest helping into a glass.

"That's not nearly enough," Helen said, outraged. She snatched the bottle from Clio, sending a stream of gin flying. She topped up her glass generously, then sloshed slimline tonic in to top it up. "I usually go for a slice of lemon," she mused. "But I can't seem to make the knife work today. Oh, well. Bottoms up." She took a long swig from the glass, tottering on her heels.

"Oh, Christ," Clio said to Tammy. "She's completely hammered."

Tammy folded her arms across her chest. "Sledgehammered," she replied with glee. "I gotta say, this is the best birthday I've had in years. The only thing that'd improve it would be if I could have a gin and tonic too."

"No way. I might not win Mother of the Year, but even I'm not that irresponsible."

Tammy shrugged. "I figured you'd say that. It was worth a shot though."

"Come here. One last hug before we go back to normal and avoid all physical affection."

"I love you, Mum."

"I love you, too, pet. Are you sure you don't mind being sent to the Reillys next weekend?

"I'm disappointed I'll miss the excitement of catching burglars in action, but as long as Ma Reilly makes her fruit cake, I'll survive. Will you look after Travis?"

Clio bent to scoop up the little puppy. He responded by giving her a generous lick on the nose. "Of course. We'll have a great time, won't we, Travis?"

CHAPTER THIRTY-TWO

....

Seán toyed with a piece of cauliflower and ignored the lump in his throat. How had he let himself get roped into spending Sunday with his aunt and uncle? Oh, yeah...Nora's pleading brown eyes, searing into his soul. An awkward situation made even more awkward by John-Joe's recent arrest over the *poitín*.

"More wine?" His aunt hovered by his side, the wine bottle poised to pour yet another dollop of disgustingly sweet white wine.

He held a hand over the glass. "No, thanks."

"But sure you're not on duty," she said, ignoring him and sloshing wine into the glass, forcing him to yank back his hand before it got wet. "Might as well enjoy it while you can."

Across the table, John-Joe's flushed face and bleary eyes indicated he'd been enjoying the drink with no qualms. "This wine tastes like shite," he said but let his wife refill his glass to the brim. "Why do you always buy the sweet stuff, Nora?"

"Because I like it. And because I'm the one doing the shopping. I didn't see you offering to shift your lazy arse off the sofa to help."

"Why should I? Aren't I the one out earning the money to buy your fancy wine?"

"And what do you think I do at the suit rental shop all week? Your money, my arse. It's *m e* keeping a roof over our heads, not you and your bloody Elvis routine. And now that you'll be up in court again, who knows what will happen?"

"The food was delicious, Nora," Seán said, cutting through the argument neatly. As instructed by his aunt, he'd brought a nice bottle of wine as part of her birthday gift. She'd immediately hidden the good wine from her husband and served cheap sweet stuff with their dinner, presumably to piss off her husband. *What a marriage.*

"More mashed potatoes? Gravy? I made it the way you always liked it when you were a boy." Nora's smile was strained, her eyes showing the tension.

Her obvious determination to make the meal a success was touching. Not for the first time since he'd moved back to Ballybeg, guilt chafed at him. Despite being married to an eejit,, Nora was a good sort, and she genuinely cared about Seán. That much was obvious. "I'm grand, thanks. I've eaten more than my fill as it is."

Her smile broadened a little. "I loved you and your brother visiting us when you were kids. Having had so many...disappointments, you were like sons to us until our own boys finally came along."

"But you understood why I stayed away."

"Yes, I do. I didn't like it, but I understood. I suppose the memories are bad enough now, even after all this time."

"Memories are unreliable," John-Joe said with a snort. "People see things differently. A child doesn't see the whole story. You think my brother was an unfaithful bastard, don't you?"

"John-Joe!" exclaimed Nora. "Leave it, for heaven's sake. Not on my birthday."

"You do think that, though, don't you?" John-Joe jabbed a thick finger in Seán's face. "I'm not even convinced there was anything serious between him and Helen Havelin, despite what your mother believed. And she was one to talk. Sure she shagged half the town."

"John-Joe," Nora clutched the crucifix around her neck as though it would ward off evil. "Stop this now. Let's forget the past and enjoy our dinner."

"His mother shot my brother, yet Johnny blames him for the situation."

Seán sat stupefied. This couldn't be true. His beautiful mother would never do such a thing. Yet memories nagged him. He saw her perfectly made-up face and gorgeous clothes. Far too fancy and expensive to be funded by a country policeman's income. He recalled being left in hotel lobbies with his little brother while his mother disappeared to meet faceless friends. He remembered babysitting Dex while his mother was out and being told not to mention her absence to his father. Was John-Joe telling the truth, or was his uncle screwing with his mind?

"You know it's true, boy. My brother shouldn't have flirted with Helen Havelin, but a man can only take so much humiliation."

"If my mother had affairs, too, why did she kill him?" *And herself...*

Nora and John-Joe exchanged a significant glance. Eventually, Nora sighed and said, "I dearly loved your mother, J—Seán, but she wasn't the most stable of characters. She suffered badly from depression after you and your brother were born. Sometimes, it was hard to get her to rouse herself to go through the motions of the daily routine. On other occasions, she was a whirlwind of hyperactivity. I've often wondered if she didn't have one of those disorders like manic depression. Bipolar, I think they call it these days."

Reeling, Seán pushed back his chair and stood. "Thanks for dinner, but I need some air."

"Seán, don't go," Nora pleaded, clinging to his arm. "I shouldn't have mentioned it, and John-Joe didn't mean what he said. You know what he's like when he's been drinking. I should have left off after the first bottle of wine. He doesn't even like the stuff."

Making fumbling excuses, Seán managed to extract himself from his aunt's clutches and make his exit. Outside the Fitzgeralds' house, he sucked salty sea air into his lungs and tried to steady his racing mind.

Walking rapidly, he headed toward the promenade and down the steps to the beach.

Blood roared through his head. He didn't need this shit. Didn't want it to be true. The sweet memories of his mother, the scent of her perfume, all tinged and tainted by John-Joe's sordid tale. *That perfume...* something expensive. Hard to pay for on his father's salary. *Damn.* Why hadn't it occurred to him before? It all made sense. What a fucking tragedy. If she had been mentally ill, why hadn't someone gotten her help? If she'd had the proper treatment, maybe she wouldn't have snapped and blasted Seán's childhood away.

He focused on the waves crashing over wet sand, the salty air, and the smell of seaweed. Here a man could think, could breathe, could gather his galloping thoughts. Why had he always fixated on the idea that his father was to blame for what his mother had done? Did he find it easier to blame the quiet, taciturn father who was hardly ever home rather than the warm and caring mother who baked biscuits and always sat down for a chat when he came home from school?

The ringing of his phone cut through his thoughts.

Superintendent O'Riordan got straight to the point. "I need you out at the halting site."

"Another attack?"

"You could say that. Someone put a knife in Blackie Murphy."

"Jaysus. Is he dead?"

"Nah, but mighty pissed."

Seán stared out at the crashing waves and forced himself to focus. "Okay. I need to collect my car, but I should be there within thirty minutes."

CHAPTER THIRTY-THREE

....

The exchange with Blackie Murphy was not going well. "Enough with the theatrics. I've got the message. You're the tough man on the halting site, and I'm not to forget it." Seán leaned forward. "For feck's sake, I'm trying to help you. I want to know who's harming your people, and I want them stopped."

Blackie cradled his sore arm and glowered at Seán. "We sort our own problems. How do we know you're not like the rest of the Guards?"

"I don't call you Tinkers, for a start."

The other man laughed. "I don't give two shites what people call us, long as they let us live in peace."

Peig shuffled into the room, leaning heavily on her cane. "You again," she said upon seeing Seán. "Would you ever give over hounding us and focus on finding whoever's behind the attacks?"

"That's what I'm trying to do. But to get to the bottom of it, a bit of cooperation from your side would help. We all want the same thing—find whoever's responsible and stop them. I know you don't want police involved, but it seems to me like you're not having much success on your own stopping the attacks."

"What are you proposing?" she asked with a sneer. "That we work together? I don't see that going well."

"It might if you'd give me a chance. So you don't trust the Guards in general, but do you trust me?"

Peig stared at him through rheumy eyes. "Oddly enough, I do."

"Ma, you can't be serious." Her son looked horrified. "We're not working with a Guard."

"Not working with him as such. Just being a little more willing to swap info."

Seán was on the alert. "Anything I should know?"

"Oh, no, Sergeant Mackey. You first."

"We've traced the air rifle I believe was used to take shots at your tires, and we've questioned people who might be responsible for the attacks. Problem is, they deny everything. I suspect we have the right men, but I'm not convinced they decided to attack your people of their own accord. Any idea who has a vendetta against you? Or some sort of agenda in driving you out of Ballybeg?" Seán leaned back in his chair. "Now it's your turn."

Blackie exchanged a glance with his mother. "We've had issues with some of the local landowners over the past few years. You know the halting site is on communal land?"

Seán nodded. This was why, ostensibly, the locals shouldn't object too loudly to the halting site's location. While the Travellers were occupying land that belonged to the community, they weren't squatting on anyone's private property.

Peig shuffled to an oak sideboard and pulled open a drawer. She extracted a pile of letters and tossed them on the table in front of Seán. "We've had several letters from the town council over the past year. They're looking to rezone this area and designate this land for building."

Seán stared, his mind in overdrive. "This is the first I've heard of this."

"That's the odd thing, Sergeant Mackey." Peig gave him a weary smile. "Very few people do seem to know about it. Aidan Gant suggested it when he joined the town council. Now that he's dead, Councilors Evans and Jobson seem particularly keen on seeing it approved."

No wonder. Evans and Jobson both owned land that bordered on the communal land. "Why are you only telling me this now?"

Peig shrugged. "We heard you had a run-in with that prick O'Shaughnessy."

"I did," he replied with caution, wondering where this was leading.

"That man was always a bigot." Peig paused to top up his tea. "And frankly, so was your father when he was on the police force."

"I'm not my father," Seán said roughly. "I'm my own man."

Peig gave him a measured look. "I can see that."

"Even if you suspect Evans and Jobson are behind the attacks on your community," he continued, "I think we can assume they're not carrying them out themselves. Are you going to give me a clue as to who is?"

Again Peig and Blackie exchanged glances. Finally, Blackie shrugged. "The only ones I recognized were Colm MacCarthy Junior and a couple of his pals. There's been bad blood between me and Colm MacCarthy Senior for years."

A confirmed sighting of the MacCarthys...excellent news. "Let me guess—dog fighting?"

Blackie gave a half smile. "As I said, we don't get on." The man leaned forward, suddenly serious. "If you don't sort this out, Mackey, we will. One phone call will rally a lot of help from our friends."

Meaning other members of the Travelling community. "Why haven't you called in the cavalry before now?"

"Believe it or not, Mackey, we just want to live our lives in peace. The moment I ask for help, I'll get it, but it'll mean an all-out war. That's a step I'd rather not take. And now that young Jimmy is getting better, simmering tempers have calmed a bit."

"I'd prefer to avoid the vigilante justice route myself," Seán said with a dry laugh, "but Jimmy was badly beaten. He deserves to have his attacker caught and punished—within the parameters of the law."

Blackie and Peig exchanged another loaded look. Finally, Blackie said, "Colm MacCarthy Junior and his pal, Ben Driscoll, are the men to question."

"Okay. Thank you for the information. I'll try my best to sort this out."

He stood to leave, and Peig escorted him to the door of her caravan, her old bones creaking with each step.

"By the way, do you know Helen Havelin's first husband's family?" he asked. "I believe they were part of your community."

Peig's rheumy eyes twinkled in amusement. "Indeed I do, Sergeant. Billy Murphy was my late husband's nephew. I've never met Billy's daughter though. She grew up in the settled community. The two lifestyles don't mix well, you know. Billy left to go on the stage, but the gypsy lifestyle was still in his blood."

He nodded good-bye and walked back to his car, deep in thought. In the days before the expected action at Clonmore House, he'd do some digging concerning the current members of the town council and their interest in the halting site.

CHAPTER THIRTY-FOUR

....

"**A**re you sure you're up for this?" Seán's handsome face creased in concern. The intensity of his gaze made Clio wish she still had the right to kiss him.

He'd called by Clonmore House a couple of hours before she needed to leave for her shift at the pub. It was the Friday before the expected burglary, and their plans were in place. Helen was staying with Superintendent O'Riordan for the weekend. Given the contented smile on her mother's face the morning after her date with the super, Clio guessed it had gone well.

Meanwhile, Tammy was on a train to Wexford. She'd been invited to spend the four-day weekend with Emma's parents. The Reillys had always made an effort to keep in touch after she'd regained custody of Tammy, and Clio appreciated that. In truth, Emma's parents had been more like traditional grandparents to Tammy than Helen or her stepfather.

"I'll be with you the whole time," Seán was saying, "and we'll have people positioned around the house. You won't be in any danger."

She nodded. "I know. I trust you." She bit her lip. "I'm so sorry about not confiding in you sooner. I should have told you the whole story that night at your house. I almost did, but..."

A small smile tugged up the corners of his mouth. "But I distracted you. I remember. Vividly."

Heat crept up her cheeks. "We haven't talked about it directly, but you've been avoiding me since my mother's party."

"Yeah. I've been busy at work—tracking down leads and verifying sources." He examined his knuckles, then turned his gaze back to her. "And I needed time to think. We all keep secrets. I know you were only trying to protect Tammy."

"I've punched Trevor O'Leary so often in my dreams. I won't deny that," she said, "but I have enough humanity not to act on that impulse. All I asked Ray to do was have his guys talk to O'Leary. I figured a show of muscle would be sufficient to send that coward scuttling."

"It's okay, Clio. Your story checked out, and I've kept my word. No one knows about this apart from you, your mother, and me."

"And Ray."

He sighed. "And Ray. I'm hoping he'll have enough to worry about after tonight not to harass you." His phone beeped. "I'd better go. I'm due for a last-minute strategy meeting with the super and the specialist team who'll be helping us tomorrow night."

At the door, they lingered, neither one wishing to say good-bye.

Finally, he dropped a kiss on her cheek. "Are you working tonight?"

"No," she whispered, inhaling his scent greedily.

"Want me to call round? I'm off duty tonight. With Colm MacCarthy Junior and Ben Driscoll in custody, I'm unlikely to be called out on an emergency. Might as well make the best of our hanging-around time before the clock starts ticking."

"That would be lovely. I finish work at eight. Is nine too late?"

He smiled. "Nine is perfect. See you then."

***

Despite her brave words from earlier, Clio was feeling the first stirrings of panic by the time Seán rang the doorbell later that evening. She cradled Travis in her arms and opened the door.

"Hey," he said, searching her face. "You look stressed."

"Just a little." She pushed a stray strand of hair back from her cheek and stood aside to let him in. "Thanks for coming round this evening. The house seems enormous all of a sudden."

That made him laugh. "This house *is* enormous."

"Well, you know what I mean. It never felt scary big before." Wrapping her shawl around her shoulders, she led the way toward the TV room. "I didn't hear your car. Did you have it on stealth mode?"

"No," he said with a grin. "I cycled. Not having a gym nearby makes it harder to keep in shape. I try to run and cycle whenever I have the time."

"Can't you use a police gym?"

"I can and I do, but the nearest one is in Cork City. I don't make it there more than twice a week. If I want to get transferred back to the NBCI, I have to be in top physical shape."

With a wide smile, she allowed herself the pleasure of raking him with her eyes. "You look very good to me. I'm happy to give you a workout later."

He moved closer, slipping the palm of his hand onto the small of her back. "And I'd be happy to let you. How's the puppy?"

"Eating us out of house and home. His appetite can be politely described as prodigious."

Seán leaned close and stroked the puppy's soft fur. "It looks like he's thriving."

Her breath caught and her pulse raced. Their eyes clashed and he bent to kiss her. The instant his lips met hers, Clio forgot all the stresses and strains of the past few months. "You sure you want to watch a film right now?" she murmured.

He nipped her earlobe playfully, making her moan. "What did you have in mind?"

She grabbed his hand and dragged him toward the staircase. "Why don't I show you?"

Up in her bedroom, Seán peered at the floral wallpaper while she settled the already sleeping Travis into his basket. "Not your choice, I take it?" he asked.

"Hell no. I'm in the process of helping Tammy redecorate her room. Once that's done, I'll concentrate on my own. My mother can let her interior designer loose on the rest of the house."

He yanked her curtains shut and took a step toward her. She trailed a finger down his chest, feeling the hard muscles beneath his shirt. She remembered running her hands over those muscles, relishing their hardness, circling taut nipples, the silky-smooth feel of his hard penis in her palms.

A flutter of anticipation rippled through her body. She felt slick wetness between her legs, an ache of longing in her pelvis.

This man had the power to turn her on like no man ever had. He was exactly the sort of guy she should avoid because she'd inevitably fuck up the relationship. But she wanted him. God, she wanted him. With all her soul, with every atom of her being. This couldn't be healthy. And it wouldn't end well. But they were together here and now, and she intended to relish every second.

"Come here," he whispered into her ear. "Lie down on the bed."

She complied, laughing when he began to unzip her skinny jeans and roll them down her legs. It tickled her feet in the most glorious fashion when he took her shoes off. He trailed kisses up her legs, pausing to lick behind her knees. By the time his hot, soft lips reached her thighs, she was a quivering mass of longing. He massaged her inner thighs and buttocks, stroking between her legs, exploring.

When he finally reached her clit, she almost shot off the bed as if electrocuted. "Oh, God," she moaned. "This feels so damn good."

Seán circled her with his tongue, tugging gently with his teeth. Fire coursed through her, an exquisite, painful pleasure that almost tipped her over the edge. "Do. Not. Stop."

He teased her for what seemed like an exquisite eternity. As if sensing how close she was to orgasm, Seán drew back, eliciting a whimper of protest. "Hurry up with the condom."

He laughed. "Impatient puss."

She heard the foil wrapper tear open, and he slid a condom over his erect shaft.

"Are you wet enough?" he asked. "Or do you need extra lube?"

"Definitely wet enough," she gasped. "Now come here."

He complied, pushing gently into her and pausing halfway to allow her to adjust to his size.

"More," she moaned.

He began to move, each thrust propelling the tension that had been mounting inside her.

She grabbed his hair as he moved, pulled him closer and deeper. Her hips matched his rhythm until finally she reached the crest of the wave and exquisite pleasure coursed through her. She heard him cry out as he matched her orgasm with his.

"God, Clio. Sex with you is amazing."

"Same with you. I wish we could do this every night."

"Why can't we?" He propped himself up on his pillow. "We're both single. There's nothing to stop us sleeping together, especially now that I'm no longer officially acting as bodyguard to your mother. Once this business tomorrow night is over, it doesn't matter who knows we're together."

"Part of me wants to say yes."

Hurt was reflected in his blue eyes. "Why does part of you want to say no?"

"Because you'll be heading back to Dublin soon. Once you catch Ray, you're bound to get the transfer you've been angling for."

A flush stained his cheekbones. "You could come with me."

Her heart lodged in her throat. If her situation were different, she'd agree in a millisecond. "I've dragged Tammy around too much. I want her to finish her secondary education at Glencoe College. That means I'll be in Ballybeg for at least three years."

He fell back on his pillow, deep in thought. "One of the guys from the homicide division in Cork mentioned —"

"Wait." She held up a finger for silence. "Do you hear that?"

Sure enough, the sound of tires on gravel rumbled outside.

Her eyes flew to Seán's.

"I take it you weren't expecting anyone tonight?" he asked.

She shook her head, numb with fear. "Ray said the fourteenth. It's only the thirteenth."

In what looked like one fluid movement, he was off the bed and over at the window. Peeking through the edge of her curtains, he abruptly withdrew. "Fuck."

She jumped out of bed and joined him at the edge of the window. Through the gap in the curtains, she saw lights in the distance. Two sets of bouncing headlights bobbed and weaved their way around the winding, hilly road that led to Clonmore House and rolled to a crunching stop in the gravel courtyard. "Fuck is right."

Seán already had his phone to his ear. "Sir, we have a problem. Two SUVs just pulled up outside Clonmore House. Judging by their builds, four men and one woman. Put it this way—they're all wearing balaclavas and the men move like pros. I'm going say they're not here for a social call. Yeah. Tell the team to hurry." He tossed the phone on the bed and hurriedly threw on his discarded clothes.

With shaking hands, Clio followed suit. "Seán." Her vocal chords croaked like a hinge in need of oil. "I can't remember if I set the alarm when you came in. We're not in the habit of putting it on during the day if we're at home."

He shook his head. "Too late to worry about that now. The ease with which they move implies to me that these guys will have no problem disabling an alarm."

"You don't have a gun?"

"No." He scowled. "Only specialized units can carry guns in Ireland. I'm going to have to improvise."

"Wait." A surge of bile reached her throat. "You can't confront them. It would be suicide. If a member of Ray's gang discovers a policeman on the premises, they'll kill you."

"I'm going to wait as long as I dare, Clio, but I can't let the chance to catch Ray Greer's gang in the act pass me by." He took her arm. "I need something I can use to defend myself. Do you have anything on this floor that would do?"

She exhaled sharply. "In my handbag." She pulled out a can of pepper spray and threw it to him. "And in my bathroom." Another two cans. "And in Tammy's." A fourth can landed on the bed.

Seán's mouth gaped. "What. The. Hell. You know it's illegal for civilians to possess pepper spray, let alone use it?"

She put her hands on her hips. "Well, *you're* not a civilian."

He let out a low whistle. "Okay. Time to improvise. If we go in there and spray that stuff around in an enclosed space, we'll be as screwed as they are. We need protection for our eyes and mouths."

"Hey, I have those eye mask thingies for on planes." She whipped a red polka dot eye mask out of the bathroom cupboard.

"Uh, no." A hint of a smile. "We need to be able to see. Ski or swim goggles would work."

"Those I have too." She rummaged through a drawer and found her prescription swim goggles. "I'm pretty sure Tammy has a pair without prescription lenses in her bathroom."

Seán disappeared and came back a minute later, armed with Tammy's goggles and a pack of surgical masks. "I found these in your mother's bathroom."

Once they'd donned mask and goggles, they snuck downstairs. The door leading down to the rooms in the cellars was ajar, light spilling out. Despite Seán's warning on the night of the housewarming party, Helen hadn't gotten around to changing the locks.

Seán placed a hand on Clio's arm and thrust a large can of pepper spray at her. "Stay here and wait for backup," he whispered. "On no account are you to follow me."

"Screw that, Mackey. If we both go down, we can ambush them with four cans of pepper spray at once. We might be two against five, but we have the element of surprise on our side."

He glared at her through the darkness. "It's too dangerous. I won't take the risk of something happening to you."

"Life is a risk, Seán. I'm coming with you whether you like it or not, so we might as well coordinate our attack."

He nodded grimly. "All right. I'll go first, but try to get down to stand beside me. We'll spray the cans with full force, then run back up the stairs. The masks and goggles will provide some protection, but not enough. Okay, on the count of three..."

They heard voices as they descended the stairs. Male voices and a woman. The woman seemed to be the one giving the orders. "Break them open, you eejit," she snapped. "We're not hauling a bunch of garden gnomes out to the cars. Extract the cash and put it in the sports bag."

Garden gnomes? What the feck? Clio exchanged a glance with Seán. He was shaking his head ruefully. He indicated they should inch forward. She obeyed. All went well until she bashed her foot on something hard. Letting out an involuntary yelp, she sprang back.

Oh, fuck.

"What was that?" The woman's voice again, alarmed now. "Did you hear something?"

"Now," Seán hissed. Cans at the ready, he sprang forward. Her heart in her throat, Clio followed suit.

The next minute or so passed in chaos. Seán and Clio emptied the cans before the intruders had time to pull their guns. Screaming in pain, four of the five fell like dominoes. One of the men, the largest of the bunch, managed to punch Seán in the chest. Thankfully, the attacker was suffering the effects of the pepper spray, and Seán was able to subdue him without much effort.

Using the rope they'd found upstairs, Seán tied up their prey. They were in the process of hauling two of the men upstairs when the backup team arrived.

The superintendent strode through the hall, Brian Glenn at his heels. "Looks like you two have the situation well under control."

Seán pulled off his mask and goggles. Clio did the same, and hacked up a cough.

Seán raised an eyebrow. "Shall we unmask them?"

"Go for it," she wheezed, searching her pocket for her inhaler.

Members of the backup team yanked off the balaclavas. Clio didn't recognize the first two men, but Seán did. "Two of Ray Greer's usual suspects."

The third man was Tank, the no-necked arsehole who'd harassed her in the pub.

The sight of the fourth man and the woman elicited a gasp from her and a strangled "No" from Seán.

"Phoebe?" Clio said, stunned at the sight of her mother's mousy PA dressed as a cat burglar.

Phoebe spat and struggled to get free. "Fuck you and your mother. I've spent four years working for that officious bitch for a pittance. Can you blame me for wanting to earn a bit of extra cash?"

"A crap job doesn't entitle you to rob your employer," Clio said, stunned. "Right, Seán?"

Seán was deathly pale, his gaze riveted on the fourth man. "Frank?"

....

CHAPTER THIRTY-FIVE

The pulse in Seán's forehead throbbed. "It was you all along. *You* were the unit mole, not Detective Inspector Connelly."

"Steady on, mate," Frank wheezed, still suffering the effects of the pepper spray. "I can explain."

"You'd fucking well better," Seán snarled, "and you'd better talk fast. Young Alan Brennan died because of you, and my reputation was left in tatters."

Clio touched his arm. "You know this guy?"

"Meet Frank Duffy, my former partner." Seán glared down at the man who, up until a minute ago, he'd considered to be one of his best friends.

Frank, still prostrate on the floor, was hauled into sitting position by two of the special unit team. "Seán, please. Let me explain."

If the man was dumb enough to talk before his lawyer got there, all the better. "I'm waiting. And it better be good."

"I got behind on my mortgage repayments," the man said, desperation oozing from his bloodshot eyes. "The job for Ray Greer was supposed to be a one-off. But one job is never enough for Greer. One thing led to another, and I ended up doing several jobs for him, always for cash payments. He gave me some useful tip-offs for our team, and in return, I kept him informed about what we knew about him and his activities. When I told him about the raid we were planning, he swore no one would get hurt."

"And you believed that?" Seán growled. "How stupid can you be?"

"I know, I know." Frank squeezed his eyes shut. "At that stage, I was in so deep I couldn't see the bottom. I was in a no-win situation. If I betrayed Ray, he'd kill me. If I continued to do as he demanded, I'd incriminate myself more and more."

"I assume the garden gnomes belonged to Aidan Gant," Seán said, naming Olivia's former husband and the victim of the murder he'd helped to solve last summer.

"Yeah." Frank gave another hacking cough. "As you know, Gant helped Greer smuggle cash out of the country. He hid the cash in various places, but mostly in the base of his garden gnome collection. Because he often traveled to competitions, it was a simple thing for him to transport them on the ferry. Controls are less strict on boats than on planes, and Gant was a respected lawyer."

"And when Gant died, Ray Greer realized he had no idea where some of his not-yet-smuggled cash was concealed," Seán finished.

Frank nodded. "You found the money he'd hidden on his own property last summer, but Ray knew there had to be more. He suspected it was in or near Clonmore House fairly early on, but couldn't find it."

"What changed? You had to remove the flooring to access the gnomes in the basement. Did someone tip you off?"

"Yeah," Frank took a drink of water offered by one of the backup team and continued talking. "Gant's former business partner, Bernard Byrne, now lives in Marbella. Ray tracked him down and...persuaded...him to reveal a few potential hiding places Gant might have used around Clonmore House. Unfortunately for us, your mother moved in just as Ray received the information. Recruiting Phoebe was an easy task. With her help, we eliminated several hiding places. Phoebe figured that Helen kept the keys to the basement in the safe, but we could have opened the door without them. The stupid cow was only supposed to take that damn antique that turned out to be a replica, but she broke into the safe too."

"Did Ray suspect Clio told us about his interest in the house?"

Frank nodded. "Yeah. That's why he brought the break-in forward by a day."

"It was a hell of a risk," Seán said, frowning. "It's not like Ray to throw caution to the wind like that. I don't understand why he pressed ahead when he must have realized we were on to him."

"Desperation," Frank said bluntly. "He's been jumpy of late. Rumor has it that he's planning on doing a runner. I was rather hoping that the rumor was true."

"I'll bet you were." Seán met his former partner's eye and stared him down.

The other man flinched and averted his gaze. "And now I'd like to speak to a lawyer."

Seán stood back and regarded the three silent goons next to Frank, plus the still sobbing Phoebe. "Where was the handover to take place?"

The no-necked Tank grunted. "On the road toward Cobh. We were supposed to meet a few of Ray's guys, and they were to take it from there."

This revelation prompted the other goons to demand legal representation, water, and—in Tank's case—a cigarette. Phoebe, after her initial outburst, clammed up and refused to say a word.

The superintendent came to stand by Seán's elbow. "Damn good work, sergeant.

He nodded grimly. "Let's get this lot to the station. I suggest we take them to Cork. There's not enough room in Ballybeg to house this many suspects."

Seán, Brian, and the team from Cork loaded Frank and his handcuffed cohorts into vans. As Seán was shoving him into a seat, Frank turned to him, a look of raw fear in his still-watery eyes. "Please, mate. For old time's sake, will you put in a good word for me? Up until the business with Ray, I was a good policeman. And even after, some of the tips he gave me helped us solve cases."

Seán stared at the man incredulously. Then, shaking his head, he slammed the door on the man and their friendship.

***

The Tuesday after the rumbled home invasion was St. Patrick's Day, the Irish national holiday. Clio was working a double shift at MacCarthy's pub, and her mother had elected to spend the day with Superintendent O'Riordan. Marcella, dressed as a leprechaun, had bedecked the pub with garish decorations that made her brother cringe.

Jayme, Ruairí's heavily pregnant American wife, was sitting at the bar, nibbling on salt and vinegar crisps. She looked pale and drawn and shifted in her seat as though she couldn't get comfortable. Even after fifteen years, Clio remembered that stage all too well.

"How are you feeling?" she asked.

The woman frowned. "I'm not sure. Odd, I guess, and kind of restless. Probably the result of weeks on bed rest. Now that I'm allowed to move about, I don't know what to do with myself. I've already sorted the nursery—several times."

Clio laughed and pushed a pint and change across the counter to a waiting customer. "I remember that antsy feeling. When is your due date?"

"Tomorrow, but given this baby's thwarted attempts to come way before her due date, she's probably decided to make me wait."

"No sign of labor?"

The other woman shook her honey-brown hair. "I've been getting Braxton-Hicks contractions for the past two weeks, but nothing more than that." She winced, shifted in her seat again, then stood. "And the constant urge to pee, but I've had that the entire pregnancy. Can you get me another orange juice while I'm in the rest room, Clio?"

"Sure." Clio loaded a drinks order onto a tray and eased her way through the crowd toward Olivia's table. She and Jonas were sitting with Fiona and Gavin at a table near the entrance. Luca, their little boy, was playing in the snug area with some of the other kids. When ordering their first round of drinks, they'd pumped her for information regarding the drama at on Saturday night. Clio had answered the questions she felt wouldn't hamper the investigation, but had left out all mention of Phoebe, Frank, and Ray Greer's possible plan to flee Ireland.

"When does Tammy get back from Wexford?" Olivia asked, helping her to unload the tray.

"Later today." Clio refilled the bowls of dry-roasted peanuts and crisps, then loaded the used glasses onto the now empty tray. "Her train gets into Cork at six o'clock. I'll collect her at the end of my shift."

"If you get a free moment, come and join us," Fiona said, twirling a long dark curl around her finger. She was sticking to mineral water and looked a little green around the gills. Clio smiled to herself. Would there be another Ballybeg baby in a few months' time?

"If I get a chance, I will, but we're run off our feet today. We'll have to do a repeat of last week's dinner.

Why don't I cook for us at my place next Friday evening?"

"Sounds like a plan," Fiona said. "Good for you, Liv?"

Olivia nodded. "Friday is perfect."

When she returned to the bar, Clio noticed Jayme's seat was still vacant. "Is Jayme still in the bathroom?" she asked Sharon.

"What?" Sharon replied distractedly, wrestling with a stubborn roll of one-euro coins. "I guess so. I haven't seen her in a while."

As if on instinct, Ruairí glanced over from the far end of the bar and frowned at his wife's empty seat.

At that moment, Bridie Byrne sallied forth from the women's toilets, a beam across her plump face. "Better get moving, Ruairí. Looks like your wife has gone into labor."

Ruairí froze, paled, and then leaped into action. "Can you hold the fort?"

"Of course," Clio said, laughing. "Take your wife to the hospital."

"And don't let her name that poor child Lucrezia," Sharon yelled.

The next few hours passed in a blur of pints, whiskies, and packets of crisps. Shortly before five o'clock, Seán ambled into the pub. Clio's heart skipped a beat at the sight of his sexy grin.

"Hey, you," he said. "I heard a rumor that you get off work in a few minutes. Want to go for a walk?"

She glanced at her watch. "I'd love to, but it'll have to be a quick one. I'm due to meet Tammy at the train station."

"Go on," Marcella said, maneuvering her leprechaun costume behind the counter. "Finish a few minutes early. You've worked through your break, so you're entitled to the time."

"Thanks. Send me a text when the baby's born."

Marcella saluted her. "Will do. Enjoy the rest of your St. Patrick's Day."

CHAPTER THIRTY-SIX

....

Seán stared out at the crashing waves, then back at the beautiful woman beside him. He should tell her the truth. He'd like to forget the whole damn sorry tale and bury it in the graveyard of bad memories, but if he didn't say something it would be a barrier between them in the future. He couldn't commit to a woman whose mother he secretly despised. The only way forward was to tell her what had happened.

He took her hand, relishing the feel of her warm fingers clasped in his. "If we're going to start a relationship, a real one, there's something I need to tell you."

The wind whipped her strawberry-blond hair around her face. "Go on. After all I've told you, it can hardly be worse."

"Maybe not worse, but different." He took a deep breath. "I don't like your mother."

"You don't say," she replied deadpan, then laughed. "I've noticed, and I appreciate your willingness to be polite despite not liking her."

"My dislike of her isn't necessarily fair."

"Care to elaborate?" Her face morphed from curious to horrified. "Oh my God. She didn't come on to you, did she?"

"What? No. God, no." Every fiber in his being revolted at the notion. "Nothing like that. It's complicated. And as I said, not entirely rational."

Clio laughed. "My whole life is complicated, and I've rarely been accused of being rational. Hit me with it."

"Something your mother did—or rather, participated in—was the catalyst for my parents' deaths."

Her eyes widened in horror. "What happened?"

"She had an affair with my father. When my mother found out, she snapped and shot him and then herself."

Clio's eyes clouded with tears. "Oh, my God. I am so sorry, Seán.

"There's no need for you to be sorry. It's hardly your fault." He touched her cheek, marveling at the softness of her skin. "If it hadn't been your mother, it would have been some other woman. My parents didn't have a happy marriage."

The memories hit him like a lash, making his eyes sting. His mother yelling and his father silent. His mother throwing objects and his father finally walking out and slamming the door.

"I say she snapped," he said in a shaky voice, "but that's not entirely accurate. On the night it...happened... she sent my brother and me to stay overnight with John-Joe and Nora. We were all under the assumption that my parents planned a date night. When John-Joe dropped us home in the morning, we found them in the kitchen."

Her hand flew to her mouth. "You poor child. I don't know what to say. How unspeakably awful."

"Don't say anything at all. Believe me, I've heard it all before. Just say nothing, but look me in the eyes. That's what most people can't do in these situations. It's why I make a point of looking people directly in the eye when I'm the bearer of bad news, not just while I'm delivering it, but afterward while they react. Too many people say all the so-called right words, but avert their eyes.

"When I left Ballybeg to live with my grandmother in Dublin, I wanted to leave the past behind me. Not seeing my aunt and uncle was one way. Not returning to Ballybeg was another. But every time I turned on the TV..."

"You saw my mother." She closed the space between them and pressed her head against his chest. "Do you think of her when you look at me?"

"What?" He drew back in surprise, touched a finger to her chin. "No, Clio. I only see you. I can't promise I'll ever be able to put the negative association between your mother and my parents' deaths fully to rest, but for your sake, I'll try."

"It's okay. I don't expect a miracle. Besides, I'd be a hypocrite if I demanded that of you. I'm not sure I'll ever forgive my mother for how she treated me when I got pregnant with Tammy. I'm moving past my resentment and trying to forge a relationship with her that's based on the present, but it will always be there."

"Whatever the truth of your parents marriage, it sounds like they both loved you and provided you with a stable home up until that point. Remember that, and don't let the way they died cloud your memories of your childhood."

"That's what I've tried to do all these years. The full impact didn't hit me until I moved back to Ballybeg. Seeing people I'd known for the first ten years of my life who no longer recognized me. I wanted the anonymity of changing my name, but it was weird introducing myself to people who'd known me as a child, never letting slip who I was. The worst was seeing my uncle again. He was my father's twin. Until he opens his mouth, he looks just like him. The one saving grace was that the house we lived in was long gone. It was knocked down to make room for the shopping center development that never happened."

Clio stood on her tippy toes and wrapped her arms around his neck. "Thanks for telling me this, Seán. I know it must have been hard for you. No wonder you looked like you'd swallowed a fish when I opened the door that first time at Clonmore House."

He gave a rueful laugh. "Seeing the gorgeous woman I'd just had sex with standing on Helen Havelin's doorstep came as a nasty shock. I thought it had to be some sort of cosmic joke."

"And then to be assigned to guard my mother. What a nightmare."

"Ah, well," he said, ruffling her hair. "It all worked out for the best in the end."

An alarm sounded on Clio's phone. She broke their embrace and pulled it out of her handbag. "Time for me to head to the train station and collect Tammy."

Still smiling she pressed a button to switch off the alarm. And then frowned. "Wait a sec. Mrs. Reilly sent me a message. I hope Tammy didn't miss her train. What the...?"

"Is something wrong?" he asked, reading panic on her face. "Is Tammy okay?"

"Mrs. Reilly sent a text message to wish me and Tammy a Happy St. Patrick's Day. She says they loved having Tammy to stay and hope she got home safely *yesterday*." With trembling hands, she hit a button on her phone, then shook her head. "Tammy's phone is switched off, and so is her voice mail."

"Call Mrs. Reilly to confirm when Tammy left yesterday."

Clio nodded and made a quick phone call to her daughter's former foster mother, followed by a call to Emma. After she ended the calls, she began to cry. "She left Wexford yesterday on the connection she was supposed to take today. They haven't seen or heard from her since. Tammy swore blind she was due back in Ballybeg yesterday, and Ma Reilly believed her. What if she's gone to meet Trevor O'Leary?"

"Isn't he still in a rehabilitation center?" Seán asked.

"I don't know," she said, wiping fresh tears from her cheeks. "I was under the impression he'd be there for a while."

"I can make a couple of calls to check. Meanwhile, phone her friends."

A few minutes later, they compared notes. "A colleague in Dublin confirmed that Trevor O'Leary went home ten days ago."

"Oh, no," Clio sobbed. "Please don't let her have run off with him. Her friends from her school in Dublin say she hasn't been in touch since we moved to Ballybeg."

"Does she have any friends at Glencoe College? I know she was having issues settling in, but did she mention anyone who spent the breaks with?"

"Olivia's brother," she said with a gasp. "A boy called Ronan. Do you know him?"

"Better than that—I know where he lives. It's only a few minutes from here. Let's go and see what he has to say. If he knows nothing, I'd suggest we go to the station to see if she shows up on today's train."

***

Seán screeched to a halt in front of the Dunne's ramshackle seaside cottage. He and Clio leaped out of the car and ran to the door. It was opened by a gangly teenage boy with gawky features and red hair. He'd be a handsome lad in a few years, once he'd had time to grow into himself.

The boy's eyes widened in surprise at the sight of a uniformed policeman and a strange woman on his doorstep.

"Hello, Ronan," Seán said. "Can we have a word?"

The boy blinked. "Uh, sure. Come on in." In the kitchen, he switched the kettle on.

"No need for that, Ronan. We don't have time. We're here about Tammy Havelin."

The boy looked at Clio curiously. "You're her mother?"

Clio nodded. "Do you know where Tammy is? She was supposed to be staying with friends in Wexford and come back to Ballybeg today. It turns out she lied to them and left yesterday. Any idea where she might have gone? Someone she might have met?"

He thought for a moment, then shook his head. "No. Tammy didn't mention running away to me. I know she had a bad breakup a while back, but she only mentioned that in passing."

"This breakup...did she mention the guy's name?"

"Terry. Or Travis. Or was that her dog's name? I think it was something beginning with T."

Seán's heart leaped. "Trevor?"

"Yeah," the boy's face cleared. "Trevor. She said he was a bit older than her and that her mother didn't approve of her seeing him."

Clio let out a bitter laugh. "Try eighteen years older."

Ronan's big blue eyes grew even larger. "What? I had no idea. She never went into specifics. To be honest, I wasn't all that interested in hearing about her boyfriend. She picked up on that. We tended to talk music and books."

"Do you have any idea where Tammy might have met him, if she'd made an arrangement to see him in Ballybeg? Somewhere she was familiar with and wouldn't be seen?"

Ronan considered for a second, then shook his head. "Not this time of year. The weather's lousy. If we go somewhere after school, it's to a café in town, but mostly Tammy and I hang out at the school library. I'd help you if I knew anything, honest. Truth be told, Tammy and I don't know each other all that well. I like her, but she's only been at Glencoe College for a few weeks."

"Is there anyone else at school she might have confided in? One of the girls, maybe?"

"No way. On that point, I'm certain. Tammy gravitated toward me because she had no friends, especially not amongst the girls. She was Jenny Cotter and Roisin Quirke's latest victim. None of the other girls wanted to be seen talking to her in case Jenny and Roisin would turn on them."

"Okay. Thanks, Ronan." Seán stood, and Clio followed suit. "We'll see ourselves out. If you think of anything, however small it might seem, give me a call." Seán slid a piece of paper onto the table.

The boy examined it before putting it into his shirt pocket. "Will do, Sergeant Mackey. Good luck finding Tammy. I hope she's okay."

So did Seán.

"Where to next?" Clio asked when they were back in the car. "Should we try the train station? She was strung so tight he thought she might snap.

He gunned the engine and pulled back out onto the road. "We have to pass Clonmore House on our way to Cork City. Let's have a look to see if she left some sort of clue in her bedroom. A diary, a note, something."

"Okay."

They were silent for the rest of the short journey back to Clonmore House. Seán keyed the security code into the gate and they drove through. Intent on reaching their destination as quickly as possible, the meandering twists and turns of the tree-lined drive failed to impress him the way they usually did.

"What the—?" Clio said from the passenger seat.

A black BMW was parked outside the house. Leaning against the side of the vehicle, sporting biker shades and leathers, stood Lar Delaney.

CHAPTER THIRTY-SEVEN

·····································

"Tammy!" Clio leaped out of Seán's car at the same time her daughter clambered out of Lar's. She threw her arms around her and hugged her tight.

"Mum," Tammy protested, "you're crushing my ribs."

"I'll crush more than your ribs by the time I'm finished with you, young lady. What were you thinking when you lied to me and the Reillys? And as for you," she glared at Lar, who was standing nonchalantly to the side, "what the hell are *you* doing here? I thought I told you to stay away."

"You did, and I obeyed." He whipped off his shades, revealing the same deep blue eyes their daughter had inherited. "Tammy showed up on my doorstep late this morning. Said she'd spent the night in my neighbor's shed and waited until she saw me come home."

Clio refrained on commenting on why Lar might be returning to his residence close to lunchtime. Knowing him, a night spent banging a random woman would be the most innocent reason on a very long list of possibilities.

"Why didn't you call Clio?" Seán demanded, coming to stand behind her. "You must have known she'd panic if Tammy didn't show up at the time she'd arranged."

"But she did get back on time." Lar's smile didn't meet his electric blue eyes. "I made damn sure of that." He turned to Clio. "How open can I be in front of the Guard?"

"Go for it. After my recent adventures, I'd trust him with my life." *Literally, figuratively, and every other way.*

"Can I have a shower, Mum," Tammy interrupted. "I feel icky after my night in the shed. I would have showered at Dad's but the only clean underwear he had to offer was a pair of his own or a scrap of lace he found in the back of a drawer that had been left by some slapper. I didn't find either option appealing."

"I can imagine," Clio said dryly.

"And he doesn't have a tumble dryer," the girl continued, an expression of horror on her pretty face, "so washing and drying the pair I had on wasn't possible."

"Clearly, my household doesn't come up to scratch," Lar said with a grin.

"All right," Clio said to her daughter. "Go up and have a shower. But don't think you're getting off this lightly. I want a full explanation later."

Tammy sighed and made to do an eye roll but caught herself in time. "Okay, Mum. Just don't yell at Dad. It's not his fault I snuck off to Dublin."

After Tammy ran upstairs, Clio led the way into the living room. She noticed Seán was very careful to position himself on the sofa beside her. The feel of his warm thigh against hers was comforting.

"Okay, spill," she demanded once Lar had settled in the armchair opposite. "Why didn't you call me the instant Tammy showed up on your doorstep?"

"Because she was crying and obviously distraught. I was more concerned about getting her in out of the rain and hearing what she had to say." He crossed his muscular arms across his equally muscular chest. "For all I knew at that moment, *you* were the cause of the problem."

"And you've since established that I wasn't the cause of her tears?"

He nodded and his mouth took on a grim twist. "She told me about that fucker O'Leary. She told me the whole damned story. And she also told me she had a shrewd notion you had something to do with him getting the shite beaten out of him."

Clio felt Seán's hand on hers. "That's right. In a moment of incredible stupidity, I called Ray Greer. I wanted his men to intimidate O'Leary. A show of muscle, that was all. I didn't expect them to beat him up."

"In that case, you've been out of the life too long, Clio." Lar's lips twisted into a grim smile. "Men like Greer's crew don't show a bit of muscle and say a few harsh words. They're trained to behave like attack dogs. Most come from backgrounds crappier than anything you experienced during your couple of years of slumming it, and you handed them a pedophile. Did you seriously think they wouldn't take that as an open invitation to work out all their childhood grievances? Frankly, I'm surprised the man is still alive."

"Want to know what's really ironic? I almost called *you* the day the police told me that prick wouldn't be brought to trial. The only reason I called Ray instead of you was because I was afraid you'd kill O'Leary."

A muscle in Lar's cheek flexed. "I probably would have."

"I didn't hear that," Seán said and put his hand over hers.

The gesture did not go unnoticed by Lar. He looked from one to the other of them and smirked. "I wouldn't have seen you hooking up with a Guard, Clio. Your taste must have changed."

"Improved at any rate," she said in a mild tone but the barb hit home.

His smirk widened. "Touché."

She gave an internal eye roll. Lar was insufferable at the best of times, and today definitely didn't qualify. "While I appreciate you bringing Tammy home, I'd rather you left."

"I'm sure you would, but I'm not going anywhere until I know my daughter is safe."

"Trevor O'Leary got out of the rehabilitation center ten days ago," Seán said, "but he's still in a bad way. I don't think Tammy has anything to fear from him."

"Hopefully by the time his physical health has improved," Clio added, "she'll have gotten over her infatuation."

"From the conversation I had with her this morning, I get the impression that she's moving on." Lar leaned forward in his seat, suddenly serious. "But O'Leary isn't the danger I'm worried about. How much do you know about Ray Greer, Sergeant Mackey?"

"Enough to know that I'd very much like to get my hands on him."

"I'm not going to tell you how I know this, so don't bother asking. Ray Greer has been winding you all up. The heat has been building on him for a while. He's a slippery bastard but a smart one. He knows it's time to get out of Ireland and try his luck elsewhere."

"We have people prepared to squeal on him," Seán said frowning, "but Greer has weathered worse scrapes than this with the help of his expensive lawyers. Why would he run this time?"

"Ah, sergeant." Lar's smug smirk was back in place. "You're an innocent lad at heart. Why do you assume the heat I'm referring to is coming from the police?"

Seán and Clio exchanged a significant look.

"He's in trouble with someone from the criminal underworld?" she asked. "Who?"

"That's a question neither of you want answered. Trust me." Lar steepled his fingers, his intense stare never wavering. "Let's just say that Greer pissed off the wrong man."

After a moment's of loaded silence, Seán asked, "What do you know about the break-in on Friday?"

"Ray plans to fly the coop, but is short of funds. To finance his getaway, he needed portable valuables such as Clio's mother's antique leopard and the cash Aidan Gant hid in Clonmore House.

"Do you have any idea where Ray is right now?" Clio asked.

Lar's grin widened. He whipped his smartphone from his shirt pocket, touched the display, and shoved it in front of their faces. "See this island? Until six months ago, it was a nature reserve. Your local council managed to push through new zoning plans to reverse the reservation order and have since sold it for a tidy sum. The new owner is building himself a holiday home, but had to put the construction on hold over the winter months. Ray paid off the security guys who are meant to be guarding the building site, and he's been using the island to hide whatever cash and portable valuables he can get his paws on."

"I had no idea Inish Glas wasn't still a nature reserve." Seán raised an eyebrow. "You don't happen to know about any other rezoning plans that the local council want to push through?"

Lar laughed. "Oh, yeah. Aidan Gant convinced several councilors to make a push to sell the communal land where there's a halting site. I don't know the particulars but they wanted to build something on it. There's supposed to be another plot of land toward Cobh where they hope to do something similar."

Clio shook her head. "And you know about all this because?"

"Nothing sinister there. Gant mentioned it to me last year."

A clever deflection if ever there was one. "Back to this island," she said. "Are you sure Ray's there at the moment?"

"Not one hundred percent, but he's definitely not in Dublin. My sources tell me that he was planning to take the proceeds of the robbery on Saturday and sail to France."

Seán handed the phone back to Lar. "It would be easy to conceal a boat on the far side of the island."

"Why are you telling us this now?" Clio demanded. "If you're willing to share the info with the police, why didn't you do so before the break-in?"

"First, I didn't know about any of this until I made a few phone calls this morning. I was aware that Ray had a mole in the National Bureau of Criminal Investigation. I did not know that said mole broke into your house on Friday night. Second, I wasn't aware that Ray was threatening Clio. I don't want that motherfucker anywhere near my daughter."

"So what's the plan?" Clio asked. "Call in the coast guard?"

Lar shook his head. "No way. I brought you the information. I want to be there when you catch Ray."

"Out of the question," Seán said. "Leave this to the police."

"Unfortunately for you," Lar said casually, "I've waited to tell you about this until the last second. If we don't find a boat within the next fifteen minutes, Ray will be long gone."

"You absolute prick," Clio exclaimed. "No wonder you took your sweet time escorting Tammy back to Ballybeg and didn't bother trying to call me. Where are we going to find a boat at such short notice?"

"Buck MacCarthy," Seán said, leaping to his feet. "Come on. There's not a second to waste."

CHAPTER THIRTY-EIGHT

....

"**H**auled away from my pint! It's a disgrace," shouted a drunk and belligerent John-Joe. "This is police brutality."

"And on St. Patrick's Day of all days," muttered Buck as he steered his boat toward Inish Glas.

"Ah, quit whining, lads," Seán said with a wink. "Sure isn't this a bit of an adventure?"

John-Joe crossed chubby arms over the orange life vest and scowled at his nephew. "I only like adventures that pay cold, hard cash. Somehow, I don't see this jaunt being to my financial benefit."

"See it as your contribution to public safety," Seán said with a grin. "And you never know, it might help to sway the judge in your favor when the guns and *poitín* business comes to court."

Lar Delaney, swagger undiminished by his bulky life vest, eyed the captain of the ship dubiously. "Is this boat seaworthy?"

"There's nothing wrong with my boat," Buck shouted over the roar of the engine. "And if that Dublin fecker disagrees, he can swim to the island."

Seán laughed. "That's you told, Delaney."

The other man gave an exaggerated sigh and sat on the seat next to Clio.

"Ugh," she moaned, clutching the side of the boat. "Are we there yet? I think I'm going to hurl."

"I told you to stay ashore with Tammy and Travis," Seán said, shaking his head. "You threw yourself onto the boat."

He could only hope that the coast guard would reach them before long. While he couldn't risk letting Ray escape to France, he wasn't keen on the idea of tackling him and his crew with a bunch of civilians as back up.

Clio grabbed his arm. "I see them. Look, they're already on the move."

Feck. Seán peered through his binoculars. Sure enough, a sailing boat was leaving Inish Glas's small dock. He adjusted the binoculars to get a better view. Ray Greer's wiry curls and thick glasses were visible on the deck. "That's them all right. Can this rust bucket move any faster, Buck?"

Buck changed gears and the elderly vessel sputtered and splashed, then lurched forward and took off at an alarming rate. "Rust bucket, my arse," Buck shouted. "Show them what you can do, *Betsy Ross*."

"You keep interesting company in Ballybeg, Clio," Delaney remarked in a sardonic tone. "First, the Guard. Now, two inebriated fishermen. And you think *I'm* a bad influence on Tammy."

"Buck and John-Joe come as a double act," Seán explained. "Buck can sail but not swim. John-Joe can't sail but can swim."

ZARA KEANE

"Between the pair of them, they have three functioning eyes and maybe half a functioning liver," Clio added, slumping against Seán's shoulder. Her complexion was green and her hair windblown, but she was still the sexiest woman he'd ever encountered.

Delaney cocked an eyebrow. "So what's the plan, sergeant? I can guarantee you that Ray and his pals are armed to the hilt. You, I assume, are a castrated Guard now that you're back in uniform."

"If you mean to say that I'm no longer permitted to carry a gun, then that's correct. However"—he got to his feet and pulled up the lid off his seat—"we just happen to have a pair of semiautomatic pistols and a couple of boxes of ammo on the boat. I suggest we use them and lose them in the sea before we get back to shore."

Delaney beamed and pulled a gun from the inside of his jacket. "Make that three semis. Give one of yours to Clio. She's a damn good shot."

Seán stared at Clio. "Do I want to know why you're a good shot?"

She smiled, picked up one of pistols, and loaded it expertly. "Let's file this particular skill under strictly-need-to-know for now."

"Jaysus," said John-Joe, swaying at the side of the deck. "Did you forget to get rid of a couple of the guns, Buck?"

"He did," Seán replied. "But if you lads cooperate, I might just forget I saw them."

360

His uncle squinted at the weapons. "Are you planning a shoot-out?"

"Much as I'd love to avoid one, I don't know see that happening." There was no need for binoculars now. They'd almost caught up with Ray's boat. He turned to his uncle. "When I tell you to hit the deck, I'll mean it. Literally."

A shout from Ray's boat indicated they'd been spotted. Crouching under the wheel, Buck got them as close to the other vessel as he dared.

On impulse, Seán grabbed Clio and kissed her hard. "In case you hadn't already realized, you've captured my heart, Clio Havelin. When we get out of this mess, I want to make a go of it with you."

Her eyes filled with tears. "Are you telling me that you love me?"

"I love you," he said, and meant it with an earnest intensity he'd never experienced before. "Now dry your eyes and don't get shot."

Lar cleared his throat. "When you two are done with the love-dovey stuff, Ray's men are prepping their guns."

They didn't need to wait long for a hail of bullets.

"Aim to incapacitate, not kill," Seán said. "After my count..."

Seán, Clio, and Delaney opened fire.

"How many of them are there?" Clio whispered after the first round of bullets had been spent.

"Unless one of them is hiding below deck, there are five including Ray."

"Four," Delaney said. "I got one."

"Injured or dead?" Seán asked, alarmed.

"If a some bastard opens fire on me, I shoot to kill, sergeant. Save your sermons for your underlings." With that, Delaney took aim and fired again, neatly eliminating two more of Ray's cohorts.

Realizing he was well and truly screwed, Ray was waving his arms around in a panicked fashion. "Stop shooting, for fuck's sake. We surrender."

Five minutes later, a disoriented Ray and the remaining member of his crew had been hauled aboard. Both had been nicked by bullets and were bleeding profusely.

In the distance, they could see the coast guard speeding toward them.

"Not much time," Delaney said. Grabbing their weapons and the remaining ammunition, he tossed them onto the deck of Ray's boat. Bending to give Clio a kiss on the cheek, he said, "Give my love to Tammy and tell her I'll be in touch."

With these parting words and a mock salute to Seán, he leaped onto the other boat. "Get moving. You won't want to be around when this baby blows."

Seán inclined his head a fraction. "Hit it, Buck."

Buck required no further invitation to put as much space as possible between him and a crazed lunatic in the possession of several weapons.

They'd almost met the coast guard when they heard the explosion.

"What the hell?" one of the coast guards exclaimed, staring in horror at the burning remains of Ray's boat. His stunned gaze switched to the occupants of the *Betsy Ross*.

"Faulty engine," Seán said, deadpan.

"It was giving us trouble from the start," Ray added, ashen-faced and bloody, but rallying.

John-Joe struggled to his feet. "If you're done blowing shite up, can I get back to my pint?"

CHAPTER THIRTY-NINE

....

W hen the coast guard escorted the *Betsy Ross* back to shore, Tammy and Travis were waiting for them on the pier along with Helen, the super, Brian Glenn, and what looked to be the entire population of Ballybeg.

"Jaysus. That's quite a welcome party," John-Joe said, delighted.

Clio snuggled against Seán's side. "I'm looking forward to getting home."

He ruffled her windblown hair. "And I'm looking forward to getting rid of everyone and having you all to myself. Preferably naked."

She was totally down with that idea, especially once she was off a moving boat and no longer seasick.

Buck was taking the *Betsy Ross's* new, bullet-ridden look rather well. "It adds a certain je-ne-say-whatsit to the vessel," he philosophized after they'd docked and Seán was assisting him down the ladder. "A bit of street cred, you know. The lads in MacCarthy's will be impressed. I might even get a few pints out of it."

"You'll be getting a free pint in any case," shouted Sharon MacCarthy from the pier, giving them a thumbs-up. "Drinks are on the house for the next hour to welcome the new addition to the family. Baby Lucy was born twenty minutes ago. So stop gawking and get to the pub."

John-Joe and Buck required no further incentive. Ignoring the squawking protests of the coast guard that they needed to be debriefed, they took off running for the pub and their promised pints.

Superintendent O'Riordan watched them go, shrugged, and went over to placate his outraged colleagues.

Brian winked when he approached. "Sharon knows how to create a distraction, clear a crowd, and make a bit of money all at the same time."

"Good for Sharon," Seán said, laughing.

"Good for Baby Lucy," Clio added with a smile.

Ray, handcuffed and subdued, was escorted down the pier by two of the reserve policemen. When Helen spotted him, she went wild.

"You blaggard," she screamed, forgetting the cultured accent and vocabulary she'd spent years acquiring. "You're a fecking disgrace. How dare you threaten my daughter?"

Abandoning a wide-eyed Tammy, Helen advanced on Ray, brandishing her handbag like a weapon. "Get out of my way, officer," she said to Reserve Garda McGarry. The man had good instincts and maneuvered himself out of danger a split second before Helen's handbag collided with Ray's face.

"Ah!" he screamed.

"And this"—Helen got in a second whack—"is for breaking into my house."

Ray staggered back, clutching his nose and yowling.

"Well done, Mother," Clio said, impressed. "I think you broke his nose."

Tammy ran to her side, clutching an excited Travis, and looking about frantically. "Where's Dad?"

Clio let go of Seán's hand, hugged her daughter, and dropped a kiss onto the puppy's furry head. "At this very moment, I'm not sure, but knowing Lar, he's perfectly fine. He said he'd be in touch with you. I think the less we say about him when we're questioned, the better."

Tammy nodded. "Understood."

"After I have a significant word with Councilors Evans and Jobson about the halting site and Travellers' rights," Seán said, giving Clio a knicker-melting smile, "we're all going to have to go to the station to be debriefed."

The only debriefing she was interested in involved removing her and Seán's underwear. Judging by his grin, the same thought had crossed his mind.

Tammy looked from one to the other and scrunched up her nose in an expression of pure adolescent disdain. "Are you two going to be getting it on the whole time now?"

Clio linked arms with her daughter. "Would you have a problem with it if we did?"

Tammy considered for a moment, then shook her head. "Nah. I like Sergeant Mackey, even if he did arrest me for attempted shoplifting."

"Eh?" Seán laughed. "Cheeky madam. I escorted you off the premises. No arrests were made."

"Won't you be going back to work in Dublin now, though?" Tammy asked, voicing the question Clio had been trying to suppress. "You're bound to get your old job back."

Seán's gaze rested on Clio, suddenly serious. Then he focused on her daughter. "That depends on you and your mother. With all the drama the pair of you have caused since your arrival in Ballybeg, the excitement of Dublin has lost its allure. Besides," he added, winking at Clio. "I hear there's a vacancy in the Cork City homicide division."

EPILOGUE

....

ONE YEAR LATER

Seán got down on bended knee in front of the hallway mirror of their newly purchased home. *Jaysus.* This position was more complicated than he'd thought. A fumble in his shirt pocket produced a fancy box, freshly procured from the jeweler that morning.

"Clio Havelin, will you make an honest man of me?"

No, that was all wrong. He sounded like he'd been gargling with acid. *Feck.* This wasn't going to cut it. How many times was he going to have to practice this damn speech before he got it right?

Deep breath.

Okay, he'd try it one more time.

Back down on bended knee, throat cleared. "Ms. Havelin, will you do me the honor of becoming my lawfully wedded wife?"

He flipped open the jewelry box with one hand. The diamond ring on which he'd just spent a small fortune shot out, spun in the air, and landed with a thud at a Doc Martin-ed foot.

A foot that did not belong to Seán's future fiancée.

368

A snort of laughter was followed by a canine whimper of delight. Cheeks burning, he looked up to see Tammy with Travis panting by her side.

The girl raised a recently pierced eyebrow. "Are you planning a polygamous marriage? 'Cause no offense, but I'm over older guys."

He retrieved the ring and got to his feet. "No, you cheeky madam. I want to propose to your mother, but I can't seem to get the wording right."

His stepdaughter nodded approvingly at the ring. "Good choice. She'll love it. What she won't love is the bumblebee-patterned tie. Definitely lose that, preferably into the nearest clothing recycling bin."

"Right." He nodded, mentally taking notes. "Ring approved, lose tie. I can do that."

"As for the wording of the proposal, keep it simple. There's nothing wrong with, 'Clio, I love you and want to spend the rest of my life with you. Will you marry me?'" Tammy smiled wide, revealing her pearly white post-braces teeth. "'Cause you know she's going to say yes."

And she did!

— THE END —

THANK YOU!

....

Thanks for reading *Love and Shamrocks*. I hope you enjoyed it!

Love and Shamrocks is the fifth book in the Ballybeg series. All the stories are designed to stand alone— Happy Ever Afters guaranteed! However, you might prefer to read them in order of publication to follow the development of the secondary characters and happenings in the town.

To find out what's next, or to sign up to my new release mailing list, check out my author website at:

http://zarakeane.com

You can also turn the page to read a blurb for *Her Treasure Hunter Ex*, the first story in the Ballybeg Bad Boys spin-off series.

ACKNOWLEDGEMENTS

....

Love and Shamrocks, or the John-Joe Book as my mother calls it, was a joy to write.

As always, many thanks go to my wonderful critique partner, Magdalen Braden; to Rhonda Helms, editor extraordinaire; to Margie Lawson for her feedback on an early draft; to Trish Slattery and April Weigele for beta reading the final draft; and to Anne and Linda at Victory Editing for the thorough proofread.

Finally, thank you to all the readers who asked for Seán's story. I hope you enjoyed it!

OTHER BOOKS BY ZARA

....

THE BALLYBEG SERIES
1. *Love and Shenanigans*
2. *Love and Blarney*
3. *Love and Leprechauns*
4. *Love and Mistletoe*
5. *Love and Shamrocks*

THE BALLYBEG BAD BOYS
1. *Her Treasure Hunter Ex*
2. *The Rock's Secret Baby*
3. *The Navy SEAL's Holiday Fling*

HER TREASURE HUNTER EX

(BALLYBEG BAD BOYS #1)

....

She'd left him in the past...
Underwater photographer Katy Ryan snags the assignment of a lifetime—the chance to explore the wreck of RMS *Lusitania*. But there's a catch: Her infuriating ex-fiancé is on the exploration team.

...He's about to blow up her future.
Declan "Dex" Fitzgerald is a treasure hunter on a mission. A priceless gem is hidden in the wreck of the *Lusitania*. With a loose idea of where to find the treasure, and even looser morals, Dex wrangles a last-minute job on the exploration team. And realizes he'll have to work alongside his uptight-but-sexy-as-hell ex.

And they're not the only ones in pursuit of the treasure...With sparks flying and oxygen tanks running low, can Dex and Katy retrieve the gem before the bad guys?

SUMMER 2015

ABOUT ZARA KEANE

....

Zara Keane grew up in Dublin, Ireland, but spent her summers in a small town very similar to the fictitious Ballybeg.

She currently lives in Switzerland with her family. When she's not writing or wrestling small people, she drinks far too much coffee, and tries—with occasional success —to resist the siren call of Swiss chocolate.

zarakeane.com

28011962R00208

Printed in Great Britain
by Amazon